About the Author

A self-confessed gypsy at heart, Peter has worked as an engineer in The Arabian Gulf, USA and Far East.

In his mid-forties, he sold his house in Hong Kong, moved onto his 43' boat, and set off to fulfil his dream of sailing round the world. Nine years later he met the love of his life, Martine, and they sailed together across the Atlantic and Pacific Oceans for the next seven years.

Peter holds sailing qualifications as skipper, engineer and radio operator, and is a British Sub-Aqua Club (BSAC) advanced diving instructor.

Charlie's Smile

Peter d'Iffanger

Charlie's Smile

Chimera

CHIMERA PAPERBACK

© Copyright 2024
Peter d'Iffanger

A CIP catalogue record for this title is
available from the British Library.

ISBN 978 1 915451 04 0

This is a work of fiction. Names, characters, businesses, places, events and incidents are either
the product of the author's imagination or used in a fictitious manner. Any resemblance to actual
persons, living or dead, or actual events is purely coincidental.

Chimera is an imprint of
Pegasus Elliot Mackenzie Publishers Ltd.
www.pegasuspublishers.com

First Published in 2024

Chimera
Sheraton House Castle Park
Cambridge England

Printed & Bound in Great Britain

For Martine

ACKNOWLEDGEMENTS

I owe a great debt of gratitude to my editors, Dr Susan P Ekins, Dr Michael B Johnson and Martine M Roux (Licence és Lettres, Université de Vincennes, Paris), for their endless patience, helpful content suggestions, as well as grammatical and spelling corrections. All remaining errors are entirely my own!

I would also like to acknowledge the excellence of the RCC Pilotage Foundation's pilot books, published by Imray Laurie and Wilson, which I used extensively in my research for the sailing areas covered in this book.

Peter d'Iffanger

ABOUT THIS BOOK

In this amazing and explicit love story, d'Iffanger challenges us to re-evaluate some previously accepted norms, and even taboos, as we follow our broad cast of well-developed characters through their rites of passage in the moral maze that is life and love in the twenty-first century.

The story is told in the first person by one of the two principal characters, Nathan Cooper, so the reader is intimately involved throughout and not a bystander or voyeur.

Nathan's family could be described as English upper-middle-class and moderately wealthy. Some of the story is set on the family yacht, based in the western Mediterranean, and might be of particular interest to sailors and would-be sailors alike.

We experience life through Nathan's eyes; both the ecstasy and the tragedy, that will test the reader's emotions to the limit. d'Iffanger confronts the explicit nature of love's sexual aspects with complete honesty, yet does not resort to any crudeness of language.

At eighty-six thousand words, *Charlie's Smile* is a good, long read, and d'Iffanger is already working on the sequel.

Would your maiden aunt enjoy this book?

You might well be surprised!

DRAMATIS PERSONAE

Maidenhead, England

Charlie

Charlise COOPER
Cambridge University student reading
Law.

Nat

Nathan COOPER
Oxford University
student reading Politics.

Paris

Paris (preferred
pronunciation Paree)
COOPER Wife of
Arthur, mother of Charlie and Nat, and
identical twin of Flo.

Flo

Florence LAROCHE
Wife of Pierre, Chef at
restaurant *Le coq en pâte*.

Arthur

Dr Arthur COOPER
Husband of Paris and
father of Charlie and Nat.
Leading paediatric
surgeon.

Pierre

Pierre LAROCHE.
Flo's husband.
French chef.

| Élodie | Baby daughter of Flo and Pierre |

| 'Harry' | COOPER family dog. Golden Retriever (adopted). |

| Frank STOKES | COOPER family solicitor and close family friend. |

OXFORD

| Adjim | Adjim ABDULLAYEV Former room-mate of Nat in hall of residence. Overseas student from Askidistan. |

| Prof. SPALDING | Head of politics department. |

CAMBRIDGE

| David | 'Camp' David gay friend of Charlie and partner of Ralph. |

| Ralph | Fashion photographer at 'Shoots' model agency. |

Lucy

Owner of 'Shoots'
agency.

Heather

Deputy Creative
Director of leading
London ad. agency.

Maggy

Charlie's former
room-mate during
fresher year. Fellow
team member of
Cambridge Ladies 2nd
Eleven Football
(soccer) team and
budding stand-up
comedian.

MARSEILLE/TOULON, FRANCE

Mathilde

Mathilde
DOVERGNE née
DELAUNAY
Close friend of Charlie
and Nat.

Aurélie

Aurélie DELAUNAY née
DOVERGNE Mother of
Mathilde. Former prima ballerina and
cosmetics model.

Alain

Alain DELAUNAY
Father of Mathilde.
Former professional

Footballer and later coach with *Athlétique Marseille*.

Anne   Aurélie's sister

Hugo Pronounced oogo.   Anne's new boyfriend

Yvette   Yvette MONTCALM
                        Mistress of Alain
                        DELAUNAY

Melanie   Melanie
                        MONTCALM
                        Daughter of Yvette
                        and Alain
                        DELAUNAY.

MAHON, CAPITAL CITY of ISLAND of MENORCA, SPAIN

Sophie   General surgeon at
                        Mateu Orfila hospital,
                        Mahon. Close
                        friend of the COOPER
                        family and fellow
                        yacht club member.

Pau   Sophie's older, retired
                        husband.

Juan (pronounced Hwon) Sophie and Pau's son.

Julia (pronounced Hoolia)   Juan's wife and
midwife at *Mateu Orfila.*

Jordi, 10yrs, and Guillem, 9yrs. Juan and Julias's football crazy sons.

Jaime (pronounced Hymee).   Wine grower friend
and neighbour of
Sophie and Pau.

Maria   Jaime's housekeeper/companion.

CHAPTER ONE

REUNION

I sat at my favourite table, overlooking the Isis from the raised veranda of The Old Trout Pub; the head on my Guinness slowly settling as the beer lost its cloudiness. It was early December, and the Oxford 'University's Michaelmas, or autumn term, had just ended. As is often the case in the shires at this time of the year, the weather was crisp and cold but also sunny, with just a light breeze ruffling the feathers of a pair of swans that were gliding past, heading downriver. The pub had lowered the screens to cut the breeze, and a gas heater was belting out hot air.

I'd left my hall of residence just after half past ten, bundled up in my thick hoodie and beanie, and walked slowly for the two miles along the towpath to the pub. I had hoped the walk would help me order my thoughts, but when I arrived I was no closer to clarity and resolved to just let events unfold.

***

The river is fairly narrow where it passes through Oxford but broadens out south of the city where the famous Oxford Academicals Rowing Club have their base. The Old Trout was south of the rowing club and just upstream of the Iffley lock.

The Isis is an alternative name for the River Thames from where it rises in the Cotswolds and flows through the City of Oxford to Dorchester, where it becomes the Thames proper, and then on to London.

My rendezvous with Charlie was set for twelve noon: less than half an hour away. My seat afforded me a view of the river end of the parking area, and hence I would see her for a few seconds before she saw me. I just wanted a few moments to take her in after our mutually agreed separation for the first term of our fresher year. I wondered in my mind if she too was suffering the same emotional turmoil as myself.

***

Both Charlie and I had started our university fresher year with the term just ending. Charlie was studying law at Cambridge, and I was doing a politics and international relations course at Oxford.

Her drive from Cambridge, about ninety miles to the northeast of Oxford, would take her around two hours.

The sun was as high as it was going to get and I took my beanie off as the heater started to win the battle against the chill. I was about to take another draught of my Guinness when I saw her old Prius hybrid park up near the veranda steps; it was five to twelve.

I watched as she stepped from the car and headed up the stairs. I sensed panic rising in me as she came onto the veranda but stood up so that she could see me. Her step faltered as she spotted me, but then quickened as she came to me. Without a moment's hesitation, she flung her arms around me and we held each other in a powerful embrace. We swayed slightly from side to side as we had always done, her face buried in my neck. I felt the emotion well up in me and could barely contain my tears. As we broke the embrace, I saw her tears were flowing freely down her lovely cheeks; she had never looked more beautiful than in that moment. I held her face between my hands and wiped her cheeks with my thumbs, our eyes locked together.

We held each other's hands across the table when we sat down, and I realised that not a word had passed between us, yet much had been said.

Our separation was over.

***

The waiter came out with lunch menus and I ordered a small Guinness for Charlie; Guinness had always been our pub drink. I tried to say her name but the lump in my throat made it more like a sob, I took a deep breath and tried again with slightly more success. Her tears now flowed again but she was smiling as she whispered my name, "Nat."

"Did you want something else?" She just shook her head.

We did not open the menus and both of us took the pub's signature dish of steamed trout with a vinaigrette of artichoke hearts, we took a half bottle of Chardonnay to help it down.

We sat in silence, sipping our beers and slowly regained our composure.

Charlie had removed her baseball cap and shook out her natural ash-blonde hair. It beautifully framed her oval face and fell to the collar of her bulky coat. She still had summer freckles across the bridge of her nose, her wide-set hazel eyes never left mine as I took in the face that I loved so much. Charlie had quite generous lips, and I longed to kiss them.

"I so want to kiss you," I said.

"Me too," said Charlie, just as our lunch arrived.

Lunch passed in a haze of both companionable silence, and it seemed, a shared understanding that what had just passed between us made small talk almost an afront.

***

Charlie went to the ladies while I paid and then waited for her at the top of the steps to the parking area, my beanie back on my head and my rucksack by my feet.

"Let's walk off a couple of units before driving," said Charlie, as we came to her car. "I'll put your bag in the boot."

With the boot open I noticed her overnight bag on the top of her case and my heart swelled with love and anticipation.

As she closed the boot I slid my arms around her and she turned into me—now we had our kiss. We held each other lightly as we kissed and my lips trembled at the contact, just the sweetest thing. We parted, kissed again, this time with the gentlest of tip-of-tongue contact, a soft promise, and we headed south along the towpath.

The towpath was paved and much wider these days than when horses towed the narrowboat barges upriver to offload produce in Oxford, and then up again to load up with the lovely mellow Cotswold stone. These days it is very popular with students and others for jogging and bike riding. We strolled hand in hand down to the lock and sat on one of the benches there.

A couple of narrow boats were moored just upriver from the lock. They had been lovingly converted to houseboats, with bright, bold, primary colour edging around the various hatches and windows.

We had hardly spoken on the way down, just happy to be together. We laughed as we both tried to speak at the same moment.

I took her hand and put it on my stomach. "I seemed to have had a weight right here, dragging me down the whole time. I can't find words to say how hard it has been." My voice had risen with the words and I just filled up. I felt no shame in my tears for they were more honest than words.

Charlie too was weeping and smiling at the same time, "Me too Nat, me too."

***

I had made contingency plans for whichever way things turned out this Saturday. I had dreaded the prospect that our love had not survived and that Charlie had found it elsewhere. I think I would have been destroyed. As things were, I could not be happier.

CHAPTER TWO

CONFIRMATION

I had hoped that we would spend this weekend together in Oxford before driving down to our family home at Maidenhead on Sunday. I had booked a room at The Cotswold Inn, a very nice four-star hotel just a twenty-minute drive away. If things had not gone as I had hoped I would have stayed there alone.

We walked back to Charlie's car with a little spring in our step. I gave Charlie directions as we came to road junctions without disclosing the destination.

As we made the last turn she realised where we were heading, "Oh Nat, that's absolutely perfect." And she squeezed my leg.

We had stayed here once before when I had attended interviews at Oxford for my course. We had loved it for lots of reasons, but mainly the country views from our room, the room itself and the excellence of the grill. The car park was mostly empty so she parked close to the entrance and popped the boot. As she leaned in to get the bags I slipped my hands around her waist and we embraced again; the frisson was palpable.

We kissed long and deep and then she broke the kiss, "We need to get to our room Nat."

***

"Nathan Cooper," I said to the receptionist.

"Welcome back, Mr Cooper, your room is ready, can I take an impression of your card please?"

I already had my card out and handed it to her. "Good memory," I said. "It's been nearly six months."

"I cheated, it's on my screen!" she said. "I've given you the same room as before, is that OK?"

"Perfect, thanks!"

She gave me the key card in a folder with the room number on it, and we headed for the lifts. Once the doors had closed Charlie threw her arms around me and we kissed again with ever increasing feeling. Her coat was open and I ran my hands under her top and released her bra. Cupping her breasts, I could feel her wonderfully hard nipples… just as I realised that the lift wasn't moving; I had not yet pressed the floor button! We laughed and for a moment, our passion paused, but just for a moment.

***

Once the door to our room was closed, we paused for a fraction of a second before trying to kiss and get out of our clothes at the same time. I fell onto the big bed first as Charlie momentarily struggled with her tight jeans. When clear of the jeans she flung herself on me.

It was an amazing joy to behold Charlie in her arousal. She lay across my right leg and wrapped her legs around it. She was wound so tight she could not hold herself back and was already moving against me. I lifted my leg just slightly to increase her contact and felt her wetness on me. In no time she started to climax in great waves and ever faster movement. She was moaning continuously, head back, eyes tight shut. "So sorry Nat… can't stop… can't stop… can't stop…"

I had my right hand just above her buttocks and rubbed the small of her back, my thumb just moving in the valley. Her orgasm spasmed with great shudders that put me on the brink of coming. Just in time she released my leg and slithered up to straddle me. I took the weight of her breasts in my hands and brushed her nipples with my thumbs as she guided me in. Charlie's vagina seemed to shiver and clench as I entered her. She cried out my name with her whole body continuously shuddering and I came, and came, and came… I cried out with each mighty pulse until they started to diminish. We were both having huge aftershocks that seemed to go on and on. It had been a long time, such a long time.

Charlie was murmuring into my neck as we came off our peaks, "…So sorry Nat — just couldn't stop — is it OK?"

I felt a mountain of tenderness and love for Charlie at such moments as this. It was not the first time she had pleasured herself like that and I found it enormously arousing. It invariably ended with us cumming together in penetration whilst she was still in orgasm.

"Don't be silly," I said. "It's one of the most erotic things we do."

We were both so spent; we kissed tenderly and I eased her to the bed beside me and held her against me. Our breathing returned to normal and after a short while her regular breathing told me she was fast asleep; it was not long before I too succumbed.

***

When I woke up Charlie was still sleeping, and my arm was numb under her neck. As gently as possible I eased my arm out and she briefly opened her eyes and rolled onto her other side so we lay as two spoons. I was bursting for a pee and slipped out of bed heading for the bathroom. My penis, legs and stomach were sticky from our love and I smiled with utter joy as I peed a powerful stream. I was the happiest I could be. I went into the shower. I would have liked to savour the scent of our passion for a little longer when Charlie slid the door open and joined me and we washed each other down with hotel gel.

"Do you know what time it is Nat? It's just after nine thirty! We need to move if we want to eat. You've given me a monster appetite!"

***

The towels were huge, as only hotel towels seem to be, and we wrapped them around us as we dried each other's hair with the hotel dryer. We returned to the bedroom; what a joyful mess the bed was! The wet patch was enormous! Charlie took the tissue box from the bedside table and put it under the sheet to make a tent of the wet bit. She then fetched the hair dryer.

While Charlie dried the bed, I put on a clean polo and underpants from my bag and dressed in the same jeans that were tangled up with the rest of our clothes on the floor. I took over the dryer while Charlie put the same jeans on and a fresh camisole and Kashmir top. She liked to go braless in the evenings and who was I to object?

***

Her hair was still a little damp and she was make-up free, but her beauty and glow from our love made her seem magical to me. She had a natural elegance that would have graced any catwalk.

I noticed several eyes following Charlie as the maître d'hôtel led us to our table, and for my sins, I glowed with pride.

The maître d' left menus for us whilst suggesting the chef's special of beef Wellington. We clasped hands across the table and held each other's eyes.

"Welcome back my love," I said. Her lovely hazel eyes were misty as she repeated my words.

The waiter came and broke the spell to take our order. We both took the chef's special. He suggested a bottle of Beaumes de Venise, a Côtes du Rhône, which was the featured wine for this month and we took that as well. The bottle was actually already on our table and we hadn't noticed. He deftly opened it and poured a taster into my glass. It was a beauty, and I nodded approval. We clinked glasses, "To us."

The waiter was soon back with a serving trolly. The Wellington was on a long cutting board, the open end, where other diners' meals had been sliced, showed the beef fillet to be a perfect a point. The beef was resting on a generous pad of foie gras and the pastry was cleverly decorated and lightly browned.

He gave us generous slices and added a garnish of tiny root veggies. He offered the jug of jus to us and we each took a handsome English-sized puddle.

We ate and chatted about our lives at uni and our roommates in our respective halls of residence. She had enjoyed her first term of law but had struggled under the stress of our separation. I had noticed in bed that she had lost some weight. She told how lucky she was with her roommate.

"Her name is Maggie and she's from Glasgow. A lady of many talents, she plays left wing for the Cambridge ladies second eleven football team, and does great stand-up. She's already a minor star in 'Footlights', that's the uni's am dram society. When I told her I had played for my high school she insisted I join her for the midweek training sessions. It's been a great way to work off my frustrations and keep fit. I'll try out for the team next term. How about your roommate?"

"Nothing like as exciting as your Maggie unfortunately, I'm so glad for you. My roommate is a great guy but certainly not much fun. He's called Adjim, and as he puts it, is from a minor 'stan, somewhere near Azerbaijan. The 'stan is nominally Muslim so he's thoroughly enjoying the freedom of association here, especially with the Oxford ladies!"

"What about extracurricular activities?"

"Well, on the fun side I go out with some guys on the course. We're trying to teach Adjim the joys of English pubs and pizza; he's a good learner and is likely to do well! On the more serious side, I've joined the Oxford student union debating society, which is great. I'm also looking at the Young this, and Young that, political groups, but the danger there is that your student affiliations can come back and bite you on the bum if you make a career in politics, and I would probably like to do that. My course has seriously spiked my interest in government."

As we finished the truly delicious meal, the waiter reappeared with the trolley.

"Perhaps a half slice?"

We both accepted. We declined the dessert and settled for a café allonge to round off the meal.

Our appetite satisfied, we headed back to the room, we embraced tenderly in the lift and Charlie rested her head on my shoulder. She was quite tall for a girl, five-feet-nine, but I was exactly six-feet, we were a perfect fit.

***

Back in the room we cleaned our teeth and then Charlie put her arms around my neck, it was a gentle embrace but after a little while I could feel her nipples against me through her Kashmir. I gently lifted it over her head and cupped her breasts beneath the camisole. Charlie undid my belt and fly and I did the same for her. I shook my jeans off leg by leg but had to kneel to pull hers off. With my head so close to her sex I could scent her musk. I pressed my face against her and she bent one leg to the side to let me in. I caressed her buttocks as I pressed my nose between her labia and she returned the pressure with her hands behind my head. My tongue softly circled her now swollen clitoris and she sighed in contentment. I slowly licked the length of her labia and back up to the nub. Charlie was getting very wet now and trembling with her arousal and the effort to stay on her feet, I took my face away and she whimpered as I picked her up and put her on the side of the bed with her legs over the edge. I again knelt between them, my arms around her hips. My tongue could now penetrate her slightly and I licked the base of her clitoris. I was mightily aroused as she started to buck against my mouth. She cried out as I took myself off and lifted her fully onto the bed. As fast as possible I moved up between her legs and entered her in a single long deep stroke. Charlie yelped as I bottomed out and I pulled back, but she pressed me in with her heels slowly so that I bottomed gently this time under her control. I stopped moving as she did her thing, gripping my penis in wonderful spasms as her climax returned. Very slowly I pulled back until the lip of my helmet just nestled under her clitoris.

"No, no!" she gasped, thinking I was pulling out entirely but cooed when she felt what I was doing. I was moving the ridge of my glans under her clitoris, just a tiny amount, and slowly increasing the depth and tempo. Charlie was coming fast now. Her movements almost a blur. I sensed her climax just in time and plunged in fully. She actually screamed with her wrist in her mouth to hush the sound. Charlie was now over the top, all control lost, massive sobs and shudders coming from her. I started to pull back again but she forced me to stay in with her heels.

"Oh Nat, I think I've died of happiness." And then, "You haven't cum yet?"

"No," I said. "Come on top."

We wriggled around and we changed positions. She was calmer now and lowered herself onto me. I found that I had better control when I concentrated on her pleasure. I still had a great stiffy which only hardened more as she started to take care of me. She moved slowly on me now and we made gentle love with the tenderness of her movements. Charlie leaned forward and put her hands on my chest while I caressed her breasts. I stretched out my fingers into fans and slowly flicked them across her nipples. I loved the feel of them hardening and the pleasure that showed on her face. I started to move with her now, sensing my control slipping. Charlie noticed it too and brought me to the brink, I wondered if she would cum again and slid my hand down to put a finger against the top of her clitoris, gently following her movement with the slightest of pressure, a low moan escaped her as we climaxed together. We met wave after wave in unison as our orgasm ebbed. Charlie then laid fully on me and slid up to brush my face with her hair first and then her breasts.

I eased her down to kiss her lips and said, "This is truly the happiest day of my life my love."

"Me too," said Charlie. "Me too!"

Charlie pulled the box of tissues off the nightstand and did a cursory clean-up of us both, put the box back and snuggled up with me. It was after midnight now and we were both exhausted, both physically and emotionally. I pulled the duvet around us as we shared a long soft kiss before drifting off to sleep… the sleep that only lovers know.

***

We woke just after nine to find ourselves tucked in together as two spoons. I kissed her neck and she turned to return it, then back to the spoons. I loved this position, the fit was perfect, my penis curled up against her bum and my hands free to roam over her from pubis to breasts. I could caress her hip and buttock and she was free to turn into me at will.

"Morning," I said.

"Best ever," said Charlie.

***

My experience of other women was somewhere between very little and non-existent, but I knew from films, literature and elsewhere that what Charlie and I had was indeed very special on every front. In our position now we both knew that the next hour could go either way, but we had stuff to do today.

"Breakfast—what do you say?"

"I know," said Charlie. "There's things we need to talk about and make some decisions, or at least a plan. Breakfast."

29

CHAPTER THREE

FAMILY

Unlike most siblings of opposite sex, Charlie and I did not experience any rivalry; we were absolutely very best friends. She played knock-about football with me and my mates, and in fact was very good at it. She still plays, and is to try out next term for a ladies' team at Cambridge. I, of course, was the heroic big brother who sorted out all the problems for her and the other little girls.

***

Charlie was eighteen months younger than me and we shared a bedroom until she was nine and I was nearly eleven. We would often sleep together in one of our twin beds, cuddled up in our innocence, our parents knew this and I expect it was rather cute to see, but equally, they realised that we should have separate rooms quite soon as we would be entering puberty in the near future.

***

By pure serendipity, it was around this time that our granddad on our father's side, Granddad Tubs to us, became less able to look after himself and voluntarily entered sheltered accommodation in Virginia Water, a short distance south of Windsor, and down-river from the family house on the Thames at Maidenhead. Granny Tubs had passed away some years earlier, and he had gone steadily downhill since. Charlie and I had only the vaguest of memories of her.

The family house was large, four bedroomed, and with a big garden running down to its much-envied river frontage. We were living then in a fairly modest two-up- two-down, in the village of Cookham Dean, not far to the north of Maidenhead.

At that time, our father, Arthur Cooper, was a junior surgeon at the famous Great Ormond Street Hospital for Children in central London, and was a protege of the celebrated cardio-thoracic (CT) surgeon, Sir Oswald (Ozzy) Hamilton.

Granddad Tubs had been a doctor too and had spent his whole career in general practice. He had joined forces with two other GPs in a group practice serving the Maidenhead area, which became something of a model for other practices.

Granddad told us how he got his nickname, Tubs. A teacher at his prep school had told the class how their family names had originated, and that a Cooper was a barrel maker. As young kids, Charlie and I jokingly started calling our dad 'Tubby', and rather surprisingly, he liked it, and it has stuck. Later on, we shortened Tubby to Tub, in the same way that children often shorten Daddy to Dad as they grow up. Dad actually did not look anything like his nickname. Always slim, five-feet-ten, with a shock of sandy light brown hair that was forever falling over his left eye. He always wore a pirate style bandana in the operating theatre to control his hair and was often given wildly patterned ones for his birthday. Dad's face was, and is, the very epitome of care and kindness. It's not hard to imagine his bedside manner.

With the family house empty and us needing more room, Tub and Granddad agreed that we should take it over in the tacit awareness that Granddad Tubs would not be needing it any more. Dad was an only child so there were no issues stopping a seamless inheritance.

Granddad Tubs had occupied only the core rooms since his wife passed away. The other two bedrooms, and a second bathroom, were in a wing at right angles to the main structure and clearly an addition at some point in time.

When our father was growing up he had had the second bedroom on the common landing with the master bedroom, the wing accommodation being largely used for guests. There was also a study on the first floor, between the bedrooms, which doubled as another bedroom when needed.

As Charlie and I were soon to become obnoxious and loud teenagers — Mum's affectionate prophecy — we got the 'new wing' and our own rooms.

***

Mum and Dad had met when he was a fresh young houseman at Great Ormond Street, and she was one of two assistants to the administrator. They had married not long after and bought their first house in Cookham Dean.

Our mum was very loving and very tactile. When we were small, and indeed ever since, the three of us would have what she called a 'love-in', where we would sit either side of her on the settee to watch the TV in a three-way cuddle. Dad was no less loving but a touch awkward on the tactile front!

Our mum came with an amazing additional benefit—her sister Florence, or Aunt Flo to us. Florence was not just her sister, but her identical twin sister, not even Dad could tell them apart when they decided to cause confusion. The pair of them were full of fun and often played amazing practical jokes on us all.

Our mum's given name was Paris, and the story goes that their parents conceived them while on their honeymoon, firstly with a few days in Paris, and then by train to Florence to binge on art. Quite where the required deed occurred was a mystery, and thereafter was enshrined in their names.

***

Mum and Dad were very Francophile and took the larger part of their summer holidays in either Corsica or on the southwest coast of France around Biarritz and the Basque region. Florence was still single during the first couple of years of Mum and Dad's married life and would often accompany them on holiday. They would usually rent a two-bedroom flat near the local beach and share the expenses on a two thirds/one third basis.

It was on such a holiday that Florence met her future husband, Pierre Laroche, and both their lives took an upswing. Pierre was nine years older than Flo and had been married before. The marriage had lasted five years and was without issue. The divorce settlement was simple, she got their original flat in Montmartre, in the eighteenth arrondissement of Paris, and Pierre the two-bedroom flat in Biarritz, plus their thirty-foot sailboat, called Soufflé, that they kept in a marina just south of Biarritz.

Flo and Pierre made a very handsome couple. Flo of course was literally the image of our mum; a slight, perhaps boyish figure, with her slim hips and modest, but perfectly adequate bosom. Mum and Flo have always kept their ash blonde hair quite short that gave them a somewhat impish look, an abiding fashion amongst young French women. At five-feet-seven, Flo was three inches shorter than Pierre.

Pierre bore an uncanny resemblance to the bilingual French actor Jean Dujardin, the Oscar winning star of the film *The Artist*. He had dark hair, high forehead and intense, broody eyes. When he smiled his whole face lit up; it was not hard to fathom his attraction for Flo.

Pierre was Parisian and had trained there before taking up his current position as sous chef at Le Ramuncho Restaurant, a high-end eatery in Biarritz. Mum tells the story of their whirlwind love affair.

They started cohabiting in Pierre's Biarritz apartment as soon as Flo had served out her notice at the law firm in Windsor where she was a paralegal; they married three months later. Weather and job permitting, Pierre and Flo would spend weekends messing about on Soufflé, with trips to the islands during longer breaks. Mum and Dad spent several summer holidays with them in their flat and fell in love with sailing at the same time.

***

Paris and Flo had hardly ever spent more than two weeks apart in their entire lives, and both found the separation very hard. Both marriages were good but their bond as twins was perhaps stronger. Flo got a job with an Anglo-French firm of financial advisors which served the considerable British expat community in southwest France, earned good money with commissions on investment plans, but became increasingly unsettled.

Their love was never in doubt, and it was Pierre who suggested that they move to England as soon as he could find a position.

***

The world of French haute cuisine has many of the attributes of a brotherhood amongst its senior practitioners. Pierre's chef, Michel Legarson, was very fond of both him and Flo and was understanding of their position. He put out the word and fielded the enquiries as to Pierre's strengths, whilst simultaneously seeking his replacement.

It was a phenomenal turn of luck that a sous chef position became available near Windsor, and in short order, Flo and Pierre flew to England and stayed with Mum and Dad at Maidenhead for the weekend of Pierre's interview with the chef, Christophe Mauger, and the owners of Le coq en Pâte, a two-star Michelin restaurant, just upriver from Eton on the north bank of the Thames, directly opposite, on the south bank, was the Royal town of Windsor. The chef was well briefed about Pierre's abilities and needed only to assure himself that they would work well together.

***

Windsor Castle is one of the queen's official residences and the restaurant often hosted minor royals. There is a photograph in the foyer of the queen's sister, Princess Margaret, and her then fiancé, Tony Armstrong-Jones, later Lord Snowden, tucking into a late supper. The place handled celebs, especially royalty, well, with discrete seating and a nearby table for close-protection officers.

There was a small studio apartment above the restaurant that Pierre and Flo could use until they found their own place.

With everything settled and all parties happy, especially Flo and Paris, Mum announced that she was pregnant!

I was on my way.

***

No child ever had such a wonderful infancy as mine. I had two mums who looked exactly the same, and two dads who did not! Auntie Flo and Uncle Pierre doted on me and so looked forward to starting their own family. Pierre flourished under chef Christophe and within a couple of years, was tacitly understood to be the crown prince for when Christophe retired in the not-too-distant future.

Flo took a job clerking for a firm of solicitors, Frank Stokes and Partners, in Eton, home of the famous school of that name, and on the north bank of the Thames opposite Windsor. She and Pierre were actively trying for a baby, and Frank Stokes, a lifelong bachelor, took a warm fatherly interest in his lovely clerk and her 'exotic' husband with the funny accent. He handled Pierre's work and residency formalities and let Flo understand that, if and when she and Pierre started a family, she could count on her job on a part-time basis to suit her needs.

Through Flo, Frank Stokes met my mum and dad, and over time became both a family friend and our solicitor.

***

Pierre had the marina take Soufflé out of the water and into storage on the hard standing. He put his flat with a holiday letting agency and settled down with Flo in a three-bedroom house in Virginia Water; the mortgage largely covered by the income from the flat in Biarritz. Pierre and Flo reserved a couple of weeks in the flat every summer, and again in early autumn, for their own or mum and dad's use, often as a foursome. They had the marina check out Soufflé, antifoul her below the water line, and put her back in the water before their first visit each year.

For the duration of Mum's pregnancy with me, and the first six months of my life, Mum and Dad did not visit France but took the opportunity to do two sail training courses at Brighton Marina, about an hour and a half drive south from Maidenhead.

The first course was the Royal Yachting Association's Competent Crew, and the second, the Day Skipper qualification. The latter was the required qualification for the International Certificate of Competence. Both courses entailed a few days at sea and some shore classes. Flo was more than happy to take care of me when they were sailing.

Everyone seemed to have the life they had ordered, except for one thing, Flo could not conceive. Pierre's sperm count was adequate, and scans showed that Flo's egg department was all in order—but the two never seemed to want to get together. IVF was discussed and discarded, they would do it the old-fashioned way, or not at all.

***

Charlise arrived a year and a half after me, never pronounced her name properly, and has never been known as other than Charlie.

Dad declared the family complete, Mum agreed, and Dad had a vasectomy.

****

Granddad Tubs passed away after three years in the retirement home; he was eighty-three. The whole event passed very naturally, with no great demonstrations of grief. Tubs' sole surviving partner in the group practice, a youngster of eighty-one, shed a tear during his eulogy, and Dad's voice caught a couple of times during his. The celebrant at the secular funeral was a humanist that Frank Stokes had arranged and was attended by several of Grandad Tubs' former patients. Music for the event was 100% Elvis!

Every Sunday for the last three years of Tubs' life, Flo would pick him up from the home in Virginia Water, not far from her and Pierre's house, and bring him to his old house for lunch and to spend the afternoon with us. Pierre rarely joined us as Sunday lunch was a very busy time at Le Coq. We changed very little at the family house during that time so as not to upset Tubs, but after his death we embarked on a major renovation, using up a sizable chunk of the proceeds from the sale of our old house in Cookham Dean.

A modern kitchen was designed and installed with Pierre as project manager, followed by a total revamp of the living/dining/patio area. Next was our turn, and Charlie and I got a new updated bathroom and bedrooms, largely to our own design.

This period was to prove very formative for Charlie and me.

****

At age thirteen my voice broke and my testes dropped. Previous attempts at self-pleasuring had climaxed in a dull ache, but now I had something to show for my efforts! Charlie was fascinated, and very much enjoyed participating.

We had both been subjected to the usual school sex education, by hugely blushing, overly fast talking, teachers, which culminated in the much-anticipated fitting of a condom over a length of broom handle. Masturbation was brushed over, no pun intended, but without any indication of the life-changing joy it engendered. Like most pubescent teenagers, we learned far more from the internet.

My elevation was very shortly followed by the onset of Charlie's menstrual periods. I wondered if her participation in my pleasure might have in some way helped to trigger her hormones. Whatever, I was more than happy both to observe, as well as to join in, as we jointly explored her new, and our joint, emerging sexuality. I sensed something akin to vulnerability in observing Charlie in her moments, and it triggered in me a much-enhanced level of tenderness for her.

We were aware, although not quite certain why, that our practice was somehow 'wrong'; for us it was a logical and loving evolution of the love we had always shared.

In common with a lot of the world's major problems, the condemnation of sibling sex largely emanated from religious dogma. The only practical reason for the taboo, as far as we could see, was the issue of children of such unions.

We were lucky that, in our family, and hence our upbringing, religious faith had never clouded our thoughts. Our evidence-based thinking thus ignored the religious aspect, but the possibility of offspring, when we were little more than emerging from childhood ourselves, was cause to ponder, especially, as we knew, the diminished genetic diversity increased the risk of deformity.

It was clear to us that the exploration of our sexuality was leading inexorably toward penetrative sex, and we were somewhat shy of taking that step. Looking back on that period, I feel quite proud of the responsibility we demonstrated.

We were, in many respects, enjoying quite a full experience in that we both regularly climaxed through our mutual self-pleasuring. I learned quite early on how the female orgasm was a deeper and more complex experience than the male, and that these early exploratory efforts of ours were actually a magic self-learning curve for our later facility at foreplay.

In terms of love and affection, Charlie and I regarded our lives as somewhat better than any norm that we knew of, but from the very start of our sex lives, we innately knew that this needed to be kept secret.

***

We waited about a year and a half before taking the final step. We knew that Charlie's hymen would break and that some pain would ensue, and that I would need to use a condom. I bought a packet from a vending machine outside a pharmacy in Maidenhead and told Charlie that the call was hers. Some days later, as she came off her climax on my leg, she straddled my thighs and had a condom in her hand. I had been concentrating on her pleasure and not cum yet, but I had a fit-to-burst erection. Charlie discarded the wrapper and unrolled the condom on me.

Shifting position above me Charlie very tentatively put the tip of my penis between her wet labia and paused. I looked up into her eyes and she locked hers on mine. Charlie's breasts were developing nicely and I now put my hands on them, the little nipples hard against my palms. With the gentlest of movements, never breaking eye contact, she started to move in tiny increments, down then up, but each time lowering herself slightly more. I felt the resistance of her hymen, she winced, and backed off slightly, before lowering herself again. I felt the resistance increase and then disappear, Charlie cried out with her hand over her mouth but kept lowering herself until I reached the limit. With a deep sigh she settled, unmoving, grinned broadly and wept. I think we were both surprised at how overwhelming this moment was. Charlie started to lift herself, and now I cried out, so she slid down again, and then again, just the twice, and in that instant I came. We would never forget this moment.

CHAPTER FOUR

SEPARATION

Charlie and I had made the decision to put our love affair on hold for the duration of our first term as freshers. We had started university at the same time due to my having to retake my A-levels. Both Oxford and Cambridge had very exacting entry standards, which I had just failed to achieve at my first attempt.

We had known for several years that the sexual aspect of our love was illicit, and indeed illegal, considering the act itself, and compounded by the age of consent in the UK being sixteen.

We talked about our future if things stayed the same. Having children was not an option for us, and the social implications, if and when our secret came out, were potentially very bad. On the other hand, if we lived our university experience to the full, we might find that the expansion of our social lives could well involve student love affairs, and all that that implied: in fact, normal life. Indeed, during this past term, I had marvelled at the sexual vigour and plurality amongst the hormone-saturated student body, but had, not yet at least, participated.

At a certain level, as the elder brother, and even though we were equals in our relationship, I felt some sense of responsibility for Charlie. There was an element in my thinking that I was releasing her to review her options, without restraint, and of course, the same applied to myself. If we did finish our sex life we would look back on our life to date with enormous affection for the rest of our lives. The prospect of separation was heart-breaking for both of us, but we were sure that we were doing the responsible thing.

In terms of avoiding contact as much as possible, we agreed to text each other with any plans for weekend visits home.

My first day at Oxford was the saddest day of my life to date.

Our separation would last ten weeks.

***

My general state of mind in those early days at Oxford was very low over the separation from Charlie. I did not think for a moment that there was anyone else for me, but we would see over the coming weeks.

Now that we were back together, our love secure, we relaxed into our relationship with greater maturity. We were studying for our future careers, and could logically expect intellectually stimulating, not to say well-paid, positions. We did however understand that we needed an equally mature attitude to the inherent risk that was the only cloud we could see on our joint horizon.

CHAPTER FIVE

NEW DAY

Charlie and I showered together, gently washing each other with a great warmth of love. We were both in a somewhat quiet and reflective mood after the amazing reaffirmation of our love yesterday, but today we needed to get serious and discuss the implications, and they were daunting.

The great thing was, that there was certainty that we would face the future together now, absolutely together, come what may.

***

We had eaten so well yesterday that we both just had a continental breakfast of yoghurt, croissants, juice and coffee.

When we got back to the room we left the 'Do not disturb' sign on the door. Once inside we embraced, rocking a little as we do. We'd misted up as we held each other, a mixture of love and trepidation messing with our emotions. We sat in the chairs by the window and looked out at the lovely rolling Cotswold hills. Charlie started.

"I want to tell you Nat how it has been for me. I was the lowest I could possibly be when I arrived at Cambridge. Not a day passed that I didn't think to call or text you to see if we could rethink what we were doing to ourselves. To be apart like that was so wrong." Charlie was weeping softly and I rose to hold her. "No Nat, sit down, I really need to get all this out." She was gazing out the window in an unfocussed way, composing her thoughts, "I think I might have been losing it had it not been for Maggie. She's an amazing friend and I had to tell her how much I was missing my 'boyfriend' to account for my depression, and that we had separated on a trial basis. Of course I never let on why, just saying it was complicated. She told me she also had someone back home. However, she has nonetheless plunged headfirst into student life and all that that entailed. Maggie had been in residence for a week before I arrived and already had a circle of drinking mates. I was drawn into her gang despite my protests. Apart from Maggie, I made a great friend of a media studies student called David," Charlie now grinned through her tears and I found I was not breathing. "David is known to all of us as Camp David…"

I breathed out! "I want you to meet David and Maggie as soon as possible. I love them dearly. They have been there for me every step throughout this awful time. You must come up to Cambridge soon next term, you'll love them too."

I was quiet now, thinking. There was much unsaid about how she had coped, but the principal message was that she had never wavered in her love for me, and at no time doubted mine.

Charlie continued, "I have never stopped loving you for a second Nat. I have been totally faithful to you, and our love, in thought and deed."

"You don't need to say that Charlie, we are as one in all that you have said." And it was true. "Do they know that we are siblings?" I asked.

"No. I don't think we can ever go down that road Nat."

There was a pregnant pause, "I agree, and that's the big question, isn't it? Do we have to spend our whole lives as if we were some sleeper cell of spies? And if so, what kind of life will it be? Lying by omission at best."

***

I looked at the time, it was noon, we should be checking out; I rang reception,

"Good morning Mr Cooper, how can I help you?"

"If at all possible, could I ask for a late checkout please?"

There was a pause and a few keyboard clicks, "How about four o'clock?"

"That's great, many thanks."

Charlie rose from her chair, "Hold me Nat."

We embraced. "More than anything Nat I want us to be in love forever, maybe we just need to be very careful—what else is there to do?"

"So, it's as simple as that, whatever happens, let's just do it!" I said. So our 'serious' conversation had not resolved anything, and yet Charlie had put it all in perspective and resolved everything!

"Let's enjoy this big bed for a while," said Charlie softly.

So we did.

CHAPTER SIX

RE-ENTRY

Charlie drove us back to Oxford where I picked up my holdall from the porter's lodge at my hall of residence.

We had spent a truly lovely afternoon in the hotel. Our high passion of yesterday, born of our ten weeks of chastity, now a glowing affirmation of the love we shared. We dozed in soft embrace and only just made the four o'clock check out.

It was less than an hour's drive to Maidenhead down the M40 motorway and we talked about this return to family, the Christmas and New Year thing. Would our parents notice the change in us, and if so comment on it? We were much more at ease than when we had left, our relationship secure, but the need for subterfuge, and the inherent dishonesty of it, was as before.

***

Both of us had visited home during the term, but never at the same time. Charlie had told me that Mum had voiced her concern about her weight loss, but she had told her not to worry, it was just poor appetite through homesickness, missing them and me. The dishonesty had actually already started, we had led our parents to believe that Charlie was driving down today to pick me up on her way back to Maidenhead.

We'd had nothing to eat since our light breakfast in the hotel this morning and were starving when we arrived home. Mum was on her own and the three of us had a stand-up love-in welcome home.

We were rudely interrupted as something thumped against our legs, I looked down to find a huge Labrador joining our embrace.

"That's Harry," Mum said. "Tub brought him home a couple of days ago. He belongs to Annie, one of his theatre techs, she's being admitted to St Barts tomorrow for breast surgery, so we're dog sitting for the duration. He's no trouble, but fingers crossed for a happy outcome for Annie."

Mum said that Tub sent his love but needed to stay at the hospital tonight. His team had been working in shifts to separate Siamese twins flown in from New Delhi with their parents. The operation had lasted nine hours. One twin was in good shape, but the other was poorly. Both were in ICU and Tub was standing by.

***

Mum was keen to hear all our news and impressions of uni, and Charlie regaled her with further stories of what she had been up to with her roommate Maggie, and of course, her good buddy, Camp David. I told her about Adjim, that we were becoming great pals, and that I already had a standing invite to visit his minor 'stan. Mum said we were free to bring our mates home on weekends, but to give a couple of days' notice. With both our roommates far from home they might welcome some home life.

Mum had made a chicken casserole from one of Uncle Pierre's recipes, and in a Le Creuset that he'd given her last Christmas.

"It's all ready to go any time you want," she said. "I just have to warm it up."

Charlie and I looked at each other, grinned, and said, "Now," in unison. Mum went to the kitchen with a broad smile and returned with a bottle of Merlot and three glasses; it was just coming up to six o'clock after all!

The meal was great, and we toasted the chef in the French manner. Harry watched us eat with great interest but was very well behaved.

"I've missed you Mum, and your wonderful grub. It's great to be home for a couple of weeks," I said.

"Thank you, kind sir, what about your sister, did you miss her too?"

I looked at Charlie. "Yes, of course, quite a lot, well... every now and again, you know... from time to time... I suppose." Charlie balled her napkin and threw it at me, we all laughed.

"We talked about that in the car on the way down, it's the first time we've been apart for all our lives, and yes, we've missed each other a lot… well a bit anyway!"

Mum laughed at the pair of us, "I'd have expected nothing less, you're very close."

"She's pretty good," I said,

"You too, turd bag!" said Charlie.

"Children, children—don't spoil it for me!" Mum laughed.

I loaded the dishwasher and boiled the kettle for tea. I took out camomile for Mum, green for Charlie and bog ordinary Tetley's for myself. The girls had settled in the lounge, chatting on one of the settees with Harry at their feet. I looked over at them; I just loved my two girls to pieces. Mum was about two inches shorter than Charlie, and still a remarkably good-looking woman. Her hair was the same ash blonde as Charlie, but with a barely discernible hint of grey mixed in, they could easily pass for sisters. I had my light brown hair from Dad, which was good, otherwise Charlie and I could have been taken for brother and sister!

As I set the tea tray on the coffee table, Mum's mobile rang. She answered, it was Tub, and we watched her face collapse: from smiling and happy to tears and sadness in just a few seconds.

"I'm so sorry my love, I was hoping on hope for the better. Yes… Give my best to the guys. Yes, they've arrived safely and we've just finished dinner. Yes, I'll tell them, try to get some sleep. I love you too."

We looked at Mum as she dabbed eyes with a tissue and blew her nose.

"I'm sorry," she said. "Very bad news from your dad, he's lost one of his babies, not entirely unexpected, but there was hope. He's just told the parents via a Hindi speaking nurse, the nurse and the parents are very upset, and he left them in tears in the ICU. He's very upset himself, and will call you in the morning, hopes you'll understand."

"Of course we do Mum," I said. "He always takes it so to heart when he loses one of his babies."

In the silence that followed I took our mugs back to the kitchen and reheated them in the microwave. Charlie was cuddled up to Mum and I joined them after I put the mugs on the table.

"Come on, tea up," I said, and we broke the love-in to sip our tea.

***

Tub was now the leading paediatric CT surgeon at Great Ormond Street, following Ozzy Hamilton's retirement last year. He and Ozzy had pioneered many paediatric surgical procedures, including micro keyhole surgery on babies still in the womb. His team now had several separations of conjoined twins under their belt, with a good proportion of them resulting in the survival of both babies. The team was in great demand, and Tub had travelled to several countries to consult with other surgeons. Great Ormond Street had charitable status, and Tub's work had featured in their appeals for donations, with Tub beaming whilst holding a twin on each arm.

***

A rather subdued Tub arrived home in the early afternoon the next day and gave us a big welcome home hug. Charlie and I expressed our sympathy for his physical and emotional ride over the last few days.

He had dark rings of fatigue around his eyes and promptly went up for a shower and nap. Pierre had a rare evening off, and he and Flo were to join us for dinner and a catch up in the evening.

As ever, Pierre brought a contribution; this time a stunning gravlax that he had marinated at Le Coq over the last three days, for our starter.

The dinner was a celebration of the return of Charlie and me after our first serious spell away from home. We spoke of our courses and first impressions of uni life.

Over dessert, Auntie Flo tapped her glass to gain our attention, she looked at Charlie and me and said, "You lovely young people have been kept out of a secret that Pierre and I want to share with you." Flo took Pierre's hand. "I'm expecting your niece or nephew this coming summer!"

While Charlie and I jumped up to hug a tearful Aunt Flo, Mum said, "Sorry to keep it from you two, but Flo wanted to wait till we were all together!"

As we broke our embrace Pierre went to the fridge and brought a bottle of bubbles to the table, while Mum set out the flutes.

Flo went on, "We know I'm a bit long in the tooth for this, but it's a dream come true for us, isn't it Pierre?"

"Certainly is," said a grinning Pierre as he popped the cork. "I thought it would never happen, but we had to keep trying, keep our hand in, so to speak!" We laughed and toasted the pair of them.

Tub chipped in, "Lots of people have babies in their forties these days, we're fully geared up—no worries!"

Pierre jumped in, "Yes, but I'm in my fifties!"

"Not to worry, we'll look after you too!" said Tub.

The dinner, the champagne and the close family camaraderie, made the evening memorable; we were all truly happy about our prospective new family member.

Tub excused himself soon after midnight. "Been a hectic couple of days," he said and kissed us all good night. To Charlie and me he said, "Great to have us all together, eh?" And he gave us a special squeeze.

Flo had taken only a sip of champagne for the toast so Pierre gave her the car keys, looked up to the heavens, and crossed himself—Flo punched him on the arm!

Charlie and I stayed up with Mum for a while, chatting about Flo and middle-age childbirth.

"Tub has strongly advised Flo to plan for a Caesarean right from the word go," said Mum. "Can't be too careful with a first baby at our age!" Charlie started yawning then and kissed us good night. Mum and I cleared the table, washed the crystal flutes by hand, and loaded up the washer with the rest.

I kissed Mum and gave her a hug. "Great evening Mum—good to be home!" And then I went to join Charlie in our 'wing'. Harry followed me and I put an old blanket on the floor for him.

***

I cleaned my teeth and found Charlie in my bed. I undressed and pulled back the duvet to find her naked except for her panties.

"Sorry Nat! I'm hors de combat for a few days." Charlie only ever wore panties in bed when she had her period.

"Not a problem, you know that, just give me a cuddle," I said, as I slipped in beside her. When our wing was renovated, we had both chosen three quarter sized beds, somewhere between a single and a double, plenty wide enough for 'joint activity' but even so, sleeping was another thing, and we usually returned to our own rooms at some point during the night. I kissed her neck and caressed her tummy and breast.

"Things might get messy Nat if you keep that up," said Charlie. "Do you want me to help you out?" she grinned. "I'm not so selfish—you know that." And it was true. Charlie gave me a sisterly kiss and went to her room. Harry stayed where he was, snoring gently!

CHAPTER SEVEN

YACHT

When Charlie and I were growing up, we would always take at least one holiday each year in Biarritz; often with Pierre and Flo. Pierre's flat had only two bedrooms, so Charlie and I would 'camp out' in the living room if all six of us were there together. One of us on the clic-clac convertible settee, and the other on a folding single bed. The six of us became too much for one car, so the two couples bought a second-hand VW Transporter seven-seater between them, a second car for both families. We would take the ferry from Portsmouth to Santander in northern Spain, just a short drive, less than three hours, from Biarritz. The ferry took exactly a day to make the crossing of the Bay of Biscay, and we would take two cabins. The short passage was a great way to start our holidays, except for the occasional rough weather that the bay was notorious for. We made much use of Soufflé, but she too was getting too small for all six of us. Charlie and I had caught the sailing bug early on, and took the RYA courses together, as soon as Charlie was old enough.

Soufflé was a good size for a couple, just about OK for two couples, but crowded with six! Pierre put Soufflé on the market with a broker in Biarritz at the end of our last summer holiday before we started at uni. We were unanimous in wanting to sail the Mediterranean and equally so in not having to sail all around the coast of Spain and Portugal to get there.

On our return home we all put our heads together and firstly agreed on the specification for a new boat, and then studied the market to establish a budget. In parallel with all that, we bought all the sailing guide books for the Med coasts of France and Spain, as well as Italy, Greece, Turkey and the Dalmatian coast of the former Yugoslavia.

Charlie and I were over the moon with this development, and spent many hours late into the night, relishing our prospects. The long holidays from uni, when we started our courses, would give us opportunities as never before when the boat was not in family use. We could go down to wherever the boat was to do chores on board, sail to new places chosen by consensus as to where we all wanted to start our next season's cruising, but mainly, it would be the first time in our life that we could be together, as a couple, for extended periods without having to worry about our secret.

Dad contacted a UK-syndicated yacht broker who put our search parameters to the market throughout western Europe.

***

The eventual purchase of our boat, a little-used, five-year-old, forty-six-foot Bavaria, and the estimated annual budget for insurance, marina fees and general maintenance, gave Charlie and me our first adult appreciation of our family's wealth; we were frankly taken aback. Tub was absolutely at the top of his game, an internationally acclaimed CT surgeon, senior member of the Royal College, and visiting professor at two top UK medical schools. Mum still worked from home on a part-time basis, largely managing the hospital's charitable efforts.

Pierre and Flo, the 'other half' of our extended family, were also doing very well. Pierre was now Chef of Le Coq, had a good salary, plus a handsome profit-sharing bonus. Flo still worked with Frank Stokes.

Our two families were equal partners in the yacht, which had all the modern facilities that made it easy to sail with just a crew of two. She was sloop rigged, with roller furling for both main and headsail, a bow thruster for easy docking, anchoring control from the cockpit, and all the modern electronics, including autopilot, radar and a GPS plotter.

The yacht was called Mathilde, and based on the south coast of France, at Le Lavandou. Tub and Pierre flew down for a three-day weekend in early September for sailing trails and price negotiation. Mathilde was taken out of the water for a survey. The local surveyor gave her a clean bill of health, and the deed was done. Mathilde was French flagged, which we kept, and the registered address changed to Pierre's flat in Biarritz. It was decided to keep Mathilde on the hard until we had plans for our first holiday.

CHAPTER EIGHT

CHRISTMAS AND STUFF

In honour of Pierre and his country, we always celebrated Christmas, as a family, on the 24th, with a traditional French dinner at Le Coq. Christmas Eve was one of the busiest nights of the year, but Pierre had booked our table for six well in advance. The six did not include Pierre, but he would visit our table when possible and join us later when the rush calmed down. We had invited Frank Stokes, still Flo's part-time boss, and a good family friend. Frank was now semi-retired but kept files for certain faithful old clients, such as ourselves, under his wing. As the senior member present, he insisted on sitting at the head of our table, and we happily humoured him with the honour. It was our custom to speak only French in Le Coq, but this year we made an exception so that Frank was not excluded from the banter. We'd left Harry at home as he was no trouble to leave for an evening.

There was a set menu for Christmas Eve with just two choices for each of the three courses.

The amuse-bouche, or palette exciter, was a lobster bisque served in a coffee cup sized bowl set in the centre of a regular dinner plate—all agreed it was stunning!

For starters, there was a choice of either pâté de foie gras, served with fig preserve and pain de mie' tiny toasted slices of brioche, or bouillabaisse. All six of us took the bouillabaisse. It was a speciality of Pierre's. Strictly speaking, it is a traditional fish stew from the Mediterranean coast of France, but Pierre had modified the recipe when he was working in Biarritz by substituting the fish for local varieties from the Bay of Biscay. Now in England, he had modified the recipe once again to use our local varieties. It had become a popular fixture on the Le Coq carte and a great choice for the Christmas menu.

The main course offered a choice of *Homard à L'Armoricaine avec riz de Camargue ou Carré d'agneau avec petits légumes.* Needless to say, Frank chose the rack of lamb while the rest of us took the lobster and it's mildly piquant sauce.

***

My position at the table gave me a clear view of the entrance, and I was curious when a smartly dressed, thirties-something man entered on his own. He was met by the head waiter, Harold, and shown to a table for two a short distance from an empty table set for four. He sat facing the entrance and unobtrusively scanned the dining room before saying a few words into a tiny mic on his lapel—only then did I notice a thin white curly cord from his ear that disappeared inside his jacket. Within a few seconds the head waiter opened the door and ushered in a party of four; all eyes turned toward them. The first couple was none other than the youngest daughter of one of the queen's first cousins, Lady Helen, and her fiancé. She had a higher public profile than most minor royals through her outspoken views on animal and human rights, in that order I believe, a nose piercing, and a tattoo only visible when wearing a thong bikini! She gracefully acknowledged the attention and wished those close to her a happy Christmas. The second couple were in the same age bracket but I did not recognise them. Last in was a young lady, in an LBD, silk jacket and low heeled 'sensible' shoes. She too had the curly cord, and joined her colleague, facing the body of the dining room. It was the first time I had seen a member of the royal family in casual circumstances, and was most impressed with the discreet close protection.

***

After a short while the happy hubbub of the diners resumed and the royal party settled down with a bottle of bubbles before their meal.

For our dessert, all except me, chose one of Pierre's creations; Surprise Mont Blanc, a delicate mix of chestnut, chocolate chips and a background of light vanilla-flavoured cream.

53

I took the cheese board, without desert, no insult to Pierre, but I rarely, if ever, took dessert.

We'd started our evening with yet another champagne toast to Flo and the baby. Pierre briefly came out from the kitchen, wearing his toque, to join us in the toast; Flo just took a token sip of hers. We took a second bottle over dessert, and Pierre came to join us, pulling up a chair from an empty table. Head waiter Harold came over to give his best wishes to Flo, and to wish us all a happy festive season. He then whispered something into Pierre's ear, and he rose immediately.

"Duty calls," Pierre said, and went over to the royal party. The dining room was now almost empty, and we saw Pierre talking to Lady Helen, and pointing towards our table.

She then raised her glass and called to Flo, "Hey Flo, best of luck to you and the baby, happy Christmas all." We all raised our glasses to return the good wishes.

The meal over, we relaxed over coffee and chatted in a companionable family way. Charlie and I had to fill Frank in on our first term at uni.

Frank said, "I hope you don't mind me saying so, but you wonderful people are the closest I'm ever going to get to having a family. I'm especially pleased with your news Flo—I even feel like I'm about to become a granddad! Thanks a lot for inviting me." I'm sure I noticed Frank's eyes mist over as he excused himself to visit the 'little boys' room! On his way back from the gents, Frank stopped by the head waiter's station and I guessed he was paying for our meal.

Lady Helen's party rose to leave and waved to us. The female protection officer went first, and the male indicated for the party to wait by the door, his finger pressed to his earpiece, in a moment he gestured that they could leave, and followed them out.

Time to go home; Tub gestured to Harold for the bill. Harold came straight away and whispered into Tub's ear.

Tub turned to Frank, "That's not right Frank—you're our guest for goodness' sake!"

"Nonsense," said Frank. "As your lawyer, Arthur Cooper, I am obliged to inform you that it is my absolute right, as head of the table, to take care of the bill—and happy Christmas one and all."

"Well, many thanks for that Frank, but I'll get you back—just wait and see!" We all thanked Frank and he rose to leave. It was less than a mile to his flat in Eton, and he decided to walk instead of taking our offer of a lift. We were already enjoying Flo's pregnancy as she was automatically the designated driver!

She drove us back to Maidenhead, a distance of about seven miles, before returning to wait for Pierre at Le Coq, as he wrapped up the kitchen for the night.

Harry woke up on our arrival home and went outside for a pee before sneaking off to my room!

***

Charlie and I spent the days between Christmas and New Year doing some preparatory stuff for the coming term at uni, and generally participating in family things. We were both enjoying the down time, and our parents, a great deal.

Tub took me aside one evening after dinner to talk about my course. He had wanted me to do medicine, and initially so did I. However, my poor A-level results the first time round gave me an extra year to ponder my future. I had decided against doing medicine and Tub was clearly none too happy about it. We had talked at great length then, and to his credit, he came around, was very understanding, and fully accepted my decision. I explained, firstly, that the length of the course, six years, seemed to stretch way too far into my future, and added to that, a year as a houseman, was just too much before starting meaningful work. I was also of the opinion that medicine was advancing at such a rate that there was just too much to learn, most of which would not be used after specialisation in whatever branch of medicine one chose to practice. Tub agreed and admitted that he now thought that medical training would need to be split into various disciplines, in much the same way as engineering was taught. After all, teeth and eye care were already separate professions.

So now we talked of my course, and where I wanted to go with it. My enthusiasm must have shown through, as we had an enjoyable and animated chat on what was wrong in the world of politics and government. Mum came to break up our antisocial absence and we joined the girls in the living room.

***

Later, in our 'wing', Charlie told me about a similar conversation she had had with Mum and Dad together, just the day before. She told me how much she had enjoyed telling them of her ideas for specialising in human rights law after graduation.

CHAPTER NINE

REVELATION

We were in Charlie's room, and I was sat leaning against the headboard while she sprawled across the bed, on her side, at my feet. I loved the enthusiastic glow from her when she talked of her passion for human rights. She looked gorgeous, wearing the same camisole and neutral coloured Kashmir she had worn at the hotel, and a midi length plaid skirt.

"Come up here," I said, and she hitched up her skirt and sat on my lap, with her knees either side of me. Charlie put her arms round my neck and we kissed. I slid my hands under both Kashmir and camisole to caress her unhindered breasts. Her nipples were already coming up as I lifted her camisole and Kashmir together over her head. Charlie rose onto her knees, so that her breasts were in my face, and I gently sucked first one then the other. I slid my hands down to her buttocks and smiled when I found she was not wearing panties.

"I left them in the bathroom when I had a pee just now!" she said, and started to unzip my jeans.

"Lie down," said Charlie, so I slipped down until I was flat on my back and Charlie removed my jeans and underpants; my penis was up and ready as Charlie wriggled round until her head was on my tummy, facing my erection.

"No Charlie," I said. "Come on top," I could see where this was going. Whilst I absolutely loved fallacio, it always seemed immensely selfish as there was little I could do for her in this position.

"Stop talking Nat, I want to have a chat with your Willy," said Charlie, as she clasped my penis around its base and licked the head in a circular motion before taking me into her lovely mouth. She used her tongue to wet my shaft before gently sucking me further in. Charlie still had her hand round the base which she now moved in conjunction with her mouth. I relaxed, lay back, and totally capitulated to Charlie's will. The sensation was uniquely erotic. Charlie perfectly measured her motion to match my rising urgency. It was impossible to moderate my need and I came massively. Charlie met each wave of my climax with a perfectly timed swallow until I was wonderfully spent. I lay back in utter bliss as she slowed her motion and withdrew. Charlie turned to face me, her face the very picture of love, a tiny dribble of my cum had escaped the corner of her mouth. She slid up to kiss me and I wiped the cum away with my thumb before we kissed deeply. While we kissed, Charlie swung her leg over me and pressed my deflating penis against her sex. She was remarkably wet and held me in place as she moved against it. Her eyes were shut tight, her head back, as her passion rose. I had my hands on her breasts and tugged gently on her nipples to meet the rhythm of her approaching climax. I was rapidly getting hard again, and Charlie helped me inside. Within a few strokes she was moaning in her ecstasy which, in turn, reignited my erection. I was fully up again but did not move as Charlie came off her peak. She settled right down on me as she absorbed her aftershocks with a beatific look on her face, her eyes locked on mine. After some moments Charlie slowly rose until I thought I might slip out. At the last moment she gently lowered herself again. She did that thing with her vagina to grip me gently. Her face told me that she would bring herself off again, and I followed her to that end. Her second climax brought me along with her, and I came with only a slightly, if at all, diminished intensity than when I had cum in her mouth.

"Wow!" said Charlie, her face the very picture of happiness.

"Wow to you too," I said.

We stayed like that for several minutes, my erection slowly diminishing inside her. We smiled into each other's eyes; the love between us did not need words. Charlie's smile transitioned to concentration, as she gently started to move again, she looked into my eyes with increasing intensity.

"I'm sorry Nat—I don't want to stop…" She started to moan almost immediately, her head back, Charlie moved faster and faster, until her moan was continuous. Remarkably, I too came to an aching, almost painful, dry climax. After a while we both had our breathing under control, and Charlie collapsed on me as I slipped out. I eased Charlie to my side as a great fatigue overwhelmed us and we slept in each other's arms. We slept right through to early dawn, and the first I knew of the new day was when Charlie kissed my nose!

"I need to pee," said Charlie. "But I think we're stuck together." Indeed we were, and we gently pulled apart and grinned at the experience. We showered together and embraced under the hot jet of water.

"That was wonderful Nat, just wonderful, I love you so much."

"Me too," I said, as I held her. We dried each other off, trying not to break contact, and went back to Charlie's bed and relaxed into a warm embrace. Charlie started to drop off so I kissed her and returned to my own bed. Harry was still fast asleep on my bedroom floor!

***

It was a few days later, and about a week before we had to return to uni. Mum, Charlie and I were sitting around the kitchen island counter. Mum looked serene and pensive and took some moments before speaking.

"You two must know that your dad and I love you more than life itself and want you to know that we do not feel judgemental, or in any way love you less, because of the way you love each other." She paused, and Charlie and I stared at each other in shock, she continued.

"I, in particular, understand what you must feel, with the necessity, as you see it, to keep things from us, and the guilt that you must feel over the deception. Let's go to the settee for a love-in, I have a little story to tell that will, I hope, both unburden me and help you." We moved to the sitting room area and sat in our usual three-way cuddle on the settee that looked out toward the river.

"I'm so pleased you haven't said a word in denial, and indeed am proud of you for that. I can see the shock in your faces, and I understand the turmoil your minds must be in," Mum took a moment before continuing.

"My story is about Flo and me. You obviously know how close Flo and I are, but I wonder if you have any conception of just how close it is for us as identical twins. Actually, we are not so much close as, in fact, one being, the same entity, but in two separate bodies. It has been so since our earliest memories. Our connection is much greater than love, I do not know the words to describe it—a oneness of both mind and body perhaps." Mum stopped, ordering her thoughts before going on.

"We have never had cause to explain ourselves to others, but with you, in the position you are in, I think the time has come. I see parallels that, at least in my eyes, give your relationship a legitimacy that others, almost certainly, would not." Mum paused again, then smiled.

"In some ways Flo and I were doubly damned, being both lesbian and siblings, these days we would be described as AC/DC, because we did have boyfriends, and indeed, we are both happily married."

Charlie and I were at a loss. A maelstrom of colliding emotions fought for conscious expression. In my mind, Mum's obvious love for us, her need to take away our guilt for the deception we had practised, and her exposure through revelation, overwhelmed all other thoughts. I could see that Charlie was as deeply moved as I was. Our love-in cuddle on the settee now took on a much deeper meaning.

"I love you so much Mum," I said, after a struggle to compose myself.

Mum ended the long silence that ensued. "So that's my story. I feel no guilt for what Flo and I were, and indeed still are. There's still more to it, but that's for another day…" Mum could not go on, great sobs now overwhelmed her, and that in turn ruined Charlie's and my own efforts at composure. The tears on all our cheeks, the deep love between us, and some enhanced kind of bonding, above and beyond any norm, kept us in silence. Mum stood up and suddenly we all smiled through our tears.

"Let's walk down to the river," said Mum. Harry followed us to the bank and became interested in the passing swans.

We sat in silence on the old bench close to the riverbank, each of us processing what had just occurred. Charlie and I sat on either side of Mum, with an arm around her. After some minutes, Mum disengaged and rose to face us.

"You guys OK?" We both nodded.

I said, "Where's Tub in all this?" Mum did not answer straight away. She turned her gaze up to the house as she considered her response.

"It's more complex for your dad," Mum said. "He and I have had your situation in our minds for a couple of years, for obvious reasons — no teenage love affairs, no boyfriends or girlfriends home for tea, and then, over the last two or three years, clear evidence — at least to me — that you were lovers. I did not share this part with him until he raised it earlier this year, and I confirmed his suspicions. We had the 'what-do-we-do-about-it' conversation, but it was difficult. For the first time in our marriage, I told him about Flo and me, and how that influenced, and indeed informed my feelings about you. He was not as shocked about Flo and me as I had feared and told me he had 'joined the dots' long ago." Another pause.

"Let's go back indoors, I'm getting cold!" Charlie and I got up and we walked back up the flagstone path with Mum, Harry following, and we entered the house via the patio doors. It had been chilly but sunny outside and we were only wearing sweaters. Now a breeze had picked up and the sun was obscured by cloud. Charlie and I had not noticed the cold, but the warmth of the living room was very welcome. Mum went to the kitchen to make tea, and Charlie and I just hugged each other wordlessly. Mum came back with the tea tray, grinning broadly.

"How bloody English we are," she said. "Any crisis—put the kettle on for tea!" We smiled at that and sat around the coffee table.

"Watching you two, so in love, is actually a sublime joy for me, I could not love you more, and wherever this thing goes, that will never change."

"And Tub?" I asked. Mum thought for a moment.

"Your dad loves you both as much as I do, but doctor that he is, has many misgivings, both medical and sociological. I told him that you had been on the pill since you were sixteen Charlie, and that allayed one of his greatest fears." Charlie's eyes looked fit to pop!

"How did you find out?"

"I found an empty pill card in your jeans when I went to put them in the washing machine!"

We drank our tea in a reflective silence. My thoughts were complex, but amongst them was a deep relief that our subterfuge, at least within the family, was over. But where to now?

***

Tub had left yesterday for a conference at Johns Hopkins teaching hospital in Baltimore and would not be back for four days. Mum had obviously chosen this opportunity for our talk, and I was glad; we all had a lot to process before we faced him with all this.

"Look, I have a little shopping to do, and you two have a lot to discuss; I'll see you a bit later."

Charlie and I just sat in silence on the settee for a while, then both of us started talking at the same moment.

"First thoughts?" said Charlie.

"Yeah, a couple; first is how fantastic our mum is, we're incredibly lucky, and second, the poopy's heading for the rotor when Tub gets back! And you?"

"Very mixed," said Charlie. "I feel an immense relief that Mum knows about us, I've hated all the lies, mainly by omission, granted, but nonetheless…" She let that hang. "What do you think's going to happen to us… what can happen?"

I thought for a short while, "If I'm brutally honest, I think nothing is going to happen, except maybe our relationship with Tub may change in some way… I don't know. We still love each other and nothing can change that. I mean, after all, what are Tub's options? He's always loved us, and I can't see that changing. That's not to say that he's happy about it," I paused as I processed that thought. "You know, the more I think this through, the more I see that the only real change will be ours, something like a gay guy coming out of the closet to his parents."

Charlie said, "Isn't that exactly what Mum just did with us, about her and Flo? What are we supposed to make of that?"

I said, "You know, I have absolutely no critical opinion about Mum's revelation to us. After all, in a certain way of thinking, what am I but a lesbian with advantages, well, one advantage anyway!" Charlie grinned at this and we started to loosen up a bit. Just then we heard Mum's car arrive and we went to help unload the shopping.

When we had helped unpacking and storing the shopping, Mum said, "So, how are we all doing?"

Charlie put her arms around her, "We think you're the greatest mum in all the world! We feel so relieved and grateful for your honesty and understanding Mum. You and Flo have nothing to reproach yourselves with." Mum couldn't speak but put out an arm for me to join in the hug, and we stayed like that for a long time.

"We should celebrate this moment Mum," I said. "You know, things suddenly seem much brighter, elevated, more bonded, I can't tell you how I feel so much… lighter somehow!"

Mum looked at us through misted eyes, "You two just overwhelm me, I'm lost for words!"

After a while Charlie broke the hug. "How about champagne and sandwiches for lunch?" she said, we all laughed in agreement. Mum and Charlie set out a smorgasbord of smoked salmon, black olives, salmon roe 'caviar', and cheeses on the island counter, while I sliced a country loaf Mum had just bought. Charlie brought over the flutes from the glass cabinet and Mum popped the champagne cork and gently poured the bubbles.

"A toast," said Mum. "Let's drink to whatever it is that happened here this morning!"

***

What a happy interlude that meal was! Mum went upstairs afterwards to do some work for the hospital, and Charlie and I were left to our own devices. We sat on the settee looking out down to the river. We both found the river a calming influence, much like sitting on a seashore and gazing out to sea, a focusing device for contemplation. Harry looked at us without comment—and went back to sleep!

Charlie said, "I'm at the point of weeping all the time, I'm so happy!" The sun was out again and I suggested we take a walk along the river. We wrapped up well and set out. Just downstream from our house, the Thames divided to flow around a very pretty pair of wooded islands. We stopped and watched the occasional river traffic and an older couple, on a narrowboat, watering their flowerpots.

***

All was well with our little world.

CHAPTER TEN

TUB

Charlie and I cooked a Shepherd's Pie for our dinner on the evening before Dad came home from the States. Pierre had suggested once, when we had made this jewel of English haute cuisine for him, to use finely diced lamb, dusted with flour and sauteed, instead of mince; it was a huge improvement.

Charlie and I were concerned over Tub's return, but not as worried as we had been earlier. Mum complimented us on our pie.

"How's tomorrow going to pan out Mum?" asked Charlie.

"Don't be too concerned. I spoke with your dad last night and he's fully up to speed on what we've been up to. Maybe best not to mention the bubbles yesterday though!" Mum smiled and our mood lifted, "I'm picking him up from Heathrow after lunch tomorrow, I'll do my best to put him in the right mood."

***

That night, Charlie and I talked for a long time in my bed, but not to much effect, we'd just take whatever happened when Tub got back tomorrow. Mum had been great, and we felt reassured that things would work out.

I saw that Charlie was grinning. "What are you thinking?" I asked.

"Just a silly thought," said Charlie. "Do you think we can ask for a bigger bed now we're out of the closet?" I laughed with her and she threw a leg over me. We often made love very gently in this position, with slower motions and deliberately long slow climaxes. It was deeply loving and very satisfying. Charlie would always kneel over me for this, and control things far better than I ever could. Her trick was to slow down as she was about to climax and stop as she came, absorbing the orgasm with slight lifts as the waves rode over her. I would gently massage her breasts all the while. She had a way of pressing down on me for maximum penetration as she came and had amazing control. Her long soft orgasms invariably brought me along with her, and I would just lay back and let it all happen.

We had a very special afterglow this time. Charlie stayed in position for a long while until my penis had shrunk to a mere shadow of his former self. I reached for the box of Kleenex and held it for her to pull out a couple of tissues which she held to her as she lifted off. I opened my legs and Charlie slipped between them. She lay fully over me and we shared a long and loving kiss before she rolled off and headed for the shower. I followed her into the shower, and afterwards we went back to my bed to sleep in each other's arms.

***

After lunch the next day Charlie and I took Harry for a long walk while Mum drove to Heathrow to pick up Tub. We deliberately avoided any further speculation about what the rest of the afternoon might bring.

Mum had left home with over an hour to spare before the expected arrival time of Tub's seven-hour flight from Baltimore. Heathrow was very close to Maidenhead, just fifteen miles, and under normal conditions would take under half an hour along the M4 motorway, and then briefly on the M25, which was London's outer ring road. Traffic on the M25 was often subject to delays from sheer volume of cars as well as accidents. It's reputation as the world's largest car park was well earned.

We'd walked for over an hour and Harry was getting very tired by the time we arrived home. We were very surprised to see Mum's car already in the driveway and rushed in to see if all was well. Mum was sitting at the kitchen island and Tub's topcoat was on the settee with his flight bag.

"Where's Tub?" Charlie asked. "Is everything OK?"

"He's fine and taking a shower," Mum replied. "His flight was early due to something about the jet stream, and I had almost no time to wait—good job I left early!"

Harry had collapsed on the kitchen floor and was already snoring when Tub came down the stairs in his dressing gown. He came straight to us and gave Charlie and me a long hug.

"Welcome back Dad," I said. "How was it?"

"Well worth the trip, I was even offered a job!" he said. "But before I tell you all about it, we all know that there's a conversation we need to have. Let's sit in the lounge and get to it."

We moved to the two settees that faced each other over the coffee table.

Tub started: "Your mum and I have had something of a roller coaster ride recently. What with your situation and other stuff about her and Flo. I know she's talked to you about all this and I've had time to collect my thoughts. The first thing I want to say is that your mum and I are solid; if anything, we are probably even stronger!" Tub looked up as Mum arrived with a tea tray and sat next to him. They linked arms and smiled as they turned their attention back to Charlie and me.

"So on to you two," he continued. "The first thing to say is that my love for you has not wavered. I must admit that your situation has not affected me as much as some might expect, indeed I only wish for your happiness no matter what the future brings," Tub paused and shared a wry smile with Mum. "We might have wished for grandchildren at some time and I know you're fully cogent that you cannot even think about that. So let me say this; we are where we are, as they say these days, and your mum and I are in full agreement that the status quo is OK with us. It's indeed very positive that things are now out between us, and you no longer need to feel any guilt. So there, you have it!"

Both Mum and Charlie had tears in their eyes. Charlie and I embraced, and I felt her tears roll down my cheek; I dared not speak over the lump in my throat. We eventually broke our hug and found Mum and Dad also hugging each other. Mum dabbed her cheeks, and we drank our tea.

Charlie broke the silence, "Thanks for all that you've said Dad—I think I'm going to cry again!" A great sob escaped her as her voice rose and I again held her.

"I've got nothing to add to that," I said. "It's all a profound relief to us, we love you both so much, thanks for everything!" My eyes brimmed over.

Tub was fading fast by dinner time as the jet lag kicked in and he yawned through an account of his trip. The paper that he had read during the formal presentations was received well and engendered some lively discussion in the ensuing debate. His topic had been ethics and logic of radical interventions, which he illustrated with his experience of conjoined twin separations.

The job offer he had alluded to earlier was an invitation to be a visiting 'fellow', or professor, to Johns Hopkins Medical School.

"I'll talk about it with you all later, but it would involve three or four trips to the States each year. There's also the issue of my work at Great Ormond Street, I seem to be moving away from day-to-day surgery—I need to get my head round where I want to go with this career of mine!" Tub rose and kissed us all goodnight. "Right now I need some shuteye before I fall over! Night all!"

It was barely eight o'clock and Mum, Charlie and I went through to the lounge area.

"So, how do you feel now?" said Mum. Charlie spoke first.

"I feel almost lightheaded with relief," she replied. "This is actually our second episode of this relief feeling."

"How so?" said Mum.

"Well, the first was over whether or not we could, or should, carry on with the way we've been living all this time."

I took over, "I wonder if you noticed Mum, that we deliberately avoided contact with each other for this first term at uni. Our idea was that we should in some way test ourselves by experiencing the student life, the expanded social aspects, and all that entailed, which we have done." Charlie took up the explanation,

"We planned to meet up at the end of term and see how we felt after such a break. We met up on the Saturday before coming home and had a fantastic reunion. We spent the weekend reaffirming our feelings, our love for each other, and stayed in a nice hotel before driving home on Sunday—sorry for the white lie about that!"

"That was the first relief Mum," I said. "We had missed each other terribly but so hated the inherent deceit of our relationship, these last few days with you, and now Dad, have been such a wonderful thing."

Mum had been smiling lovingly while Charlie and I had been trying to explain ourselves, and now just opened her arms for us to join her. We snuggled up in a silent love-in for some while.

"Your dad and I did notice the changes; the avoidance of joint visits home being the most obvious," Mum said. "But it was the way you were with each other, the glow if you like, when you came home that gave me the resolve to have the conversation that we had while he was in the States."

"Both you and Dad have been amazing," said Charlie. "What fantastic parents, if I had a god or two I'd feel blessed!"

I got up to make our various teas. I felt quite drained and was continuously yawning.

"I'm off to bed soon," I said, as I put the tray on the coffee table. "I feel like I've run a marathon!"

"I'm off too," said Mum. "What a day, what a wonderful day!" We drank our tea, kissed Mum good night, and went to our 'wing'.

CHAPTER ELEVEN

BACK TO SCHOOL

Charlie and I started our second term at uni in mid-January. Our lives had changed dramatically over the winter break and we were still dizzy with admiration for the way in which our parents had handled our 'situation'.

Our 'outing' with Mum and Dad had lifted the heavy load of guilt that we had felt for several years, and at least within the family, legitimised our love. However, we well understood that nothing had changed with regard to our interaction with the rest of the world.

***

Charlie and I spent the majority of our weekends at home and effectively became weekly boarders at university. Charlie became a reserve player for the second eleven football team at Cambridge and was required, on occasion, to sit on the substitute bench for Saturday matches. The first time she played during that term I was there to cheer from the side lines. It was the third weekend of the new term and Charlie played midfield in the second half as substitute for an injured centre half. I was very proud of her performance. Cambridge won with the only goal of the match early in the second half, and it was Charlie who set it up from the right wing for the centre forward to head home. I joined the players and supporters at the pub after the game and met Maggie and Camp David for the first time. I liked them both immediately. The beer flowed freely but I largely abstained as I had the family VW van with me and needed to drive us home after the pub. David was a wonderful guy and I had a good chat with him before the beer and noise made conversation impossible. Maggie and Charlie were arm in arm and very merry. The captain called for order to offer a toast to Charlie as the star of the game.

Charlie was required to down a pint in salute as the group chanted, "Down, down, down…" Until her glass was empty! Maggie again called for order to announce that she would be performing in a stand-up fringe event at this year's Edinburgh Festival; the 'mob' shouted for her to tell a joke!

"That's good timing as I need to test a new joke," said Maggie after a swig of her beer. "Here goes! So Thor, the god of thunder, was over Scotland directing a mighty storm over the lowlands, when he spotted a crofter's daughter, herding her sheep to shelter. Thor fell instantly in love, and breaking all the godly laws, descended to appear before her. She too fell in love with him at first sight and they went into the croft. After an evening and night of endless love the crofter's daughter looked into Thor's eyes and said, 'I never dreamed I'd meet such a lover as you, I'm completely overwhelmed.'

Thor said, 'I have something I must admit to you, you see, I'm Thor!' The crofter's daughter laughed, 'I'm nay surprised, me… I can hardly walk!'" Maggie sat and basked in the raucous approval and the landlord declared a free round on the house! Charlie had introduced me as her brother and Maggie drunkenly did her best to chat me up!

***

The drive from Cambridge to Maidenhead would normally take less than two hours for the eighty-mile trip directly down the A1(M), but Charlie started to feel unwell early in the trip and went very pale. I pulled into the next services and Charlie only just managed to get her door open before she vomited. I held her from the side and gently rubbed her back until she had got rid of a stomach full of beer. I reached into the van for tissues and a bottle of water from the door pocket and wiped her mouth with a tissue as I guided her away from the smelly puddle.

"I'm so sorry Nat, I feel awful!" Charlie rinsed her mouth with the water, took a couple of deep breaths and looked up sheepishly. We walked around the car park for a while, and I kept my arm around her.

"Better out than in," I said. "You'll feel better soon."

"It was that last pint that did it… but what could I do?" said Charlie. "I'm hungry now!" We walked slowly to the coffee shop and I sat Charlie down at a table overlooking the car park. At the cafeteria-style display I bought a couple of ham and cheese submarines and two paper cups of coffee from a vending machine. While Charlie tucked into her sandwich, I called home to say we were running a bit late and to start dinner without us. "Not to worry," said Mum. "We had a late lunch with Flo and Pierre, so we'll wait for you." Charlie reclined her seat in the van and slept for the rest of the ride.

***

We eventually arrived home just before nine o'clock and Mum immediately served the cold dinner of pastrami, mixed salad and fresh country bread. The pastrami and bread were from Le Coq that Pierre had brought over when he and Flo had come for lunch earlier. Mum and Dad were very pleased with Charlie's account of the match and her 'stardom' for setting up the winning goal. She made an awful attempt at telling Maggie's joke to such a degree that no one 'got it'! We didn't mention Charlie's minor mishap on the way home!

***

"I met Camp David and Maggie for the first time," I said. "They're both great, I liked them straight away, Charlie is very lucky to have such mates close to her."

"What's the team's attitude to heading the ball?" said Tub, "You know it's getting a lot of attention these days—several famous retired players have gone down with early-onset dementia."

"Yeah, we're aware of that, our coach is encouraging us to practice Wayne Rooney style overhead kicks, especially the forwards, to limit it. For midfielders like me, the main problem is intercepting balls from the goalie at the other end. The men can take it on the chest but that's also a problem for us girls. I don't know where the conversation will go—maybe some type of helmet. The Americans have the same issue with their version of the game, and they already have helmets! I absolutely avoid heading as much as I can, but can you imagine football without it?"

"We'll see—just be aware that's all!" said Tub.

71

Charlie started yawning. "I'm off," she said. "A bit knackered from the game!" Harry followed Charlie to our wing and I asked Tub how Annie was doing after her surgery.

"Could be better, I'm afraid," he said. "I'm actually quite concerned. She's had a radical mastectomy and now she's undergoing radiotherapy to neutralise remaining traces in her lymphatic system. The trouble is that the lymphatic system is often the conduit for metathesis. She could have traces elsewhere in her organs that could pop up anytime in the future."

"Is she still in hospital?"

"No, she's at home and goes back in a couple of times a week for the radiotherapy. I go round to see her at least once a week, as do others on the team. She always asks after Harry but she's too weak to have him back yet. She's in the trade, so to speak, and knows exactly where she's at. We might have Harry for some time."

"I'm so sorry to hear that, Dad; I know what a softy you are!" I was so pleased to have Tub unload on me like this. I think it was a first; something like a rite of passage in our relationship.

"I only met Annie once when you had all your team here for a BBQ last year. She was very jolly. I remember her putting on her original Jamaican accent to tell some very fruity jokes!

"We all miss her enormous smile around the theatre. You know, this doctoring job has much in common with the police. We deal with tragedy on an almost daily basis. We try to be very professional but it's very hard sometimes, especially when it's one of your own."

The emotion was starting to drag down the lines around his eyes and he was quiet for some moments.

He continued, "You know, cancer treatment has made much progress during my career but it's still almost mediaeval in some regards. In the black humour jargon of the trade, we call it 'slash, burn and poison' for surgery, radiotherapy and chemo—it's not far wrong!"

"Sad as this is, Dad, I'm very pleased with this chat. You're a good man Tub Cooper, and a great father."

Tub gave a grim smile, kissed my forehead, and said, "I'm off to bed; sorry to burden you!"

"No burden at all, Dad, sleep well!"

***

I hung around for a while before following Charlie; she was fast asleep and snoring softly, when I looked in her room.

I took a quick shower before going to bed and slept right through until I heard Charlie in the shower. She came naked to my bed and tucked in with me.

"I'm a dirty cow," she said. "I was too tired to even brush my teeth last night! So, what did you think of my chums yesterday?"

"As I said over dinner, I think they're great, I'm so pleased to have met them."

"Oh! I forgot that—what else can't I remember about dinner?" she giggled and snuggled up to me. "Maybe it's the heading!" Charlie put a hand on my penis. "I'm not after anything, honestly!" she said, and slipped on top; a happy playful grin on her lips.

***

Breakfast is a bit of a rolling feast at home and Mum and Dad had already finished when we turned up. They sat with us as we drank a whole cafetière of Lavazza between us and nibbled some toast and marmalade.

"How's Flo doing?" I asked.

"Doing very well I'm relieved to say," said Mum. "She's absolutely blooming, and her baby bump is coming along nicely."

"Do we have a likely date yet?" said Charlie.

"She can tell you all about it herself, she should be here for lunch soon, Pierre is working of course."

A very happy looking Flo arrived at noon and gave us a big hug. We sat facing out to the river as she regaled us with all her baby news.

"The provisional date is the last week of July. That's pretty accurate as my Caesarean is pre-booked. It needs to be a little premature as they don't want me to start labour."

"Do you know the sex yet?" said Charlie.

"I've told the hospital that we don't want to know! We'll take whatever comes; we are looking forward so much!" Flo was the happiest we had ever seen her.

Mum came in from the utility room with our washing in two paper bags, ready to take back.

Mum said, "We talked yesterday over lunch about going down to Mathilde over Easter. Flo and Pierre won't make it, just to be careful, but what about you two—shall we go as a foursome?"

Charlie and I grinned at each other. "You bet!" we said in unison.

"Give some thought to possible trips to familiarize ourselves with the boat, and so will we."

***

Mum had defrosted some spanakopita that she had made some weeks earlier. She made them in batches to an original Greek recipe, even the pastry! The filling was mainly spinach, lots of feta cheese, an egg, a generous drizzle of olive oil, and whatever fresh herbs were available from her array of pots outside the kitchen door. She'd cut the pastry in squares, put the filling in the centre, and fold up the angles to make individual parcels, rather than use a traditional pie dish. It had become a family favourite, even Pierre approved! It could be heated up, but we all preferred it cold. Mum and Flo made a sort-of Greek salad, no red onion and just a sprinkle of feta to go with it.

***

Charlie and I had discussed how we wanted to manage our weekends and decided that Charlie would pick me up in Oxford on the Friday after lectures, except for when she had a match on Saturday, then I would drive up to watch the game before coming home together on Saturday evening. We would have to work out a plan B if Charlie had an away game. Everyone was pleased with all this as they would see far more of us in the future. We didn't mention that this was the only way we could sleep together on a regular basis!

CHAPTER TWELVE

SETTLED

I had the VW van pretty much to myself these days and was becoming quite fond of it. Its footprint was about that of a midsized car and the higher driving position suited me fine. The fact that it could hold half a football team, and all their kit, was part of the attraction for Charlie as well.

On our drive up to Oxford I filled Charlie in on the amazing conversation I'd had with Dad yesterday; she was equally moved.

"Wow! What a thing! You know, I'm so amazed at the evolution we've gone through over the past month or so. We've gone from naughty teenagers, deceiving our parents over what we're doing, to a lovingly accepted item. Mum has come out to us about her early AC/DC and incestuous life with Flo, and if I understood what she said correctly, there's more to come; what can that be I wonder?" I let all that sink in before I responded.

"I have no idea what Mum meant by that, but you're right, she did say something to that effect. I'm happy not to speculate, I've enough to process!"

Charlie came back, "You know, between the two of them, I'm most impressed with Dad. Remember when he and Ozzy Hamilton did Dad's first heart transplant as lead surgeon. He told us how he froze when he held the child's new heart in his hand for a moment, then Ozzy said his name quietly and he carried on with the procedure. We were just kids, but I remember he was overcome in relating the experience and went out to walk round the garden. That, and his dad's funeral, were the only times I can remember him being emotional—till now, that is!" Charlie was right, I remembered it well.

"Yeah, well remembered. It was just before we moved house I think. He keeps his feelings very close normally, maybe he's coming out as well, he was clearly upset over Annie's cancer."

***

We were arriving at my hall of residence; Charlie would take the van on to Cambridge.

We both got out and Charlie said, "Maybe we're being treated as adults, what do you think?" Charlie smiled and put her arms around my neck.

"Looks like it," I said. "And I'm very happy about it, let's try to live up to it, eh?" I put my arms around her as well and we kissed in a brotherly way. "See you Friday." I pulled my bag out of the van and Charlie hopped into the driver's seat.

"I'll call when I arrive."

I dumped my bag in the room and took a stroll down to the river; I was very pensive, but in a happy way; so much was slipping into place in our lives. I could see a very pleasant routine evolving and was glad.

***

My course was getting more and more interesting as it developed, and I began to attend some of the student political societies' events. I decided not to become a member of any of them until I was certain of my own direction, but my inclination tended towards the young conservatives. On paper I was clearly Tory material; private day school, Oxford degree course, and moderately wealthy family, but I was fully aware, and critical, of the inherent class structure that underlay the political divide in the UK.

Charlie was also very happy with her course. It was clear that her passion for human rights would inform her choices. We followed current affairs closely and talked endlessly about justice and political issues of the day. As well as her football training and playing, Charlie had started to run. At weekends we would often run together. As my stamina increased so did my love of running. I also ran during the week, along the Isis towpath, and found it wonderfully meditative. I was never much of a team player, so the

76

individuality of running was perfect for me. Charlie was called to play for the team approximately every other Saturday. I always attended her games and Mum came up when she could. Dad came a few times, but work dictated his availability. Mum got on very well with Charlie's mates and especially enjoyed the after-match pub sessions. We made a subgroup of ourselves with Maggie and Camp David, and took it in turns to be the designated driver.

***

As Easter approached, our plans for the first trip to Mathilde took shape. Charlie and I had the longest break so would fly down a week before Mum and Dad to prepare her for sailing. We had only seen photos of the boat to date so Dad and Pierre prepped us as to what needed doing. Marseille was the closest airport with direct flights from Heathrow, so we booked our one-way ticket early. Mum and Dad would follow in a week. Flo and Pierre would not come due to Flo's pregnancy and they would take Harry for the duration.

***

The love that Charlie and I shared deepened and matured greatly now that we were accepted as an item in the family. The need for secrecy outside the family was, however, always there. We wanted to invite our friends from uni for weekends, but were unsure as to how we could manage that and maintain our secret. I suggested that I could return to Oxford after a Friday night at home and Maggie or Camp David could have my room for the Saturday night. Charlie was somewhat reluctant but agreed with the logic; we would try it after the Easter break.

***

I went up to Cambridge for Charlie's last match of the term. They were playing a team from Chelmsford, and just before halftime, Charlie went down in a tackle and was accidentally kicked on her lower back. The referee blew his whistle to stop play and the Cambridge coach and I rushed to her.

She was in a lot of pain and the coach made her lie still as she signalled for a stretcher. I held her hand in the ambulance, and tried to reassure her, but I was very worried. The duty doctor in A & E sent her straight for X-rays. Thankfully they indicated no fractures, but she was very badly bruised. He gave her a shot for the pain. I asked if she could sit up for the ride home to Maidenhead.

"Let's wheel her to the nurse's break room and try one of the easy chairs," said the nurse. We eased her off the trolly very carefully but she still yelped and could not get comfortable in the easy chair.

"Would a fully reclined car seat do?" I asked.

"We can but try, otherwise she'll have to go by ambulance. I'm not sure I can find one for such a long trip!"

I took a taxi to the football pitch car park and returned with the van in short order. I parked as close as possible to the A & E entrance and reclined the front passenger seat as far as it would go. The rear seats were a bit spartan, but upfront the seats were more like a saloon car. I helped a porter roll the trolly down the entrance ramp to the van and he and I set Charlie on the passenger seat.

She fidgeted around a little before forcing a grim smile, "I'm good for the ride Nat, let's get it over with!" Charlie was still in her football kit, so I drove to the club house to get her holdall. The match was over, and the team was showering in the locker room. Maggie and the captain came out to the van. Charlie played down her injury but did not try to sit up. Maggie gave Charlie a gentle hug and told her how much they had missed her, they had lost two-nil without their star half back. Commiserations over, I asked if they had a blanket to put over Charlie as it would probably be too painful to change her into street clothes. The captain went in search of a blanket. Maggie gave me a hug and kissed my cheek.

"Give me a call on how you're doing Charlie," she said. "I guess you've got the good doctor to care for her when you get home, but drive carefully Nat, she's very precious to us!"

I tucked the blanket around Charlie and reset her seatbelt. I leant over and kissed her before closing her door and going round to the driver's side.

***

I drove slowly, avoiding potholes and bumps as much as possible until we were on the motorway. I kept to the speed of traffic in the slower lanes and passed my phone to Charlie to call home and report our situation. Dad said he had some stuff for the bruising and to beep the horn on arrival so he could meet us and help unload Charlie. After the call I was pleased to see that Charlie had dozed off, the doctor had told us that his shot might make her drowsy.

Once home, Dad and I carried Charlie between us to our wing. He advised a hot bath and then he would take a look at her injury. Mum stayed and helped me strip her while the bath filled.

"Boy!" said Charlie. "I so need a pee but I don't think I can sit on the can!"

"Not to worry," said Mum as she lifted the seat. "face the toilet and bend your knees astride the can as much as possible, and just let it go." Charlie did as instructed and got most of it in the bowl!

I grinned at her after the exercise; she saw the funny side and managed to grin back. "Good job I don't need a poopy, eh?"

Mum and I laughed with her, I gave her a tissue to blot herself, and between us, Mum and I lowered Charlie into the bath. Mum had put some scented salts in the water and Charlie relished the feeling after a brief wriggle to get comfortable. Mum left me to clean Charlie up.

I washed her all over and shampooed her hair, Charlie said, with a warm smile, "Don't get too fruity washing my bits, a turn-on would cripple me!"

I managed to lift her out on my own and she stood holding the wash basin while I towelled her dry and used the dryer on her hair. After I had brushed her hair she managed to turn to face me and put her arms around my neck, we slowly, and very gently, shared a warm kiss.

The bath had done wonders for her and she managed to walk slowly as I supported her to her room. We managed to get her night shirt on and to lie flat on the bed. Mum and Dad came in at that moment and Dad asked how she felt.

"A lot better for the bath thanks, but still very sore!"

"You'll need to turn over so I can look at the damage, put a pillow under your tummy, it'll be comfier."

Dad helped her turn over while I manouvered a pillow under her. Dad lifted her night shirt to have a look.

"That's quite a bruise, must have been a hell of a kick," said Dad. "It's already a very pretty array of colours. It covers half the width of your lower back and the top part of your right buttock! It'll take at least a week or two to fade. Did they put a cold pack on it in the ambulance?"

"No, the trainer did that before the ambulance arrived, Dad."

"Good man!" said Dad.

"Woman!" said Charlie over her shoulder. Dad gave me a tub of cream.

"This is a very old remedy for bruises, Grandad Tubs used it on me as a kid and it works just as well, if not better, than anything in our pharmacy. It's called Arnica and you very gently apply it to the bruise and surrounding area, OK? One last thing, check for any blood in your pee Charlie, just in case the kidney under the bruise is involved."

Mum and Dad left us to it. Charlie asked, "Can you put another pillow under my tummy Nat, I think it will be more comfortable for me?" I lifted her with one hand and slipped the extra pillow in.

"How's that?"

"Better, much better!" said Charlie. Her bum was now raised even more, and I found the view both gorgeous and funny!

"Not a view I often have of you Charlie, but you look fantastic."

"Are you taking the pee-pee Nat, you're looking straight at my anus?"

"I know, and it's a perfect sight, honestly. A bit like a bowling ball but with only one hole instead of three!" Despite herself, Charlie laughed with me.

"Just get on with it Nat Cooper!" said Charlie, still giggling as I put the first blob of Arnica on the bruise.

"That's cold!" she said.

"Don't worry, it'll soon warm up!" I replied, as I very gently massaged it in circles over her back and bum. Charlie relaxed under my ministrations and after a while she half turned her face to me.

"While you're there Nat, can you get our cream from the bathroom and give me a back rub?"

I fetched the tube and put a dollop on my hand to warm it up. I started at her neck and shoulders, smoothing the cream onto her skin and massaging it in with firm but reasonable pressure. I slowly moved down

Charlie's back but avoided the bruised area. I massaged deeply on the uninjured buttock and beneath the bruise on the injured side.

Using both hands I moved to her hips and outer thighs, Charlie sighed, "You're hired Nat, feel's wonderful, no pain… hmmm!" Charlie very slightly opened the gap between her legs in a clear invitation and I could smell her arousal.

"Are you sure you want this?" I asked.

"Mmm… yes please, Nat… hmm… very gently though!"

I worked her inner thighs now and the crease between bum and thighs, edging ever closer until I lightly brushed the soft down between anus and vagina. Charlie cooed and tried to press her bum toward me. She was wet and I slipped my thumb in just under her clitoris. If the g-spot existed I was right on it. With my other hand I undid my belt and fly to release the pressure! Charlie was moving on my thumb in gentle little strokes.

"Oo… Nat, can you get inside from there?" I opened her legs enough to get close and very gently pulled her hips back to meet me. Charlie yelped and I stopped trying to bring her any closer to me.

"Sorry Nat!" I could just get close enough to rub my helmet on her labia and clitoris if I held my penis in place, and that was good enough for both of us. Charlie slowed down as her climax arrived and I pressed my penis harder against her as I came with her. I slipped my thumb back in and Charlie shuddered on it as the waves rolled over her. I had hold of myself and continued to come all over her bum until I was spent. Charlie's breathing slowed down.

"Have we hurt your back, my love?" I said.

"No!" said Charlie. "But if we had it would have been worth it!"

***

Dad advised Charlie not to attend the last week of term and to take only light exercise. Maggie copied her lecture notes to her via email and we made our preparations for the trip to Le Lavandou.

Charlie's bruise deepened in colour to rich shades of black and blue and Mum gave it a daily rub with the Arnica while I returned to Oxford for the closing days of the term.

***

It was eleven days since Charlie's injury when Mum dropped us off at Heathrow airport for our midday flight to Marseille. The bruise was just starting to fade and Charlie was feeling much better, but the two-hour budget flight had not been comfortable for her. We had pre-booked a Citroën C4 hire car which we picked up at the airport. We entered our destination on the GPS and took the A50 autoroute for the ninety-minute drive to Le Lavandou. We had both driven our family van in France but this was my first time in a left-hand drive car. It all came very naturally to me and was a huge improvement on driving our right-hand drive van here. The marina was easy to find being right in the centre of the Le Lavandou seafront.

The weather had been quite overcast in Marseille and we were pleased that it brightened up as we approached the beginning of the Côte d'Azur at Hyeres. By the time we reached Le Lavandou the clouds had dispersed and the sky assumed the wonderful duck egg blue that it was so famous for, and which Winston Churchill had loved as a backdrop for many of his watercolours.

The town itself rose sharply from the seafront road in pastel shades typical of the region. The shops on the north side of the beach road were exactly what one would expect of a popular holiday destination; restaurants to suit all tastes and purses, interspersed with beach wear and sand toy boutiques. Parking was impossible at the roadside, but we were lucky to find a slot in a Pay and Display car park within easy walking distance of the marina. The capitainerie itself was on an island in the centre of the moorings and linked to the land by a short hump-backed bridge. The control tower had a panoramic view of the extensive moorings as well as the marina's sea entrance. The layout of the marina was very characterful, we would certainly need a harbour plan to find Mathilde!

Dad had emailed the capitainerie to say we were coming and had full authority regarding Mathilde. The receptionist welcomed us in heavily-accented English and was visibly relieved when we responded in French. She gave us a brochure of the marina facilities, which included a moorings plan, and the door code for the toilet and shower block. She gave us the key to the boat and marked Mathilde's berth on the plan.

Our first sighting of Mathilde stopped us in our tracks!

She seemed huge in every dimension, length, beam and mast height, as well as deck height above the pontoon! We looked at each other in awe and I walked along the finger to see her name on the transom just to make sure!

We boarded via the swimming platform and into the cockpit. I unlocked the companionway washboard and placed it on a cockpit seat. I let Charlie precede me down the companionway steps to the interior. If anything, the interior looked bigger than the outside, and we marvelled anew at this stunning yacht.

From the bottom of the companionway steps, the view forward was amazing. To starboard, or right, there was first a chart table and then a U-shaped dinette and an island settee, it could probably seat six comfortably and eight at a pinch. Opposite the table was the galley, with a three-burner hob and oven under. There was a bathroom, or head, aft of the galley with an electric toilet and full shower. Wow! I'd always found it amazing how the volume of a yacht seemed to increase disproportionately to increments of the length, but the maths was right, this boat was fifty percent longer than Soufflé but had more than double the volume!

We sat at the saloon table and I took out the notes I had made during our briefing with Dad and Pierre. There was also a note on the table from the yard to say that the engine and galley sea cocks were open but the toilet one was closed, as the output was diverted to the holding tank. Charlie and I looked at each other in wonderment and gazed around our home for the next four weeks.

"I'm not prepared for this Nat. How on earth can we sail such a boat?"

"It will be much smaller at sea," I said, somewhat hopefully!

We had not yet explored the accommodation and rose to check out the cabins. Either side of the companionway there were double cabins under the cockpit seats. The height above the bunks was restricted over half the width by the cockpit seats above, but Charlie thought we could manage if we kept our activity to the outer half! Foreword of the saloon was the master cabin. We looked at each other and knew at once that this was our bedroom until Mum and Dad joined us. The double bed was massive and tapered to the narrowing of the hull toward the bow.

"What a playpen," said Charlie, and I smiled and nodded in agreement.

There was another head with shower adjacent to the fore cabin and yet more single bunks on the port side aft of the master cabin. We left the saloon and went up to the cockpit.

"This is so much more than I had thought," I said. "I'm shy of even thinking about taking her out."

We'd lost track of time and the sun was well down; I looked at my watch.

"We should think about dinner soon, it's half past seven," I said.

"Eight!" said Charlie. I put my watch on an hour for the time difference.

"So, even more reason to think about dinner!" said Charlie.

"How's your back?" I said. "Could you manage a walk into town?"

"I'm still sore from the flight Nat, maybe tomorrow, eh?"

"Fine by me. Dad mentioned a restaurant just opposite the marina that he and Pierre enjoyed, I'll get my notes." I took our bags down from where we'd left them in the cockpit and called up to Charlie, "Do you want anything from here or shall we go as we are?"

"I just need a sweater, so will you, it's getting a bit chilly."

We walked slowly toward the marina exit and it was clear that Charlie was hurting. There were some restaurants tucked in amongst the brokers and chandlers in the marina itself, so we chose a pizzeria there instead of walking any further, Charlie was well pleased! We sat at an outside table overlooking the moorings; plenty of time to explore the town tomorrow.

***

We at last relaxed after our busy day and soaked up the atmosphere. Charlie was smiling at me.

"What are you grinning at?" I asked.

"You, Nathan Cooper, 'cos I love you!" I leaned over for a kiss.

"Love you too!" I said.

"Just look at us Nat, enjoying an al fresco pizza on the Côte d'Azur, with our forty-six-foot luxury yacht just over there!"

"Yeah! I could get used to this! Let's get you back in shape—first priority. We have a week before they arrive which is plenty of time to go through the list. I think I'll go get the car and bring it to the marina car park, the Pay and Display ran out about half an hour ago!"

The pizza was pretty good and we washed it down with a half-litre carafe of the local red which was quite drinkable. I'd actually forgotten about the car and hoped I didn't have a fine. I left Charlie to finish the wine and collected the car; no fine! I rejoined Charlie and we finished our simple meal with a coffee before going back to the boat. Charlie rang home to check in while I made up our bunk in the fore cabin. I laid a beach towel on it so that I could give Charlie's bruise it's daily dose of Arnica. She was very sore so I was particularly gentle this time. I was also careful not to precipitate any other activity. I handed her nightshirt to her and folded the towel. She lay on her side, bruise up, and I crawled in beside her so we lay as spoons.

"Thanks Nat, I know you understand. Not to worry, I'll be back in leg-over form in no time!"

CHAPTER THIRTEEN

DREAMS REALLY DO COME TRUE

Charlie lay on my arm and I put my free hand on her breast over her nightshirt.

"Good night Nat, sweet dreams!"

"I think I will have a good night, I'm quite knackered, sweet dreams to you too sweetheart." Charlie lay her hand on mine, and that's exactly how we woke for our first full day on Mathilde. The first thing I knew about the new day was Charlie sliding off the bunk for her morning pee. I just caught a glimpse of her as she entered the head. I had once told her that the sexiest thing she ever wore was one of my shirts, and nothing else; since then, she has worn nothing else, if anything, in bed!

I was boiling the electric kettle in the galley when she came out and put three measures of coffee in the cafetiere. She stood behind me and put her hands around me and her head between my shoulder blades; she had obviously left my shirt in the head.

"What are the priorities?" said Charlie.

"How's your bruise?" I replied. Charlie slid her hands down my front and cupped my balls with one hand and my penis in the other. "Much, much, much better—I think I know the first of our priorities now!"

I turned off the kettle.

I had a pee and joined Charlie on the bunk. We made wonderful but careful love with Charlie on top controlling events. She slowed to a stop at the moment of her climax and put her head down as I gently squeezed her nipples. Charlie let out a long low groan and looked very serious as she concentrated on her pleasure and I joined her on the second wave and came with her. When she raised her head I saw she had tears on her cheeks.

"OK?" I asked.

"Absolutely," said Charlie. "It's just that I'm sometimes overwhelmed, I love you so much!"

"Come down here," I said. She lifted off and lay between my legs, her lovely face against my chest. I caressed her back and gently over her bruise.

"How is it?"

"It's a very happy bruise now, thank you!"

"It was my most incredible pleasure, ma'am!"

***

We had not showered since we arrived and decided to use the marina facilities until we had worked out how to use the onboard system. We took our shower kit, shorts and tops to the ablution block and afterwards strolled to a coffee shop near where we had our pizza last night. The coffee and fresh croissants were great; what a perfect start to our day!

We returned to Mathilde and I brought up the cockpit cushions from below and switched the kettle back on before coming back up with my notes and a fresh pad. When the kettle boiled Charlie went down to make the coffee and came back with a full cafetiere and two full-sized French coffee bowls.

Yachting is all about lists: checklists for fuel, water, canned and frozen food before leaving port; lists for first aid stuff, sun cream, alcohol and mixers, tea, coffee and fresh food bought as late as possible.

And yet there was always something left out!

We sat with our coffee and gazed at the rich array of craft around us.

"Do you think we should dress up in fancy dress today, you know, like when boats cross the equator?" Charlie asked.

"Why on earth do you say that?" I replied.

"Well, we had a first today, didn't we?" Charlie said with a wide grin on her lovely face.

"Indeed, we did," I smiled and leant over the cockpit table to kiss her.

***

Before starting our lists, I wanted to test run the engine. After starting I leant over the stern to check that cooling water was exiting OK and let her idle while I finished my coffee. When she was up to working temperature, I checked the mooring lines were tight and engaged the propeller in forward gear. Mathilde eased forward as the stern lines tightened and Charlie went to the bow to check we still had some room up front; I increased the revs and the prop wash aft was impressive! I noted that the stern pulled to port under the paddle wheel effect of a left-handed propeller. I did the same in reverse and the stern went to starboard as the bow lines tightened. I let her run in reverse for ten minutes before checking instruments, all was well and I switched off. Next was the bow thruster. I'd never used one before but the principle was obvious, a small electric prop at the bow could thrust the bow to port or starboard as a mooring aid. The control switch simply had two arrows! I pushed it to the left and the bow pulled to port, right and it pulled to starboard. What a boon that was going to be in parking this big boat!

***

So now to the lists.

The galley needed virtually everything, from cooking oil to, well, everything! We also needed shopping for our day-to-day usage and for the first few days after Mum and Dad arrived. By two in the afternoon, we had our lists and were feeling hungry.

"How's your back for a little walk?" I asked. "We can have a baguette sandwich from the pizza joint and then go shopping."

"I'm good but I'll avoid any heavy lifting if that's OK."

"Sure, let's go."

There were two chain supermarkets in town, an Inter Marché and a Carrefour, we chose the latter as we had liked the one in Biarritz.

Two full shopping trolleys later, our boot was full. We used the marina's own trolleys to bring it all to the boat and by six we had most of it stowed and made a storage plan of where things were. The fridge ran on either mains or the onboard batteries and we had put it on mains before leaving. The ice tray was almost frozen and we put four beers in the freezer for a little later. We'd bought a freshly cooked chicken from the supermarket's rotisserie for our dinner and plenty of salad to go with it. We were too tired anyway to go out!

First thing tomorrow we would try out the dinghy and it's little outboard motor; a potter round the moorings would be pleasant.

We turned in pretty early and slept like logs. We had always enjoyed sleeping on Soufflé, the slight motion from wind or passing traffic seemed to lull us to sleep; Mathilde was even better!

****

The sky was cloudless the next day as I went in search of a fresh baguette while Charlie made coffee. We had our simple breakfast in the cockpit and decided to work on a tan while we did our job list.

The dinghy was a small RIB, or rigid inflatable boat, tied down on the foredeck. We launched it over the stern and lowered the motor from its bracket on the aft pulpit to the dinghy's transom. The motor, a 4hp four-stroke, seemed new and started on the second pull of the cord. We were in our swimming costumes and well lathered up with sun oil as we set off for our test drive. Charlie's bikini was modest by modern standards being high cut but nothing like the latest ones with just a thong in the bum cleavage, Charlie had once tried one on and hated it! I very much-admired Charlie's attitude to fashion trends. At five-feet-nine inches tall and slim figure, she did not need high heels and has never had any. The male trend for designer stubble was also a no-no with her.

"I don't want a wire brush on my bits, thank you very much!" she once told me when I hadn't shaved for a couple of days!

****

We pottered slowly around the marina for a while and then had the confidence to venture outside. The sea was flat calm so I opened the throttle slowly to its maximum. The little boat responded well, due to the fibreglass hull, and was fast for such a small engine. Charlie moved to the bow and she rode even better.

When we returned to Mathilde it was nearly midday. We had a cold beer each in the cockpit and then Charlie brought up the remains of our chicken from last night and our baguette from breakfast.

"Have you noticed that this boat gets slightly smaller every day?" said Charlie.

"It does, how about we take her out this afternoon? There's no wind so we can see how she goes under engine and test the autopilot!"

Charlie grinned, "Yeah! Let's do it!"

Charlie cleared the cockpit table while I stowed the outboard engine back on the aft pulpit, and the dinghy on the foredeck. We discussed how we'd reverse out of our berth. I would do the helm and Charlie would watch clearances from the bow, with a boat hook handy, and take in the fenders as we headed out. I called the capitainerie from my mobile to tell them our plan and they said to call when we were re-entering; they'd have a marinero on the dock to take our lines.

With the engine warmed up, I released the stern line and spring while Charlie did the same at the bow and signalled when we were clear. I very gently eased into reverse with the engine just at idle and Mathilde eased out of her slot. As soon as we started to move back I shifted into neutral and let her momentum carry her out. Charlie signalled from the bow when we were clear of the finger and I used the bow thruster to turn the boat through ninety degrees and headed toward the exit in forward gear and still at idle revs. Charlie came aft pulling fenders over the lifelines as she came.

We were both very tense during the undocking but now, clear of the marina, we relaxed and I headed due south for about a mile opening the throttle as we went. I practised with the helm, steering in circles forward and then in reverse. I handed the helm to Charlie for her to try and she grinned broadly.

"Wow! How about that Captain Nat?"

"Absolutely perfect Captain Charlie—and wow to you too!" I looked around for other traffic while Charlie played with the helm and then went below for a couple of cold beers.

We'd looked at the chart before leaving and now headed west toward another small marina at La Favière. There was a bay on the other side of the marina which looked ideal to try out our ground tackle. Charlie engaged the autopilot and increased our speed to six knots; the throttle still had plenty to go but this was fast enough for our first outing.

The bay was picture perfect with two white sand beaches separated by a small promontory.

Charlie had disengaged the autopilot and brought Mathilde to a stop in five metres of water. I watched from the bow as Charlie released the plough anchor from the cockpit control and let out a few metres of chain, stopped, and then raised the anchor.

"Just checking we can bring it back up!" And sent it back down. Charlie idled back as the chain paid out until the bow dipped to say the anchor had dug in, then increased the revs to ensure we were secure, the bow dipped again as the chain tightened; we were well dug in.

Charlie switched off the engine and we relaxed on the cockpit cushions.

"How about a skinny dip?" said Charlie. "I can see people swimming from the beach!"

"OK," I said, with some trepidation, and went below for towels and soap.

After lowering the swimming ladder, we stripped and dived in from the swimming platform.

"Holy shit! That's cold, cold!" cried Charlie as we surfaced.

"Once round the boat and out," I said.

On our return to the stern, we found the temperature almost pleasant but still got up onto the platform and used the swimming shower and soap to wash off. Wrapped in our towels we dried off in the cockpit and I called the capitainerie at Le Lavandou on their working channel to test our VHF radio, it worked fine.

"How about a beer, some more sun cream and head back fairly soon?" I asked.

"Sounds like a plan!" said Charlie.

When we were a little off the marina entrance Charlie checked in on the VHF working channel, and sure enough, there was a marinero waiting on our finger. Charlie had the helm and perfectly lined us up using the bow thruster, then gently eased us in without even squeezing a fender on the finger or our neighbour. A touch of reverse and we were home! The marinero clapped his hands and bowed to Charlie and then took her stern line. I wasn't sure if he was applauding her boat handling or her bikini, maybe a bit of both!

***

After hosing the sand and weed off the anchor, Charlie and I once again used the swimming shower for our evening ablutions.

We'd decided to treat ourselves to a meal ashore and went to the restaurant that Dad and Pierre had recommended.

The meal was great and good value considering the location. We lingered over the remains of our carafe of local white after finishing the meal and held hands across the table.

"What a perfect day, and what an amazing boat, eh?" said Charlie.

"I agree, and you brought her in absolutely perfectly, I hope I can do as well next time out.

"If there's any breeze tomorrow let's go out and air the sails, what do you say?" I asked.

"Oh yes. How about going to the islands just out there," said Charlie, pointing through the restaurant windows towards the islands just offshore. "Looks about a two-hour sail, we'll look at the chart over coffee aboard."

Back onboard, with a bowl of coffee each, we studied the chart. Charlie was right, the Ile du Levant, the aptly named island to the east of the Ile de Porquerolles, was eight nautical miles to the south of us, an easy sail of less than two hours. I checked the weather forecast on my phone app; sunny, with a light breeze from the northwest for the next three days; perfect!

***

The prevailing wind throughout much of the Med is from the north to northwest, with occasional red-sand-bearing southerlies, called Sirocco, from Africa. The Golf de Lyon also has unpredictable violent winds, also from the northwest, called Mistral, which can gust up to fifty knots from seemingly nowhere. The old adage that yachts in the Med need small sails and big engines was well founded.

Charlie's earlier comment that Mathilde was getting smaller became truer by the day as our confidence grew.

While I topped up the fresh-water tanks, Charlie called home to report on our progress. Mum and Dad were well pleased with our efforts and really looking forward to coming out. We too were pleased with ourselves.

Charlie could barely keep her eyes open and kissed me goodnight. We were both feeling the effects of the fresh air and sunshine, the beers during the day and the wine over dinner.

After a last look around the deck I followed her down and left the chart on the saloon table. Charlie was already fast asleep, snoring gently, and looking absolutely beautiful. Her ash blonde hair was splayed around her head like a halo and her arms and legs flung out to occupy the entire width of the bunk; there was no room for me! Sometimes I feel overwhelmed when I look at her like this. This lovely woman filled every part of me with love and I shed a tear of happiness for her. I had not the heart to disturb her so gently pulled the sheet over her perfect sun-kissed body and retreated to the saloon where I wrapped a double sheet around me and slept with a cushion under my head in the saloon.

I woke just before first light with Charlie gently stroking my cheek. "Time for bed," said Charlie.

Still half asleep, I let Charlie take my hand and lead me to the bunk.

"I was having a dream," said Charlie. "That I was masturbating, and as I came in the dream I woke up to find my hand there, I was very wet and reached out to you… but…" As she related her dream Charlie was sliding onto me. "And now I want to share my dream with you." My penis was awake slightly before the rest of me and Charlie gently lowered herself onto me. There was indeed a dreamlike quality to the feel of being inside her. She put her hands on my shoulders, her head down and moved very gently on me. I caressed her swaying breasts and gripped her nipples between my fingers. I could feel she was ahead of me. "Let it go my love," I whispered, and flicked her nipples. She was bursting and threw her head back as the climax hit her. She kept still and I could feel her spasms through the muscles in her vagina as they gripped and released with every wave.

"I so love you Nat…"

Charlie's moments had brought me along with her and I could feel a wonderful anticipation of my orgasm. I gasped as my ejaculation erupted deep inside her. Charlie quickened her movements as if milking me and I kept on coming as she continued to cum with me.

"Sorry to disturb your sleep Nat!" said Charlie with a wicked grin, as a wonderful post-coital relaxation enveloped us.

"I'll forgive you this time!" I said and held her to me as we drifted off.

***

We showered in the ablution block and took breakfast where we had done so yesterday. Charlie took my hands.

"Dreams really do come true, eh?" she said, and I smiled broadly in response.

"You seem to prefer being on top more than the missionary position, is that OK with you?"

"It is, and anyway, who says there weren't any female missionaries?" There was no smart answer to that, so I just smiled with her.

"This is by no means a complaint, you understand!"

The café sold us a couple of baguettes to tide us over the day's sailing and I checked the weather forecast on the app. "Still good," I said. "Wind up to twelve knots."

CHAPTER FOURTEEN

ILE DU LEVANT

Charlie backed us out of our slot and headed for the exit while I phoned the capitainerie with our plan for the day. By the time we were clear of the marina I had the fenders stowed in their rack on the pulpit and was loosening the mainsail sheets ready to pull it out from the in-mast furling system. I'd never used such a system before and was very impressed at the ease with which the sail deployed, a comfortable one-man operation.

Charlie took a course for the eastern end of Ile du Levant and engaged the autopilot as I tightened the mainsheet. Mathilde heeled slightly as the main filled and Charlie cut the engine. It's always a magic moment in sailing when the boat is under sail alone, the silence broken only by the hiss of the water on the hull. Mathilde was showing four knots on the meter under main alone.

Charlie paid out the headsail furling line as I winched in the port gib sheet and Mathilde leapt to six-and-half knots in no time.

Charlie and I sat down on the helm seat and looked up in awe at how she sailed in so little wind. The relative wind on the sails must be only around six knots as we were doing over six with the forecast wind of twelve knots coming from over our right shoulder.

When we rounded the eastern tip of the island the wind dropped to next to nothing under the lee of the island and I put the engine back on. We motored slowly along the south coast with just the main catching what little gusts there were, and the headsail safely rolled up on the fore stay. There was a small bay to starboard with two other yachts at anchor, and we turned in and anchored behind them in six metres of water.

With the anchor well set I rolled up the main and went below for two beers, the jar of Arnica, and some sun cream while Charlie set the bimini sunshade over the cockpit.

Charlie had removed her bikini top and I could not resist the urge to embrace her. A familiar warmth suffused me and Charlie pressed her hands against my chest.

"Down boy, down! Our beer will get warm!"

"If you rebuff my advances again Miss Cooper I shall go on a sex strike!"

"Hmm, how long a sex strike?"

I pondered for a few seconds, "Oh, maybe up to an hour or so!"

We grinned and chinked bottles.

"To life!" said Charlie.

"Indeed," I replied.

***

We spent a lovely afternoon in the bay and decided to stay the night. Charlie's bruise had faded under my daily Arnica administrations and I pulled her bikini bottoms to half-mast for today's application.

My penis had obviously not got the memo about any sex strike. When Charlie turned to me, and fully removed her bikini, the case was already lost!

Mathilde's cockpit was probably the most uncomfortable place on the boat for love-making, but Charlie straddled me as I sat and seemed to do just fine. It was surely a measure of my great love for her that I put up with it!

We had a chilly skinny dip before the sun was down and washed off the Arnica, sun cream and detritus of our love-making.

We were quite peckish, so Charlie went down to rustle up an impromptu meal while I called the capitainerie with our change of plan. I then called home to report. I told Mum we were in this lovely bay and how much we were enjoying Mathilde, indeed, with all the mod cons she had she could be single handed! Mum was impressed and then advised that they had invited the previous owners, via email, for apéro on the Sunday, the day after they arrived, and would text us a shopping list tomorrow. Just then Charlie popped her head out of the companionway to put some olives and anchovies in the cockpit and took the phone below to talk to Mum.

Charlie came back up with our apéro—a plastic measuring jug of box wine; we'd have to do better than this on Sunday!

***

The next day we continued our circumnavigation of the two islands and sailed home fairly close hauled. Mathilde was superb on the wind and did just over eight knots in an apparent breeze of eighteen knots a little forward of the beam.

I docked Mathilde without drama and hosed the deck and anchor. Charlie reconnected our mains cable and went below to switch the fridge from battery to mains and bring up a couple of cold beers. We'd had plenty of sun on the sail back so now put up the bimini shade over the cockpit. Tomorrow was Thursday and Mum and Dad were arriving on Saturday. It was a great feeling to know that we had their complete confidence and we resolved to have Mathilde in perfect shape and preparations for our entertaining on Sunday well in hand.

***

There was an open market every Thursday just outside Le Lavandou on the road to La Favière that was highly recommended. We decided to go there and were advised not to drive as parking was normally impossible.

We left early in the morning for the two-kilometre walk with our backpacks ready for whatever took our fancy. Two hours later we returned with an assortment of olives and cheeses for Sunday, two portions of paella for our dinner that evening, and a top for Charlie.

***

On Friday we took breakfast at our 'usual' cafe and drove to the supermarket to get Mum's list plus our own.

We had a take-away sushi lunch from the supermarket and gave Mathilde a good going-over before making up the bunk for them in the forward cabin. We used our sheets to make our own bunk in the port aft cabin.

When we were happy with our efforts we went for our shower in the ablution block and on for a pizza where we'd had our first dinner.

"Did you notice something this afternoon Nat?" said Charlie as we drained the carafe. I thought for a moment.

"Nothing comes to mind… what?"

"It's the first time we've actually made up a double bed for ourselves without thought about Mum and Dad!"

"Wow! You're right—what does it tell you?"

"Good things," said Charlie. "Good things!"

***

We arrived at Marseille Provence airport in good time for Mum and Dad's flight from Heathrow. I visited the car hire desk to tell them I would be giving the car back at their office in Le Lavandou later in the afternoon.

Charlie and I sat in the arrivals area and talked about our ideas for the holiday. We'd studied the charts and sailing guides and decided we would prefer to go west to Barcelona and then the Balearic Islands of Mallorca, Menorca and Ibiza. The only other option was to turn east along the Cote d'Azur toward Corsica and Sardinia with options for the Italian mainland and Sicily. Both were tempting and we would be happy to go along with Mum and Dad's wishes.

***

Mum's first reaction to Mathilde was exactly the same as ours and Charlie reassured her that Mathilde shrank a little every day!

By the time Mum and Dad had showered in the ablution block and changed into lighter clothes it was after six. Charlie and I left them in the cockpit to relax while we went below to prepare our own welcome-aboard apéro.

We had bought a case of Mumm champagne for Sunday and had three of the six chilling in the fridge. We agreed that five was more than enough for tomorrow!

Charlie reached up to put the nibbles in the cockpit and I came up with the bubbles and four acrylic flutes that we had bought in the chandlers; they looked exactly like crystal but of course did not 'chink'!

Pierre had introduced us to Mumm saying how it was up there with the best but significantly less expensive; it had been our 'house' champagne ever since.

Charlie and I had always enjoyed our own company but it was great to have us all together.

We 'thunked' our flutes, cheered 'to life' and swapped all our news. Dad asked what our views were for the holiday and we asked them to go first.

"No, you two first."

I looked at Charlie and she nodded for me to go ahead.

I explained how we saw the options as being just east to Corsica and then south for Sardinia and Sicily or, west to Barcelona and the Balearics, and that we were 'slightly leaning' toward the latter!

We looked at our parents in anticipation and they smiled at each other and then us.

"You've weighed the options in the same way we did," said Mum. "And we've come to exactly the same conclusion!"

Charlie and I 'high-fived' and I topped up our flutes with the remaining bubbles.

"What have you made for dinner?" Dad asked.

"Reservations!" said Charlie.

CHAPTER FIFTEEN

APÉRO

I left Charlie in our new bunk early the next morning to get fresh croissants from a bakers a short walk from the marina. On my return everybody was up, the bimini set, and a welcome cafetiere steaming on the cockpit table.

"First thing's first," said Mum. "I'm going to go over the plans for this evening and prepare what I can in advance."

Charlie said she'd help Mum as she knew where everything was stowed, Dad and I decided to enter the waypoints for Barcelona on the plotter. I got out the sailing guide and showed Dad the harbour plan for Barcelona. Of the three marinas, I'd chosen the one that was right up inside the commercial harbour, Port Vell. It was a short walk to the town centre and all amenities. Dad cast an eye over the plan and agreed.

"No competition really, looks great, Now, when shall we leave?"

"We could leave tomorrow," I said. "I thought it might be an idea to go first to the bay Charlie and I were in on Ile du Levant to start our holiday—nice swim, a bit of sun and relax. It'll be Mum's first time out on Mathilde and an easy intro."

We calculated that at six knots we would need around thirty to thirty-five hours for the trip to Barcelona with the probability of going a little faster. We would of course sail overnight, a first for all of us. I checked the wind app on my phone — north westerlies twelve/eighteen knots for three days — we'll take that!

The girls finished all the things that could be prepared beforehand by lunchtime and we all went for pizza. Mum was still dazzled by Mathilde and agreed that our idea to overnight in the bay would be very good for her.

***

Our guests for apéro, Aurelie and Alain Delaunay, arrived at six-thirty. Dad had met Alain when he and Pierre had visited last year. He was about Dad's age and looked very fit. Pierre had recognised him as a former player for Athlétique Marseille who had retired after ongoing hamstring issues. Aurelie Delaunay was quite a shock. She looked to be about twenty years older than Alain and in poor health. Dad helped Alain in getting her aboard and settled under the bimini. She smiled graciously for the help and relaxed with a sigh on the cockpit cushions. She was clearly a lady of some breeding and without doubt a great beauty in her day. She wore a full-length wraparound sundress that only seemed to emphasise her fragility and pallor; she also carried a thick shawl over her arm for when we lost the sun.

We were a surprisingly convivial party. Aurelie, in particular, was enjoying her outing and was the one who suggested we drop the formal French Madam and Messier for our given names, and *vous* for the informal *tue*. She had been a professional ballet dancer and later the face of a well-known French cosmetics company. Alain was still with Athlétique Marseille as a coach/tactician and was impressed with Charlie's interest in the game. He said how he saw a great future for ladies' football but to be careful not to overtrain her leg muscles! He demonstrated his point by pulling his cargo pants tight over his enormously developed muscles.

"Not so feminine, eh!"

We were all genuinely enjoying this lovely couple. Aurelie was clearly very poorly yet still the star of our little party. She amused us greatly with her anecdotes about the French fashion scene in her day and only once referred to her condition as 'ma maladie', but did not elaborate. Alain was very attentive and held her hand for most of the evening. She drank less than half of her glass of champagne but enjoyed several of Mum's canapes.

We had just started the third bottle of bubbles when we heard a little voice from the dock.

"*Bonsoir tout le monde!*" Alain turned his head to the bow.

"Mathilde!" he called.

"*C'est moi!*" she called back.

"It's our daughter, we thought she was spending the weekend at her university!" Alain explained.

"Come aboard!" called Mum.

Dad had not known that the yacht was named after their daughter so it was a pleasant surprise for us all. As soon as she came into the cockpit it was clear how much she resembled her mother; Aurelie would have looked exactly like this in her day, just a little taller. Mathilde kissed her parents and shook hands with the rest of us.

"I am sorry to crash your gates like this," Mathilde said in English. "But I decided I wanted to say goodbye to myself!"

"We're all OK with French," said Mum. "champagne?"

I popped below for another flute and brought the bottle with me. Mathilde had extremely short dark hair which suited her fine features very well. She was slim with a rather boyish figure and a good bit shorter than Charlie.

She sat between Charlie and I at the forward end of the cockpit and whispered, "I was hoping to practice my English with you but my father only speaks a little."

Dad had noticed that Aurelie was holding her shawl tightly around her thin shoulders and suggested we all go down to the saloon. Dad went first to give a hand to Aurelie down the companionway and they all settled around the saloon table. Charlie asked if they would mind if we stayed in the cockpit for a while so that we could speak English with Mathilde; nobody objected.

Charlie and I were delighted with Mathilde and we got on extremely well. We all had a good laugh when I explained the difference between 'crashing our gates' and 'gate-crashing'! Mathilde was very friendly and forthcoming. We exchanged information about our university courses and families and learned that she was in her second year studying English and human sciences at the University of Aix en Provence.

She explained that she was very close to her mother and spent most weekends at the family home helping with her care. Her mother suffered from a form of blood cancer called myeloma. Tears rolled down Mathilde's cheeks as she told us that her mother's life expectancy would not be very long.

We had just exchanged invitations to visit each other when Mum called for us to join them. We quickly swapped phone numbers and joined the 'oldies'!

Mum had made coffee for us all and had some dark chocolates on the saloon table. Aurelie was looking very tired and Alain said how much they had enjoyed meeting us but it was time to drive home. They lived in the hills above Toulon and the drive home would take around three-quarters of an hour.

Dad and Alain carefully helped Aurelie into the cockpit and onto the dock where we said our goodbyes. No handshakes this time, just gentle hugs and kisses on both cheeks. Charlie and I gave Mathilde a special hug and quietly wished her bon courage.

***

We were a little sombre as we sat around the table with our coffees. We told Mum and Dad what Mathilde had told us about Aurelie's illness and Dad explained.

"It's a form of blood cancer, a bit like leukaemia, but it affects the plasma cells—she's actually a very sick lady by the look of her."

"So sad," said Mum. "She's such a lovely person."

We all agreed that we would treat the apéro as our dinner and just finish off the remaining canapes.

We went over the plan for tomorrow and on to Barcelona.

Dad had spoken with the capitainerie for them to keep our mooring open for us and we would let them know if our plans changed. We all agreed that we would likely make a decision to moor Mathilde somewhere in southern Spain after this holiday.

Mum called Flo on her mobile and put it on loud speaker. Pierre was at work; Flo was in great shape, but complained that she wanted to pee all the time!

We told her of our plans and she looked forward to our next instalment. She also said that she had googled the options for Mathilde's next medium-term mooring and for us to look-up Cartagena as an option.

CHAPTER SIXTEEN

SOUTH

I did my usual run to the bakery for our breakfast and topped up the fresh-water tanks. Charlie and I had hardly used any diesel, so we had plenty for all contingencies. Charlie took us out while Dad and I stowed fenders and mooring lines. Mum sat in the cockpit and took it all in!

After we were well clear of the marina, Mum and Dad played with the engine, autopilot and bow thruster controls until they were familiar.

Charlie was elected captain for the day and put Mum on the helm while Dad and I deployed the sails. I took a picture of Mum grinning from ear to ear as Mathilde took the wind and Charlie cut the engine.

Mum was so enjoying the sailing and Charlie let her steer until around halfway to the island before suggesting the autopilot. Mum lifted her hands off the wheel and marvelled as the wheel made fine course adjustments for our waypoint off the eastern end of the island. Mum took us into the bay and anchored us firmly a little closer to the shore than Charlie and I had done last week; we had the bay to ourselves this time.

Mum was experiencing the same first impressions that Charlie and I had had and gave Dad a big hug and kiss.

"Boy! You and Pierre sure chose the right boat, I'm in awe!"

Charlie and I made submarines from the baguettes I had bought this morning and handed them up with four cold beers.

Over our lunch we discussed a watch system for the trip to Barcelona and agreed that Dad and Charlie would alternate with Mum and me for four-hour watches. Dad had called Port Vell on Saturday to book our berth and we would confirm it in the morning after checking the weather app.

We were all excited about our first overnight passage. We tested the lights and whistles on our life jackets and checked that the gas inflator cylinders were in date. We agreed to wear the jackets at all times on deck.

Mum and Dad talked about their conversation with Alain and Aurelie last night. It transpired that Aurelie was the sailor of the family and came from a family of 'old money' who had had yachts for three generations. Mathilde was also a keen sailor but Alain not so much. Without Aurelie there was little point in keeping Mathilde.

Alain's life revolved around football and he spent most of his day at a video editing suite in his home office where he studied the tactics of teams that Marseilles was scheduled to play. He would then conduct strategy planning sessions with his players for upcoming matches using his video clips for illustration.

Charlie spoke about how we had so enjoyed Mathilde and hoped she would be our friend in the future.

Overall, the evening had been a little depressing over Aurelie's condition, but this was moderated to some extent by the prospect of Mathilde coming into our lives.

***

With a good forecast for the next few days, we left our bay at eight o'clock in the morning. Mum and I had the first watch but everybody was on deck and helped set the sails.

We had programmed a waypoint into the plotter for a straight line to Barcelona and would check during each watch that we were on the line and make course corrections as needed. Mum and I sat on either side of the cockpit so that we had no blind spots and settled down with the autopilot doing all the work. After an hour, Mum checked the plotter and found we were a few degrees south of our course due to leeway being slightly more than anticipated and corrected on the autopilot by pointing us a little higher; we made two more minor corrections during the rest of our watch and handed over to Dad and Charlie at noon; Mum sat at the chart table and noted our GPS position in the log and marked it on the paper chart with a soft pencil. Our average speed over our watch was six-point-five knots, if we kept that up we would arrive in Barcelona in under thirty hours.

With no land in sight and the wind steady at fifteen knots from the northwest, we fed the crew on watch and rested on our bunks until our watch at four in the afternoon. Dad and Charlie had made only one minor course correction and we were right on our plotter line.

Mathilde was equipped with AIS, Automated Identification System, which showed the identity, course and speed of other vessels in our vicinity on our plotter screen. Mathilde also had a transponder which showed our own information to other vessels. Mum and I had never used the system but when we started our watch we studied the plotter to understand. We saw that we had three vessels in our vicinity, none on a course that was of interest to us. It would be dark by the end of our watch and we wanted to compare the plotter screen with our own observations. We switched on Mathilde's navigation lights early and watched the screen. At eight o'clock Dad came up with our dinner of cold chicken and salad and we showed him the vessels on the screen and pointed out their navigation lights that we could see. What a boon this would be in poor visibility—almost like radar. After dinner Mum and I made up the log and went to our bunks; we would be on watch again at midnight till four.

***

We arrived at our waypoint off the entrance to Barcelona port just before two in the afternoon and rolled up the sails in preparation for motoring through the mile long channel of the commercial harbour to the Port Vell Marina. Dad called the marina to give our ETA and received directions to the visitors' dock. Mum and I deployed our fenders and got the mooring lines ready.

A maninero with a bike was waiting on the visitor dock and directed us to a mooring, he then peddled off and was waiting there to take our lines as we nosed into the slot with Mum at the helm and Charlie ready to help if required. Mum did a perfect job with just a tentative touch of bow thruster—a first for her! While Dad took our ship's papers and passports to the capitainerie to check-in, we gazed around at what was clearly a very high-end marina. There were several enormous super yachts with deckhands busy polishing anything that didn't move, one even had a helicopter sitting on its landing pad above the fan deck at the stern.

"And I thought Mathilde was huge!" said Mum.

When Dad got back, we had prepared a simple late lunch of cheese, crackers, olives and beer. It was noticeably warmer here than southern France and the cold beer was most welcome.

We had the bimini up as Mum and Dad were being very careful of their exposure; Charlie and I already had a good start with our tan. Our conversation started with our trip to Barcelona and any lessons learned. We had been lucky with the weather and agreed that we had had a pretty easy time with our first overnight sail, so we discussed several what-if scenarios. A serious topic was the ultimate catastrophe of being forced to abandon ship through collision with a floating object, such as a shipping container. They tended to be only just buoyant and not easy to see, especially at night. Our radar had not been used yet apart from testing, it had an alarm for targets in our direction of travel and we resolved to use it on our next trip to see what it picked up that we had missed visually, if anything. In terms of actually abandoning Mathilde, we'd make up a 'grab bag' that we would take into the life-raft with us, containing two days' food and water, a handheld VHF radio, a waterproof case for at least one of our cell phones, and our essential papers.

***

Charlie and I decided to go for a run, our first since her back injury. The bruise was still visible, but Charlie had full movement without any discomfort. We left the marina and ran the length of the rambla, a wide pedestrian path that started near the marina and ran through much of the centre of Barcelona. The rambla was popular with locals for their Sunday walkabouts, when families would dress in their finest for this typical Spanish ritual. Another interesting feature of the rambla was the 'statues'. These were actually people dressed up overall as famous or amusing characters. Two of the best that we saw were a 'Statue of Liberty' and a 'Laurel and Hardy' tableau. Of course, each 'statue' had a bowl for passers-by to show their appreciation.

***

When we got back to Mathilde we found a note to say that Mum and Dad had gone out for a walk and a little shopping. The companionway key was in its prearranged place under a cockpit cushion and Charlie went below for our towels and returned wearing her bikini. We showered on the swimming platform and dried off in the cockpit before going to our cabin. Charlie's lovely bum was several shades lighter than the rest of her body when she removed her bikini and I could not resist taking her into my arms. It was our first intimacy since leaving France and our embrace was sheer bliss. The feel of her breasts and the brush of her pubic hair against me were pure joy; I was quickly aroused. Charlie put one foot on the bunk to allow me to touch her with my hand. She was clearly aroused as well, and I laid her on the bunk and put my face between her welcoming thighs. Charlie's labia were hot to my touch and her clitoris high as I gently ran my tongue over them. She pushed my face harder to her and moved slowly against my tongue. Her motions quickened and I slid up to fully enter her. Our movement stopped completely for just a second or two as we savoured that magic moment before I started to move inside her. The need for release was on us in no time and Charlie's first spasm brought me to the first ejaculation of my own orgasm. She continued to clench her muscles around my penis with each wave of her climax and I continued to cum in perfect time with her. I was on my elbows still and watched as Charlie's tears of joy rolled toward her ears. I leant over and licked them away before kissing first her nose and then her lips. We shared the sweetest kiss as I slowly withdrew my deflating penis. Charlie let out a smiling, "Ooh!" As my helmet popped past her clitoris and we lay side by side in a gentle embrace. We had started to doze just as the boat tilted slightly and Mum and Dad came aboard.

"Ahoy Mathilde," Mum called.

"Ahoy yourselves!" we responded in unison. After a perfunctory wet-wiping, Charlie put on a fresh bikini and I a pair of shorts before joining them in the cockpit.

"We were just having a bit of a siesta," Charlie explained as she tried to cover a blush by taking the shopping bag below.

Mum and Dad went to the facilities for a shower while we finished up with the wet wipes. We decided that we should celebrate our first night sail and safe arrival in Spain with some bubbles, so I laid out the cockpit table while Charlie knocked up some simple canapes below.

Mum's face lit up when she saw our preparations and Dad said, "Great idea, and we've found a lovely family bistro for our dinner tonight—table booked for nine!"

***

We'd been warned that Spaniards took their evening meal very late, with few restaurants open before eight-thirty, that suited us just fine today as it was already seven-thirty.

We toasted Mathilde and then each other for our efforts and talked about what to do tomorrow. Charlie and I related a chat we had had with a marinero who highly recommended a visit to the Miró Foundation complex. It was located on the top of a hill toward the southern side of the city and best reached via a very characterful funicular railway. The foundation contained not only the world's largest collection of the artist's work, but many works by other artists. Dad fetched the tourist brochures that the capitainerie had given him on arrival and all agreed that that was our plan for tomorrow sorted.

***

Even at nine o'clock we were only the second group to sit down for dinner; we could hear the conversation from the other table and realised that they were in fact German tourists! The first Spanish diners arrived at nearly ten o'clock.

The restaurant specialised in paella and Dad had ordered a mixed seafood and chicken one when he had booked our table. We knew nothing of the local wines and Mum ordered something dry, white, local and well chilled for our dinner wine. The waiter grinned when he presented their best house white and poured a taster for Mum to try.

"Perfect!" Mum declared, and the waiter half-filled our glasses before putting the bottle in an aluminium ice bucket. The wine was truly great and chilled to a near Arctic temperature! Mum noted the name; Barbadillo, from the Cádiz region in southwestern Spain.

The risotto, which looked and smelled fantastic, arrived in a large, shallow, black-iron pan; we tucked in immediately and found it was just as good as it looked—a great introduction to traditional Spanish cuisine.

Dad talked about some decisions that he and Mum had made during the week that Charlie and I had been in France, and wanted to run them past us before taking any action. They first concerned the offer from Johns Hopkins to be a visiting fellow, and Mum had agreed that he should take the position. It involved four trips per year of five days duration. He would have the use of an apartment on campus, and they would welcome Mum if she chose to join him at any time; an offer that Mum said she'd take up at least once a year. The money was much more that he had anticipated, and the position would certainly be a feather in his CV. The contract would be on a renewable two-year basis. Charlie and I looked at each other and nodded.

"I think it's great and you should certainly do it, Dad," I said. "And thanks a lot for involving us in the decision!"

Charlie chipped in, "I'm really proud of you Dad, we're so lucky to have you, and equally, it's right that others should benefit from what you have achieved."

"I'll take that as a yes then!" said Dad with a broad smile, and we raised our glasses to him.

"The other thing that your Mum and I have been going over is our family finances. Frank Stokes has a finance guy on his staff who advises on tax aspects of wills, trust funds and such and I've asked him to run his eye over our situation. As you know, we have no mortgage on the house, or Mathilde, and we have a very healthy sum in our savings account; now, with the income from this Johns Hopkins job, Frank thinks we should take a serious look at our options," Dad paused for a sip from his wine glass. "Frank's man will report by the time we get back, but in the meantime, any ideas you might have can be put on the table."

"Wow!" said Charlie. "What sort of ballpark are we talking about?"

"Upper six figures," said Dad.

"Wow again!" I said.

Dad explained that the hospital would offer him a 'working consultancy' contract for a fixed annual sum plus extra for work above a certain minimum. He would now confirm his acceptance of the Johns Hopkins, and Great Ormond Street contracts by email.

Business over, we headed off to the Miró Foundation!

***

For me, the two best things about the Miró visit was the view over the whole of Barcelona from the top of the hill, and a stunning 'fountain' in stainless steel by the sculptor Calder. The fountain was unique in that the liquid cascading through the stainless steel was not water but mercury—quite mesmerising! Miro's work I just did not 'get'; Mum was our art 'expert' and she felt the same as me!

After the ride down on the funicular we headed for the Cathedral (church) of Sagrada Familia. This was the crazy looking church designed by the Catalán modernist architect Antoni Gaudí—the man who gave his name to the English language in the word 'gaudy', meaning tastelessly showy! The building was indeed 'gaudy', but I liked it!

We had a simple beer and sandwich lunch and then headed back to the marina for showers before coffee in the cockpit.

Dad got out the sailing guide so we could think about the next leg of our holiday. The days were ticking by and next Sunday week Dad needed to be back ready for work on the Monday.

Mum said, "I want to get my bum brown and sandy, let's head for Mallorca and find a nice anchorage off a white sand beach!"

None of us could argue with that!

CHAPTER SEVENTEEN

MALLORCA

The chart showed that we could sail to Puerto Sóller on the northwest coast of Mallorca in daylight if we left Barcelona at first light. There was a small marina tucked up in the northern end of the resort under a promontory that offered good protection from the prevailing wind. The sailing guide gave the phone number of the marina and Charlie rang them to book a slot.

***

The wind had stiffened to twenty knots with gusts to twenty-five shortly after leaving Barcelona. Fortunately, the wind was well aft of our port beam and Mathilde took off like a rocket even though we had not fully deployed either sail. I figured we had reduced our sail area by around thirty percent. The moderate waves were with us and Mathilde rode them majestically at over eight knots.

We had entered our waypoint in the middle of the bay of Porto Sóller and kept tight on our course except for bearing off to starboard when an approaching ferry, obviously bound for Barcelona, passed us port-to-port. We had corrected by three degrees to port and could now see the island. Dad had been skipper for the day and had made up the log and entered our position on the chart every four hours.

We were about an hour out when the wind and sea moderated and we unrolled the remaining sail area. Mum came up with beer and sandwiches for lunch.

Dad had the helm and switched off the autopilot after lunch and started the engine, he ordered sails rolled up, fenders deployed, and mooring lines readied.

Mum called the capitainerie on their VHF working channel and directed Dad to the visitors dock as advised. A marinero met us and directed us to turn into the second pontoon and raced round to meet us there.

When we were settled, I took our papers and passports to the capitainerie to check in.

When I returned Mum and Charlie were already in bikinis and rubbing sun protection into each other; Dad was in his swimming shorts and studying the Balearics Sailing Guide. Mum 'shooed' Dad and me to the aft end of the cockpit so she and Charlie could sunbathe on the cushions down the long sides; they both lay on their tummies with bra straps undone.

Dad nudged me, smiled, and said in a stage whisper, "Not bad for an old fart of forty-three, eh?"

I could see that Mum was grinning as she stuck her fingers in her ears. Charlie turned over onto her back holding her bra in place.

"Anyone around?" she asked. There was no one who could see the girls lying down so Charlie put her bra aside and massaged some sun cream into her breasts—I just had to look away!

Mum turned over and I wondered if she would do the same as Charlie. I had no time to wonder as she removed her bra, waved it in the air, and threw it to Dad!

I had seen Mum and Flo topless many times on Soufflé but this was the first for at least two years. She truly looked wonderful. Her breasts spread just slightly more than Charlie's but they could still have been sisters. My eyes met Dad's and we grinned like naughty boys!

***

After a lazy afternoon, we all showered on the swimming platform before a late apéro. We discussed our objectives and all agreed that we did not seek to be tourists but would rather enjoy the sailing and anchorages for which the Balearics were renowned. We'd all read the sailing guide and tourist brochures and realised that it would be too rushed to visit all the islands; we would concentrate on Mallorca, Ibiza and Formentera. Our direction of travel was clearly southwest toward the Spanish mainland and Dad phoned the marina at Le Lavandou to cancel our mooring there.

Dad suggested we go clockwise around Mallorca, enjoying the many sheltered bays and recommended eateries along the way and on to Puerto Cristo where we could visit the amazing Caves of Drach which were a short walk from the marina there.

We enjoyed a walk along the white sand beach of Puerto Sóller before having a fun dinner wandering around the many tapas bars, sampling their tasty wares. As advised by the maninero, we only visited the busiest bars!

On our walk back we noticed that the sea was breaking against the marina outer wall and I checked my weather app. The wind had strengthened since our arrival to thirty knots and would not die down until late tomorrow; we were here for at least two nights.

The wind did not moderate until late Sunday so we left early Monday morning. Mum and Charlie had done enough shopping on Saturday so that we would be independent of shore facilities for a few days and could enjoy one or two nice anchorages on the way to Puerto Cristo.

The strong wind over the last few days had left a very lumpy sea for our sail round the northern coast of Mallorca. As soon as we turned more southwards the sea calmed and we had perfect conditions. It was amazing how the days had slipped by; Dad needed to be home next Sunday—just six days away after leaving Puerto Sóller. Mum and Dad had decided that Dad would fly back on Sunday from Palma and booked an afternoon flight to London Gatwick; there was a direct bus service from Puerto Cristo to the airport. Mum had no need to rush back as she could do her work for the hospital on her laptop. Mum called Flo later that evening with Dad's flight details and she agreed to pick him up at Gatwick.

***

In the event we only anchored once on the way to Puerto Cristo. We stayed for four nights in the picture-perfect bay of Cala Guya, anchored in four metres just off a totally unspoiled white sand beach in the northern end of the bay. The southern end was clearly being developed as a holiday resort.

Our stay in Cala Guya was the most perfect holiday the four of us had ever spent together. The mornings were greeted with the smell of fresh baked bread that Mum made from premixed packets, left to rise in the cockpit overnight; the days spent in glorious relaxation, Dad in particular benefited enormously.

***

On the second day, while Mum and Charlie took the dinghy ashore to get their 'bums sandy', Dad and I had a long and wide-ranging conversation. We ran the engine for an hour to charge Mathilde's domestic batteries—the fridge being the main draw. To cool off, we swam to the bow and hung onto the anchor chain while we talked.

"Your Mum and I have noticed that you and Charlie never call me 'Tub' these days. This is in no way a complaint, but why's that?"

"Interesting," I said. "Charlie and I talked about this on our way back after the Christmas break, and of course, after all the revelations, mainly about Charlie and me, but also about Mum and Flo. We both came out of all that feeling much more adult, more responsible, and more bonded than ever with you and Mum; you could say it was a renaissance for us in our relationship with each other, as well as with you two. It was truly massive for us," I laughed. "But in answer to your question, I think 'Tub' went out the window with what remained of our childhood!" Dad now laughed as well.

"We too did much soul searching over those days and subsequently. We, just like you and Charlie, are very happy with the evolution of our situation; the honesty and maturity on all sides has truly enhanced our lot." We were both quiet for some seconds and then spontaneously, albeit rather clumsily, we embraced with the anchor chain sandwiched between us. It was the first time in our lives that we had done that.

Back on-board we turned the engine off, and Dad brought us up a couple of cold San Miguel beers. Dad talked about how excited he was about the changes in his career. He wanted to explore the Darwinian and ethical aspects of his work and especially the modern idea that parenthood was a human right and that the medical profession was obliged to facilitate conception in the most unlikely of circumstances. He thought the world's most pressing problem, after climate change, was overpopulation and all the ills from the knock-on effects of resource depletion and loss of habitat.

Off the top of his head, he suggested that two-to-three billion would be an optimal world population.

"I think Darwin would nod sagely if he could hear you Dad," I said. "Now, shall we solve another world problem or swim ashore with the small cold box full of beer for our ladies?"

The girls were alone on the beach, face down on their towels, and completely naked. We each took a cold beer from the box and crept up on them to place the bottles between their shoulder blades—their screams could have been heard in Palma! We were eventually forgiven and enjoyed the beer with them before heading back in the dinghy.

***

We arrived in Puerto Cristo in the late afternoon of Friday; we had been reluctant to leave our anchorage, but the real world beckoned!

Our Saturday visit to the Cuevas del Drach, or Dragon's Caves, was absolutely amazing; a vast network of caves, most as big, if not bigger, than a cathedral, festooned with huge stalagmites and stalactites. The highlight of the visit was a huge underground lake where visitors were serenaded with a modest recital of classical music by a small orchestra carried on rowboats. Easily our best day ashore to date.

It was Dad's last evening with us so we enjoyed some homemade tapas for our apéro before going ashore to a nice seafood restaurant recommended by the capitainerie. Dad checked with Flo that she was still on to pick him up at Gatwick and Mum gave her an update on our lazy days at anchor; Flo was suitably jealous!

In the morning we all went to see Dad off at the bus station and settled in the cockpit afterwards to plan our next move. Mum would stay with us for our remaining week before we all returned. She insisted that Charlie and I move back into the fore cabin!

***

Our original idea had been to head southwest toward Cartagena on the Spanish mainland, via Ibiza, the renowned 'party island', but now, after a more in-depth study of the sailing guides, we realised that that was probably not our best option. Cartagena looked like the perfect place to spend the winter but was quite a way from any decent sailing and anchoring areas; in fact, the closest good cruising was exactly where we were—in the Balearic Islands!

Mum confirmed that she wanted to continue the holiday and Charlie and I heartily agreed. Our only issue was where to leave Mathilde until the summer holidays.

The most promising was the island of Menorca, just a day-sail away from Puerto Cristo to the northeast. The capital of the island, Mahon, was uniquely situated on a long narrow inlet, much like a fjord, and had multiple yacht clubs and marinas; Mahon also had direct flights to Gatwick.

Decision made, we checked out at the capitainerie for an early departure the next day; Mum and Charlie did some last-minute shopping, and I topped up the water tanks. I put a note in the log to pump out the holding tank when we were well offshore in the morning.

Dad called to report his safe arrival and Mum related our plans for the coming week to which he agreed wholeheartedly. Flo was with him and had brought their dinner, Pierre of course was working.

Mum and Flo chatted for ages so Charlie and I went below for drinks and nibbles. They were still at it when we came up!

The call eventually ended, and Mum brought us up to date. Flo was huge and really looking forward to the end of her pregnancy and would feed Dad for the week! When Mum told her of our plan to leave Mathilde in Mahon, Flo said Pierre would be jealous; he had always wanted to visit the town to pay homage to the French chef who had invented mayonnaise there and named the source in honour of the town. The corruption in spelling is largely due to the local Catalán language name for Mahon being Mao.

After dinner ashore we sat in the cockpit and checked the weather on my app—light to variable, mainly from the north. We chose a bay on the southwestern shore of Menorca as our destination. It was less than forty miles away, about six hours; we elected Charlie as our skipper for the day. The bay was called Calas Coves because of the large number of caves in the area and considered the most beautiful bay in the Balearics.

CHAPTER EIGHTEEN

MENORCA

The light breeze was forward of our port beam but too little to be of much use to us. We ran the engine to increase the apparent wind across the sails and motor-sailed the whole way to Calas Coves. The pilot showed that the bay was long but very narrow, just two hundred metres wide. Sailors were advised to anchor and run a stern line ashore to stop the boat swinging to the anchor. We had never done this before, but Mathilde already had a spool of buoyant line on the aft pulpit for this purpose, and I prepared it for deployment after pumping out our holding tank.

There were four other yachts in the bay, all with stern lines, and we followed their mooring pattern without any drama; had there been a crosswind it might have been another story! I had taken our line ashore in the dinghy and looped it over an embedded post provided for the purpose.

The bay was well worthy of its reputation—the most beautiful anchorage we had ever seen. The water was crystal clear, and we could see perfectly the small and not so small fish that came to check us out. The bay terminated in a wide white sand beach that stretched the full width of the inlet.

With anchor and stern line well secured, and bimini set, we settled in the shade for a late lunch of sandwiches and beer. I sat at the helm and watched my topless 'girls' at ease and just loved them. Charlie saw me grinning and came over to sit on my lap and embrace me—what more could a man wish for?

"If you two want to get a room that's OK with me!" said Mum with a laugh, and Charlie unhanded me to return to her seat.

"Something your dad and I learned when we sailed with Flo and Pierre on Soufflé was to allow what privacy we could for each other's intimacy, and ignore without comment any accompanying sounds," said Mum.

"Mathilde is a lot bigger but you need never feel inhibited on our account—and vice versa of course." This latter with a huge grin!

"Got it!" said Charlie and I in unison, and we all laughed.

Charlie and I had never flaunted the physical aspect of our love but this latest from Mum totally evaporated any vestigial misgivings that we might have harboured.

The cell phone signal was quite strong and Mum called a small marina in Mahon that we had noted from the pilot. She booked a slot for Thursday and Friday night with an option open for a three month stay until our summer holiday. That done, we all took a shower on the swimming platform and relaxed in the cockpit till sunset.

With the engine compartment still warm, Mum made up two loaves from the bread mix and left them to rise next to the engine.

****

Our closest neighbour was a Spanish flagged power boat with an older couple and two young boys, probably grandchildren, on board. As I went below to prepare our apéro, the elderly gentleman came alongside in his dinghy and addressed Mum and Charlie in heavily accented French. He explained that he and his grandsons had been fishing and caught a Tuna of around four kilos which they would cook on a gas BBQ on their aft deck and wondered if we would care to join them. Mum invited him on board to have a drink with us as she graciously accepted the BBQ invite. I popped up to join in the introductions; our visitor was called Pau.

Charlie asked if Pau would like to collect his family for drinks with us, but he explained that his wife, Sophie, was showing the boys how to fillet the tuna and marinate it for the BBQ.

I asked Pau in French what he would like to drink and Mum and Charlie in English.

Pau said, in English, "Ah, so you speak English as well, good, my English is a lot better than my French!"

Everybody dithered over what to drink so I suggested a cold bottle of Barbadillo—all agreed!

Charlie came below with me and made up a plate of local rough cut serrano ham. Serrano is rather chewy by English or French standards, but the flavour is amazing and well worth the effort. I put some gherkins in a bowl, and voila, instant apéro!

When we passed up the drinks and ham, Mum had already explained that we were in fact English and happy to speak either language; Pau was clearly happier in English.

Pau admired Mathilde and I gave him a short tour. He explained that he and Sophie had always had sailing boats until they had sold their last one, a Swedish built forty-two-footer, two years ago.

"We became aware of our position on the age curve," Pau explained. "And are now very pleased with our move to power. Our boat is very easy to handle, and we do a lot of fishing!"

Pau's mobile rang and he excused himself to answer it. After a short exchange he lowered the phone. "It is Sophie; she is asking about dinner and I say you are all coming, yes?"

"Yes indeed," Mum said. "And many thanks."

Charlie asked, "What language were you speaking to your wife, Pau?"

"It was Catalán, we are both from these islands and love our old language, but most people here speak Spanish as well."

Pau finished his glass and rose, "Shall we say eight o'clock?"

I held his painter tight as he climbed into his dinghy from our swimming platform and pushed him clear to row back.

I shared out the remaining wine and said, "What shall we take with us?"

"How about another Barbadillo," said Charlie. "And some French cheese?"

"Done!" said Mum.

***

At eight o'clock I rowed us across to Pau's boat and the elder grandson took my painter.

"Good evening, my name is Guillem, welcome aboard Claris." Guillem was about ten years old and we suspected that his welcome had been well rehearsed.

"It is our pleasure, Guillem, thank you," replied Charlie.

Guillem held our painter as we stepped onto Claris' swimming platform and I watched as he let out a few metres before making it off on a stern cleat.

"Is OK?" he asked.

"Perfect!" I replied, and we followed the girls onto the aft deck.

Pau's wife, Sophie, looked a good ten years younger than Pau. She had a lovely round face and wide-set dark eyes that flashed with humour. In contrast to Mum and Charlie she was quite buxom—voluptuous even!

Guillem and Jordi were eleven and nine respectively and had a handsome olive complexion topped by curly black hair—much like their grandmother!

Mum presented our dinner contribution and Pau suggested we open the Barbadillo for our predinner drink. We had brought two French cheeses with us, a firm Tomme from the Basque region of France, which Mum advised should not go in the fridge, and a Camembert that we could put on the BBQ after dinner—Mum would show how!

We were a relaxed and convivial party. The boys were encouraged to participate with their schoolboy English and were most impressed that Charlie shared their enthusiasm for football. They immediately insisted that she join them on the beach in the morning for a 'training session'!

Sophie's English was excellent; she explained that she was a general surgeon at Mahon's largest hospital, the Mateu Orfila, and did a shift in the Urgencias, when there was no one to chop up!

"Like the tuna?" said Jordi.

"Exactly," said Sophie. "Except Tuna is more difficult!"

The boys giggled and Mum raised her eyebrows.

"What a pity, my husband is a CT surgeon at Great Ormond Street but flew home yesterday from Palma."

Sophie enquired after our family name and smiled broadly when Mum told her.

"Anything to do with the Cooper-Hamilton retractor by any chance?" Sophie asked.

"Wow", said Charlie. "Dad's famous!"

"Indeed," said Mum. "He's the co-inventor."

The conversation flowed as if we were old friends, and I was reminded of our apéro with Mathilde and her parents; this boating life was getting more agreeable by the day!

Sophie and the boys maintained a steady supply of nibbles, including our serrano, until nearly ten o'clock when Pau lit the gas BBQ. Our Barbadillo had miraculously all evaporated! The BBQ was clearly designed for boats; made of stainless steel, it was circular with a domed lid and clamped to the aft pulpit.

Pau closed the lid to heat the grill and Sophie brought up the tuna. She was clearly a gifted surgeon and had cut perfect fillets instead of the usual steaks cut crosswise. We could smell the aromatic herbs and olive oil as Pau put them on the hot grill. The fillets were just a centimetre thick and Pau flicked them over after about thirty seconds to do the other side. In no time the tuna was on our plates and a huge bowl of mixed salad put on the table to help ourselves. I had never tasted tuna as good as this!

The red wine was served from a bottle without a label and was a perfect match for the tuna.

"This is the best yet," said Mum. "And the anonymous wine is perfect!"

Pau explained, "We have great wine on the islands. This is from our neighbour's vineyard in the low hills above Mahon. He gives us a five litre can from time to time and we put it into bottles. If you buy this wine in a Bodega it would cost over twelve euros; it is one of the best from Menorca."

"So, how do you BBQ Camembert, I want to know?" asked Sophie.

"I need some of the fresh herbs you used for the tuna and some thin slices of garlic," said Mum.

"Coming up," said Sophie.

"I normally do this in an oven so you should put the lid on the BBQ and set it to the lowest heat."

Pau followed Mum's instructions.

"Now, remove the cheese from the wooden tub and discard the paper wrapping. Put the lid on the bottom and put the cheese back in the box. Now cut several slits in the top of the cheese, stuff with herbs and garlic and put on the BBQ for around ten to fifteen minutes."

Pau followed Mum's orders and after ten minutes Mum checked the cheese with a knife.

"It's almost there, do you have any bread or crackers?"

Sophie got the bread and Mum tested the cheese again, "Perfect!"

Pau used an oven glove to put the cheese on the table and Mum opened up the top to reveal the hot semi-liquid Camembert.

"Dip in!"

***

Over breakfast the next morning we chatted happily about our wonderful evening with Pau, Sophie and the boys. I had made a note on my phone with the make of the BBQ and wrote 'fishing tackle?'

Charlie's phone rang, "*Buenas días,* Charlie," said Sophie. "I can see you have finished breakfast and the boys are keen for their 'training session' with you—what time would suit you?"

"*Buenos días* to you too, any time from now on," Charlie replied.

"OK, the boys will pick you up now, bye and thanks!"

Charlie went below for a top to put over her bikini, trainers and a plastic bag for her phone. When she reappeared, the boys were just arriving, Guillem was rowing.

"Good morning everyone!" shouted Jordi.

"Buenos días!" we shouted back.

Mum and I could see Charlie and her 'students' on the beach; there was just one other family on the whole wide beach.

Mum's phone rang; it was Pau.

"Good morning, Paris, I want to talk with you about your plans to leave Mathilde in Mahon, can you come over for coffee?"

"No!" said Mum. "I pick you up and we have coffee here, OK!"

"OK, we are ready any time now."

Mum took the dinghy across while I made coffee and set the cockpit table with mugs and a plate of biscuits.

When we were settled with our coffees, Pau laid out a Mahon harbour plan on the table.

"Which marina have you booked for this week?" he asked. Mum and I studied the plan and indicated the marina.

"So, that marina is quite good, but it is a commercial enterprise and quite expensive—I have another idea for you." Pau pointed to a small yacht club a little further down.

"We are members of this club. It's a private members club and we do not rent out space on our pontoons. However, my friend has a slot here, but his boat is out of the water for an osmosis treatment and must dry out for another four months. I have spoken to him this morning and he says you are welcome to it until he goes back in the water."

"Wow, that's amazing Pau, thank you so much!" said Mum.

"There is a catch of course," said Pau. "You will need to become members and your application must be seconded by two members—that will be myself and my friend who owns the mooring. The annual membership fee is nine-hundred euros—less than half what you would pay for three months in the marina!"

"That's great Pau, but your friend must want something for our use of his mooring?"

"Not to worry," said Pau. "He is not a poor man, in fact he owns the vineyard of our wine last night! He wants nothing from any friend of ours."

"I'm overwhelmed," said Mum. "Of course we accept his generous offer and look forward very much to thanking him in person."

"Of course, you must stay in the marina for the two nights you have booked and on Friday I will come with you to our club."

"I'm so moved that you should treat us as such friends after just one evening together," said Mum.

"Pau and I talked about that last night," said Sophie. "We think you are a lovely family, and of course, it did help that you are married to one of my heroes!" she grinned.

We sat in the cockpit till midday while Sophie and Pau marked our pilot with all their favourite anchorages. I asked Pau about his fishing equipment and made some notes; it looked like something I could get quite interested in.

When Charlie and her 'pupils' returned I put beers on the table for us and cold water for the boys—we had no other non-alcoholic drink! Charlie was wiped out.

"These two have run me ragged!" she said, and Sophie translated for the boys. A rapid exchange in Catalán followed and Sophie said how much they had enjoyed themselves.

Mum invited them all back for dinner this evening. "I have no idea what it will be—probably a pie!" she said.

***

After a quick lunch of Mum's fresh bread and cheese, Charlie curled up on the cockpit cushions for a nap while Mum and I went below to plan the dinner.

In the end it was a toss-up between a Shepherd's pie and spaghetti bolognaise, as both used fundamentally the same ingredients!

Charlie had heard our conversation and called down, "Spag bol if we have some nutmeg!"

We did have nutmeg, so that was that!

Our guests brought two 'anonymous' bottles of the red that we had enjoyed last night and a dessert of Pan de Calatrava, a Spanish type of bread pudding but about a thousand times better than ours!

The atmosphere in our cockpit was an amiable continuum of the previous evening. Sophie wanted to know what was in the sauce that was so nice and different from usual.

"Nutmeg and finely chopped celery," Mum replied.

"I'm going to try that next time," said Sophie.

They were going fishing early in the morning and invited us to join them. Mum and Charlie wanted to spend our last day on the beach, but I was keen to go. Sophie asked if she could stay with the girls, and so it was.

Claris carried four fishing rods which clipped to the ceiling of the saloon when not in use. On the aft deck they fitted into sockets for fishing. Pau motored at about eight knots with the four lines trawling behind at varying distances.

I took lots of photos with my phone and a video of Jordi bringing in a good-sized tuna which Guillem helped bring aboard with a gaff hook and sprayed something into the gills—the fish died immediately.

"What was in that spray?" I asked

"Alcohol!" replied Guillem.

I learned a lot that morning and resolved to buy some kit for Mathilde.

"We will go back to Mahon this afternoon," said Pau. "Please call me when you arrive in the marina tomorrow and I will take you to the club for your membership paperwork."

***

We left Calas Coves after breakfast the next morning for the thirty-mile sail to Mahon. There was just enough breeze to fill our sails for the first couple of hours until we rounded the southernmost tip of Menorca and then motored northeast for Mahon with sails furled. I called the marina with our estimated arrival time and was advised to tie up to the fuel dock before being allocated a slot. That was perfect for us as we needed to completely fill Mathilde's diesel tank before leaving her for three months; any air space in the tank could cause bacterial scum to form which might block the fuel filter.

Mum called Pau after we had topped up on diesel and were tucked into our slot; he would take us all to his club for lunch and membership formalities at noon tomorrow. Pau also recommended a local, non-touristy, restaurant for our dinner tonight with apologies for not being available to join us.

Mum booked our flight home for Sunday morning and checked-in with Dad and Flo with all our news. Pierre was delighted with our choice of Mahon for Mathilde's temporary home.

Charlie and I called Mathilde in France and had a very long and pleasant chat with her. She would start her new term next week, the same as us. Her mother's illness had plateaued for a while, but the trajectory was still inexorably downward. Charlie and I reiterated our open invitation for the summer, but we all knew that Aurelie's condition would dictate Mathilde's availability.

***

Pau arrived promptly at noon the next day and took us by Land Rover to his club. The club was small with about fifty moorings on two pontoons and a bar/restaurant over an office and workshop. Pau introduced us to the secretary and Mum completed the paperwork for our family membership with Pau translating the forms which were in both Spanish and Catalán. The secretary welcomed us in the bar with a round of drinks while Mum and Pau did the formalities. Mum used her phone banking app to transfer the fees to the club's IBAN.

Business over, Pau took us down to see Mathilde's new mooring and would join us in the morning to help bring her to her new home. Pau introduced us to Pedro, the club's caretaker, who would take our lines on arrival.

After a lunch of perhaps the best fish soup I'd ever tasted, Pau drove us back to the marina. Mum had wanted to invite Pau and his family for a nice dinner in town, but Pau got in first saying that Sophie had planned our evening with some home cooking, the boys were looking forward to seeing their trainer, Charlie, and they had invited the owner of our mooring, their neighbour, Jaime, pronounced more like Hymee, to join us - what could we say?

***

We were all quite overcome by the amazing hospitality that we were experiencing. The evening with our new friends was memorable in many ways: Jaime was a delight! He was about the same age as Pau but shorter and corpulent. His completely bald head was deeply scored with lines that told us that his default expression was a broad smile, and his big red nose that he was probably his own best wine taster! He had been a widower for many years and was without issue. It seemed that Jaime was a full member of Sophie and Pau's extended family. The two boys were having an excited conversation with Jaime in Catalán and Sophie told us how they were telling him what a famous footballer Charlie was!

Sophie was helped by Jaime's housekeeper, Maria, who kept up a continuous stream of small delicacies from the islands, much like an extended tapas meal. Every morsel was a delight and were mostly new to us.

The wine flowed freely but we noticed that Sophie was abstaining. She had explained that she was on-call for major incidents and would be our designated driver. Mum thanked Sophie and Pau profusely for their many kindnesses and asked her to express our gratitude to Jaime for the use of his mooring. Jaime looked embarrassed after Sophie's translation and waved his hand in a 'not-at-all' gesture!

On the drive back to the marina, Sophie explained that their son and daughter-in-law would be arriving on Sunday after spending the Easter holiday with her parents in Barcelona, and that they were temporarily living with them while their new house was being built close by.

Like Mum, Sophie was a very tactile and affectionate woman, and we had a major 'hug-in' when she left us at the marina entrance.

Back on board I made coffee and we sat in the cockpit to reflect on our good fortune in meeting this lovely family.

"I feel quite humbled by this whole experience," said Mum. "Is it the camaraderie of like-minded yachties or have we been unusually lucky?"

"I think it's both," said Charlie. "This holiday has been an eye-opener for me too. Look at how we enjoyed Mathilde and her parents and how welcoming the club here has been, not to mention Jaime's generosity toward us."

"I think you've both got it," I said. "This boating thing cuts across, or perhaps through, all professions and nationalities. We've lucked into something truly special!"

***

Charlie was a little weepy when we cuddled up in our bunk, a combination of the many kindnesses we'd been subject to, a hint of Jaime's wine perhaps, and the fact that our holiday would be over in just thirty-six hours. Charlie had a leg over me in our embrace and started to gently press her sex against my thigh. I placed my hand on the small of her back to help her, but her slight movements tailed off and her steady breathing told me that she had drifted-off; I stifled a chuckle at the realisation that this must be the female equivalent of 'brewers droop'!

After breakfast, Charlie and I checked us out at the capitainerie and Pau and the boys arrived as we returned to Mathilde. We let Pau take us round to the club and both the boys had a go at steering, he handed the helm to me to ease her into Jaime's slot. Pedro took our lines and I ensured we were well moored for the months ahead. Pau said he would check Matilde regularly and Mum gave him our spare key so that he could run the engine from time to time.

Charlie made us coffee and I set the bimini to shade us in the cockpit. The boys went off with Pedro to 'help' him with his chores.

Pau was a founder member of the club and pointed out some interesting boats. He was especially proud to point out three beautiful, traditional looking power boats that had been built by a small yard right here in Mahon. The boats were handmade on fibreglass hulls, much sought after and quite expensive.

We chatted amiably until one o'clock when Sophie joined us and suggested lunch in the club. We had much to do after lunch to put Mathilde to 'bed' and Mum suggested they join us for dinner in the club tonight as a modest leaving party, and for Jaime to join us if possible. Pau said that the cook could prepare his speciality seafood paella and we all agreed that it would be the perfect send-off for us.

The club had a washing machine and tumble dryer adjacent to the toilets where Charlie did all our laundry while Mum and I cleared the fridge and lockers of perishable food which we gave to Pedro.

When Charlie returned, we put clean sheets on our bunks and packed our bags for the morning.

Happy with our preparations, we enjoyed a last beer before taking our showers in the club facilities.

***

Mum had told the cook that we would be having an 'early' dinner at nine o'clock and everyone, including Jaime, turned up shortly after the hour.

Two tables had been put together alongside the window overlooking the moorings and the town beyond. The paella for eight was in two black, iron pans that left just enough room for our plates; the wine, curiously, came in unlabelled bottles!

Our happy evening was frequently interrupted as Pau introduced us to other members, but there was also a touch of sadness for our leaving these lovely people in the morning.

Sophie would not countenance our taking the bus to the airport and would pick us up in the morning for the fifteen-minute ride.

CHAPTER NINETEEN

BACK TO THE WORLD

Dad, Flo and Pierre were all waiting for us in the arrivals hall at Gatwick: Flo seemed at least twice as big as when we had left just four weeks ago, so big in fact that she was hard to hug over her baby bump! Dad had brought the VW van to accommodate us all and we were home in no time. Pierre had prepared a cold lunch and we all sat around the kitchen island updating each other. Dad thought we had good reason to celebrate our 'maiden' voyage on Mathilde and popped the cork of a bottle of Mumm. Flo, it seemed, was a little further on than first calculated and her C-section was brought forward to the second week of July.

I brought my laptop to the table and plugged our phones into it in order to see our photos. Charlie, Mum, Dad and I looked so happy and tanned and our pictures of all our friends, the club and our anchorages spoke for themselves. We raised our flutes and toasted Mathilde and our best holiday ever; Flo just raised her glass but did not drink!

***

After Flo and Pierre had left, Dad detailed his career changes which were all now confirmed. He then asked if Charlie and I had had any thoughts about our family wealth and how we might do something useful with it.

"The only thing we came up with was that we had all we could personally wish for and especially so now that we had Mathilde," I said. "You already fund our debit cards and I'm happy with the van for my personal use. Charlie's Prius is quite knackered and could do with being replaced but there's no rush for that."

"Actually, I hardly need a car, we do most things together anyway," said Charlie. "And the van is usually available for us."

"How about your student accommodation after your fresher year?" asked Dad. "Frank's money guy is very pro-property and knows your situation. What would you say to us buying a two-bedroom student flat in both Oxford and Cambridge. Firstly, for your use for the remainder of your courses, and afterwards to keep as a buy-to-let for student accommodation?"

"Do we have enough for that?" asked Charlie.

"The short answer is no, but Frank says we could start a holding company with this house as the major asset and surety for loans to buy the flats," said Dad. "Oh! And Mum and I want a swimming pool!"

"Wow," exclaimed Charlie. "That is such a great idea!"

"I agree… and a wow from me too!" I said. "What's the next step? Do Charlie and I start gazing in estate agent windows, or the online equivalent, or what?"

"Nothing for you to do at this stage," said Dad.

"Frank's guy, his name is Ed by the way, has connections and will look for both new-builds and conversions in both towns, sort the wheat from the chaff, and give us a short list. As for the pool, Frank has recommended an architect to visit and guide our decision-making process with some sketches. I think Frank's as keen as we are, maybe he'll join us for an inaugural dip!"

***

Charlie and I went back to our wing to get ready for our return to uni for the last term of our fresher year. There was something of a strangeness about our coming back after such a great time on Mathilde and our being together twenty-four-seven for four solid weeks.

"Penny for your thoughts?" asked Charlie.

"Sorry, I was miles away," I replied. "It just seems a little strange to be back after such a great holiday."

"Yeah, and the conversation about a swimming pool, it's like we've followed Alice through the looking glass! And what about having our own flats?"

"The idea of the flats is sound and very practical; interest rates are low, student rents in both towns are high, and property values over the next three years are bound to go up a good bit." I thought for a minute. "What do you make of this two-bedrooms thing? Will we be expected to get flat mates?"

"Interesting thing to ponder, I think I'd rather not have a flat mate," said Charlie. "In fact, if that's the deal, I'd rather have a one-bedroom or studio. How would we explain ourselves when we visit each other if there's someone else there?"

"Not if, it's when!" I said. "Although two bedrooms would make sense for letting after we finish our courses; let's put it to them over dinner tonight."

We had little to pack and our laundry from the holiday had mostly been done at the club in Mahon.

Charlie decided to have a shower before dinner and undressed in my room. I never tired of watching her as she removed each item to put on the bed. Her tan was all over perfect, her bum perhaps a shade lighter! She must have felt my eyes on her and turned to me.

"You look great my love," I said, my tone betraying my feelings. Charlie came to me and put her arms around my neck.

"And do I feel as good as I look?" She gently pressed against me.

"I can feel how pleased you are Nat." And she kissed me as she undid my jeans, and I pulled my polo over my head. Charlie laid on her back on the bed and I kissed her deeply while my hand roamed over her tummy and slowly downwards. I just brushed her sex and thighs and back again and up to her lovely, tanned breasts. Charlie moved her free hand down to her vagina and I could feel her nipples rise under my hand as she caressed herself. I broke our kiss and moved my mouth to her breasts and gently sucked first one then the other. Charlie brought up her hand and put her finger in my mouth. The scent and taste of her almost brought me to climax.

"Come inside Nat… now… please!"

I slid over her and she guided me in, raising her hips to take me to the fullest depth of her. We were both well on our way and I failed to hold back as I came powerfully. After my second wave Charlie shuddered to orgasm herself and held me in the way she does until we were both spent.

We lay like that for some time just smiling our love for each other, our eyes moist from the sheer joy of it… until my penis slid out of his own accord!

"Oops!" said Charlie, and laughed. "Shower time, eh?"

As we got back to the living room Flo was just arriving with a large Le Creuset and a fresh loaf balanced on top.

"Lamb ragout take-away!" she announced. Dad took the heavy pot from Flo.

"You should not be carrying heavy stuff at this stage Flo!"

As the stew heated up in the oven Charlie and I made a simple apéro of cheese and crackers. All of us had a bottle of Guinness except Flo who had an apple juice.

It was a warm evening, and we had the patio doors open as we sat around the coffee table with our drinks.

"So, what do you two think about getting your own flats?" asked Flo.

"It's amazing!" said Charlie. "And a pool—wow!"

"Yeah, I think I might move in when the pool's finished!" joked Flo.

"Just one thing about the flats," I said. "What's the thinking behind two bedrooms?"

"So you can have friends stay over or even have a flat-mate," said Mum.

"We just talked about that," said Charlie. "And thought a flat-mate might be a problem when we visit each other. We may even come under some friendly pressure about having a spare bedroom."

"What about equipping the second bedroom as a study with a clic-clac for occasional use?" Dad suggested.

"We had thought that a one-bedroom or even a studio might be better— and indeed cheaper to buy," I said.

"A one-bedroom flat could still have a clic-clac in the living-room," said Charlie. Mum and Dad looked at each other with the briefest of nods.

"You raise a good point," said Mum. "Talk it over between yourselves and we'll go along with whatever you decide and let Ed know your wishes." Charlie and I looked at each other and nodded our agreement.

Pierre had modified his recipe for the ragout to include more potatoes to suit our 'Englishness' and we enjoyed it all the more! The lamb melted in the mouth and the potatoes remained firm and took on the amazing flavour of the jus. Pierre called just after eleven to say that Le Coq was empty and that Flo could pick him up as soon as she liked.

We all kissed Flo goodnight as she went to collect Pierre, and then each other as we went to our beds. Flo had brought Harry back at lunchtime and he happily followed Charlie and I to our wing after a lengthy pee on the lawn.

Harry settled contentedly on his pad and Charlie and I cuddled up in my bed.

"I still think a one-bed flat is best," said Charlie. "What do you think?"

"I agree, we'll tell them in the morning."

Charlie showed no sign of leaving for her room and was soon gently snoring in sync with Harry. The next thing I knew was waking at first light with no sign of Charlie in my bed. After a satisfying pee, I went to her bedroom and slipped under the covers to cuddle her awake!

***

Over an early breakfast we told Mum and Dad about our decision to go for single-bed flats and Dad said he'd ring Ed later in the morning. We needed to be on our way by nine o'clock as we both had to be checked in by lunchtime and Charlie had a two-hour drive to Cambridge after dropping me off in Oxford. I was trying to look forward to resuming my studies but for some reason I could not focus. Charlie was more buoyant and looking forward to her friends and I reflected that over the previous two terms I had not made any real mates other than in the rather shallow 'pub and pizza' community; I resolved to be more active in the more serious extracurricular activities of the university.

***

After giving Charlie a brotherly kiss outside my hall of residence I went up to my room and changed into running kit; a run might be just the ticket to lift my mood.

I jogged through the city and out onto the Isis towpath where I quickened my pace. At the Iffley lock I felt quite winded and sat for a while on the same bench that Charlie and I had shared on the day of our reunion.

Remembering that time lifted my mood and I reflected on all that had occurred since then. Our outing with Mum and Dad, Mum's revelation about her and Flo, our wonderful holiday on Mathilde and the new friends we had made, and now plans for a swimming pool and independent living for the rest of our university life!

I ran another mile before turning back to Oxford. I was in a better frame of mind, more grounded about slipping back into student mode; it felt good.

CHAPTER TWENTY

REALITY

After a shower I went to the admin office to check in and returned to get my stuff ready for the first lecture of the summer term.

I checked the time; Charlie should be back in Cambridge in about an hour and I wanted to hear her voice and remind her of our bench at Iffley lock.

Adjim arrived with just a few minutes left before the check in deadline and rushed off to the admin office after dropping his bag.

We shook hands and bumped shoulders when he returned.

"Wow Nat, you look like an Arab with that tan!"

"And you still look like an Arab!" I joked and we laughed together. I was surprised at being quite pleased to see him. He told me of spending the first and last week of the Easter break in London with his cousin, a second secretary at his embassy, and the middle two weeks at home in his 'stan. The cousin was ten years older than Adjim and had a very nice embassy flat in the Bayswater Road, one of the swankiest addresses in London.

"I have to admit, Nat, that I enjoyed my time in London more than being at home. I've been corrupted and seduced by your Western decadence—and loved every minute of it!" He laughed again but sobered to describe his time at home.

"My father is now a deputy minister in our equivalent of your foreign office and taking his position very seriously. He insists that my sister and I behave accordingly, no fun at all!" Adjim paused. "Women do not have equal rights at home and my sister will soon be seventeen. She would like to follow me to an English university, but my father is strongly opposed. I love her dearly and I wish I could help; she's not a happy rabbit."

"Bunny!" I corrected him.

"Yes, bunny, I remember now!"

***

Our first lecture of the new term was a lot like an American style business presentation: a review of where we'd been, where we wanted to go and how we were going to get there. The stark difference with law, medicine and the sciences was that there were few, if any, laws, facts or formulae to learn and be examined. Lots of history of political systems to be studied and discussed, what worked and what didn't. Foreign relations, treaties, pacts, and conventions were as close as we would come to sets of rules, Geneva and Vienna conventions and Maritime law excepted.

At the end of this term, I would be 25% through the course and was consciously avoiding any postgraduate career thoughts; that said, I was an avid student of current affairs and especially foreign relations.

***

Charlie and I talked almost daily; like me, she had settled back into the student groove but our Easter break was never far from our minds. She and Mathilde chatted frequently, and it was clear that Mathilde derived much comfort from the friendship in her distress over the decline in her mother's condition.

The improved and strengthened relationship with our parents was an enormous boon to us and we resolved to spend most, if not all, of our weekends at home, not out of a sense of duty, but because we genuinely wanted to.

***

The architect had visited the house on the Monday following our return to uni and had taken about a 'million' photos of the available area for the pool to develop his suggestions. Charlie did not have a match on the first Saturday of the new term, so she picked me up on the Friday after lectures and we were home by dinner time.

Flo was already at our place helping Mum with the dinner and as usual had brought a contribution from Le Coq—a gravlax that we had so enjoyed before. During the meal I caught Mum's eye and we shared a knowing nod and smile, no words needed.

The conversation flowed companionably as we updated each other, and Dad advised that the architect would visit in the morning with some sketches. He had asked if we had a smart TV that he could use and we confirmed that we did.

Flo left at eleven to collect Pierre from work and we continued chatting over coffee. Charlie floated the idea of inviting Mathilde over for the next long weekend.

"To be frank," said Charlie. "The next bank holiday will almost certainly be her last opportunity for a break during this awful period."

"I can move up to the spare bedroom and she can have my room," I suggested and all agreed.

"It's curious," said Charlie. "We've only had a few hours together with her, and subsequent phone calls, but I really feel some affinity with her."

"That's actually great," said Mum. "This could well be the most important time in her life so far and a close friend will be a great boon."

Charlie was a little subdued following our chat about Mathilde and what she was going through; we resolved to call her in the morning with our invite. We had a gentle cuddle in Charlie's bed after our showers and I kissed her goodnight before going to my room.

***

The architect arrived just after eleven, a rather gangly 'ageing teenager' in his late thirties, and introduced himself to Charlie and me as Robert Wright, "Call me Bob."

Bob connected his laptop to our telly, and we gathered round to watch his show.

The presentation was stunning; Bob explained that he used a CAD, Computer Aided Design, software package to superimpose pools of various sizes and configurations onto the photos that he had taken on his previous visit. Each image had a pretty bikini-clad girl sitting on the side of the pool to help our sense of scale.

The images were so good that they seemed to show the pool already in use!

"And now for the sordid bit!" said Bob. "I've chosen a size and configuration that, from an architectural point of view, I think suits your wishes and available space. You can change any aspect of this plan, but I'll use it to give you an idea of the basic costs involved and pricing of options."

We were all most impressed and the image on the screen seemed as though the pool was exactly where it should be.

"I'm most impressed Bob," said Dad. "What size is that?"

"Six by three-and-a-half metres," Bob replied.

"So, let's talk about options," said Dad. Bob listed the most common options: springboard, underwater lights, sliding cover and several more.

"What about heating?" asked Dad.

"Glad you asked! We're just finishing a similar sized pool in Windsor which will be heated by a geothermal heat pump. If ordered at the same time as the pool, the groundwork, which involves buried pipes for the heat exchange, can be done with the pool excavation at a modest incremental cost. I can take you to see the work any time you say."

Bob handed Dad a folder with pool and option prices all laid out, as well as a thumb drive copy of his presentation.

"I'll leave all this with you to discuss amongst yourselves and you can get back to me at your convenience."

Bob took his leave, and Mum and Dad took a swift look at the costings. Dad looked at Mum whose mouth hadn't closed yet!

"It's only money, my love!" Dad said, and they both grinned.

"Let's go outside to picture our pool and see if we agree with young Bob," said Mum.

We all agreed that his plan was optimal. I paced out six metres—a perfect fit for the river side of our patio.

"OK, now leave it with me!" said Dad.

CHAPTER TWENTY-ONE

FLAT HUNTING

Charlie and I drove up to Oxford after an early Sunday dinner at home. Charlie had called Mathilde yesterday with our invite to visit and Mathilde had happily accepted. She had rightly pointed out that if there wasn't a common long weekend, she would be happy to fly up on a Friday evening and back on Sunday evening.

"Mathilde sounded very keen to come over sooner rather than later. Her Mum was still on a kind of plateau, but they knew that might not last very long," said Charlie. "I have a match on the Saturday after next and I thought it might be nice for her to visit then. We could all drive up in the morning, see a bit of Cambridge, have a nice pub lunch before the match—what do you think?"

"I like it—a nice high-intensity slice of our lives, let's do it!"

"OK, I'll call her when I get back to the hall this evening."

***

After a week back in the uni 'groove', Charlie and I were clearly settling into a happy pattern that nicely combined our student and family lives. One of our more mundane problems had been where to park our van during the week. This was solved by Charlie's friend, Camp David, who rented a flat with his partner, on the outskirts of Cambridge. The flat had a parking place which Charlie had free use of.

David's partner, Ralph, was a fashion photographer and was frequently away on shoots. It was through the parking arrangement that Charlie met Ralph in the last week of the spring term. Charlie thought that Ralph was a good ten years older than David, taller and rakishly good looking. Ralph, according to David, was a talented cook and promised to invite Charlie and Maggie for dinner sometime soon.

***

Charlie called me later to report on her calls to Mum and Mathilde; Mum was pleased with our plan and Mathilde very excited; she would text her flight details when booked.

"Maggie just told me that we're invited for dinner on Wednesday with David and Ralph. Maggie hasn't met Ralph yet and we're both looking forward to it; it's a first for both of us!" Charlie said. "And how nice it will be to have an entertaining evening without guys 'hitting' on Maggie and me all the time—not that Maggie minds that much!"

"I look forward to hearing all about it, enjoy the dinner! Sweet dreams."

"You too!"

***

Dad texted both of us on Wednesday to say he was going with Bob to visit the pool installation in Windsor on Saturday morning and that all would be welcome. Ed, Frank's financial wizard, also had some preliminary stuff to run by us regarding our student flats and would visit after lunch on Saturday. Charlie called on Thursday.

"Wow, things are hotting up, eh!" Said Charlie.

"Indeed, how was your dinner last night?"

"Fantastic! They are so good together and the food was great. I took a bottle of Mumm in a cold bag for apéro. Ralph is a pescatarian and made a bouillabaisse that was just as good as Pierre's—don't tell Pierre I said that!" Charlie had obviously had a great evening and was positively bubbling with her news.

"Ralph insisted on taking some photos of Maggie and me with a professional looking camera and told us we had supermodel potential—we guess he says that to everyone!"

"I must admit I'm a little jealous—I don't think I've any prospect of something similar here," I responded. "But I'm happy for you!"

141

"Hmm… there's a couple of ladies on my team who are *very* close, maybe I'll introduce you!" We laughed together; it was lovely to hear Charlie so happy.

***

Charlie picked me up as usual on Friday and we chatted on the way home about the meetings tomorrow. The pool would be great for all of us, Flo and Pierre included, but it was the idea of independent living in our future flats that really caught our imagination.

Dad would be a little late for dinner, so we waited for him. Mum explained that he and one of the theatre nurses were visiting Annie on their way home. Dad was a little down when he arrived.

"Annie's news is not so good I'm afraid," he explained. "Her radiotherapy is not helping and she's having a CAT scan next week to see what's going on. She looks a bit jaundiced to me which could be seriously bad news; we'll know more next week."

"How is she holding up?" asked Mum.

"She's remarkable really, very tired and her speech is an effort due to the radio, but her famous smile is never far away; we can only hope!"

Dad's mood lifted a little over dinner as we talked about our meetings tomorrow. We all decided to go and see the pool project in Windsor with young Bob, and Charlie and I were excited about whatever Ed had found for us.

***

The house in Windsor, a new construction, was finished and the groundwork for the pool was at an advanced state. The pool was not yet installed and was a one-piece fibreglass moulding resting in a wooden frame on its side near the excavation of its final position. Bob indicated the trench for the heat-exchange tubing, and it was clear that the pool and geothermal groundwork were best done hand in hand. The pool was the same model that Bob had recommended for us but looked huge out of the ground—much like a yacht when out of the water. When installed, the pool would rest in a layer of insulating cement-like material to conserve heat.

142

The contractor was using a mini-digger for the trench and pool excavation and I was impressed with the minimal disturbance to the surroundings. The excavated earth for the pool was loaded directly onto a trailer whilst the soil from the trench was already neatly deposited on plastic sheets ready for the backfill.

Back at home, Bob joined us for a simple beer and sandwich lunch and Dad confirmed that we would go ahead with Bob's recommendation in every respect. Bob explained that he would be our project manager and that the same contractors currently working in Windsor would start here as soon as the current groundwork was completed—probably within the next two weeks, weather permitting.

***

We sat around the coffee table with a cafetiere and imagined the view with a pool just the other side of the patio!

"I'm so looking forward to this," said Mum. "With the heating and cover we can make use of it all year round." Before she could gush further there was a ring at the door which Charlie answered.

She came back with a smart but casually dressed gentleman in his fifties carrying an extra-wide document case.

Charlie did the introductions and we settled back on the sofas and got a coffee mug for Ed.

"By way of introduction, let me say that in my former life I was an accountant with a large estate agency with offices throughout the shires, but I'm going straight now that I work for Frank!"

We enjoyed his joke but had the distinct impression that this was not the first time he'd used it!

"I've used my contacts in both Oxford and Cambridge to develop a short list based on the brief that Frank gave me," said Ed. "You'll notice that I have an A-list of three properties in Oxford and two in Cambridge and a B-list if you need a greater choice. The A-list properties are all in purpose-built, well-managed apartment buildings. Conversions can be problematic and there are none on either list." Ed unzipped his case and produced the agents' brochures for the A-list flats.

"I suggest the following," said Ed. "Drive or walk around to see the outside of these properties and the local area to get a feel for the locations. All the flats are within a mile of the central cluster of colleges and thus in easy walking distance. My B-list takes the radius out to two miles. For investment purposes after your courses, flats in this property sector are very popular, particularly with overseas students from wealthier backgrounds, and hence command top rents."

Charlie and I eagerly spread the brochures over the coffee table and flicked through them.

"This is so exciting!" said Charlie.

"So," said Ed. "I'll leave all this with you. When and if you want to view one of these please allow me to make the arrangements and absolutely do not make an offer—that'll be my job after a careful and emotionless evaluation; any questions?"

Dad looked around the table, no hands went up!

"Well, that's great Ed. Thank you very much, we'll be in touch when these two get back to me."

Heedless to say, Charlie and I did very little else other than study the brochures for the remainder of the afternoon.

***

After Charlie dropped me off in Oxford on Sunday evening, I Immediately changed into my running gear and marked a town plan with my three addresses, put the brochures in a small backpack, and set off. At each address I took out the brochure and tried to identify the flat by the floor level, and description of the view from the windows.

There was in fact little to choose between the first two but the third was a new-build. All had just city views and all had allocated parking. The decision would be made based on building management's reputation, the interiors and price, and there was always Ed's B-list if nothing 'clicked'.

Charlie called later to report her safe arrival and I told her about my jog round Oxford to see my A-list flats.

"I'm doing the exact same thing tomorrow," said Charlie. "Shall I call Dad tomorrow about any flats we want to view?"

"Yes please, I want to view all my three, there's really nothing to choose between them from the outside," I answered. "Any evening around five is good."

The agent for two of my flats called at five the next day and we arranged to visit both flats on Tuesday evening. Within five minutes, I had a call from the agent of my third flat and made a similar arrangement for Wednesday.

The first of my Tuesday flats had a Chinese post-grad medical student tenant who was returning to China after this term. The agent explained that he was also the letting agent for the two flats and that both were owned by the same family who were going to resettle in Australia where their daughter lived. Both flats were available with contents.

There was little to choose between the two flats except that the second was slightly more modern, with bigger windows and a better equipped kitchen.

I thanked the agent and told him that Ed would be in touch.

I felt a little melancholy as I strolled slowly back to the hall. After all our excitement in the run-up to visiting the flats, I now felt rather lonely as the reality set in. I resolved to go for a run and not mention my feelings to Charlie until she has seen her two flats.

***

I ran my favourite route down the towpath and pushed myself to go a further two miles past the Iffley lock.

The run did the trick and I felt more positive on my return. I called Charlie after a shower to report on my two flats but did not mention my feelings. Charlie would see her first flat tomorrow at the same time as I was seeing my third; she'd call after her visit.

***

Adjim came in as I finished my call and suggested we go out for a kebab and beer dinner. I was pleased to see him and my mood improved over the meal; the kebab was great but I dreaded to think of the calories!

"Have you any ideas about how to help my sister Nat?" Adjim asked as we drank our beers straight from the bottle.

"Why not wait till next year when she takes her university entrance exams, and in the meantime, try to convince your father to relax a bit; can your mother help, would she even want to?" I warmed to my thought process. "And anyway, your father's in the foreign ministry, if he gently moved to a more liberal attitude he would gain kudos with his western counterparts, be seen as a reformer even. If your sister passed her exams you could show the courses available to her — you could present a compelling case for her to realise her ambitions — and another thing, if she chose a course at Oxford, you would still be around for her first couple of years."

"Wow Nat!" said Adjim. "You give me a lot to think about! Another beer?"

Adjim got the next round and was lost in thought as he drank his beer.

***

My third flat was a new-build with a fully equipped, modern kitchen and a breakfast bar island similar to the one at home, only smaller. The brochure only had a floor plan of the flat but no photos and now that I stood in the empty areas I had none of my depressing thoughts of yesterday. The bedroom was bigger than in the other two flats and the bathroom seemed bigger as it had just a shower and no bath—fine by me! The flat was on the top floor of the four-storey block and had a view of the roofs of some of the lovely Cotswold stone buildings in the college area of town.

I didn't need to go to Ed's plan-B!

***

Charlie rang about an hour after my return to hall.

"Hi Nat!" said Charlie. "I need to be cheered up, my flat was so depressing and I could never see myself living in such a place!"

"Well, you've come to just the right place my love," I said. "I felt exactly like that yesterday after seeing my first two flats, but the flat I've just seen has greatly lifted my spirits. The other two were pokey with

146

depressing cheap furniture, whereas today's flat is an open plan new-build and even has a breakfast bar just like at home. I'm going to tell Dad I've made my choice!"

"Wow, you're so lucky, I wish I had a new-build to look at, maybe I'll ask Dad to see if Ed can come up with something a bit more modern. The flat today didn't even have cable!"

"How does tomorrow's flat look from the brochure?"

"More of the same, I'm afraid. I'll go and see it anyway but I think I'll pin my hopes on something from Ed's plan-B, something new would be great!"

"Well, have I cheered you up?"

"Actually yes! I'm very pleased for you and you've given me hope for my quest as well. By the way, Mathilde texted me—she's arriving at eight-fifteen on Friday evening at Gatwick and her return flight is at ten Sunday night. I texted her to say we'll pick her up and not to eat anything on the plane!"

"I wish we were together," I said. "I'd love to cheer you up properly!"

"Oh, stop it Nat, I have actually been feeling a bit horny just listening to your voice, I think I might do something about it when we've finished."

"Why not do something now, I'd love to hear you. What are you wearing, I want to picture you?"

"Oh Nat, I'm only wearing one of your shirts, and I've already started… I'm just sliding my finger over my labia… I'm already wet… talk to me Nat!"

"I can just picture you my love, I've got a great stiffy and have it in hand… I wish it were you…"

"My clitoris is so swollen, Nat… I'm imagining my finger is your tongue and I'm doing what you do… I'm a little inside now… Oh, it feels so good Nat… I've put the phone down… I'm caressing my breast… can you hear me OK?"

"Perfectly… you're bringing me with you… I wish it really was my tongue… I'm almost there… you?"

Charlie's moan told me all I needed to know and I came strongly, my semen shooting up to my chest. Charlie was still coming and I could hear her stifling the cries with her hand.

"Oh Nat… I'm still coming… coming… you OK?"

"Right with you my love!"

"I've crossed my legs with my hand still there Nat… squeezing tight… I love you so much!"

I could hear Charlie coming off her highs and see her perfectly in my mind.

"Me too my love… me too!"

CHAPTER TWENTY-TWO

MATHILDE

Charlie and I took Mum and Dad's Lexus to meet Mathilde at Gatwick. Her plane was on time and we just had twenty minutes to wait. The M25 London ring road had usually calmed down by this time of an evening and we had not added much of a contingency to our estimation of travel time from home.

The arrivals area was pretty busy and we saw her well before she saw us waving like lunatics!

Mathilde was a small woman, her hair perhaps even shorter than when we had last seen her. She was wearing a Breton striped T-shirt, skinny blue jeans, and towing a small 'wheelie-bin' carry-on case.

Her face lit-up when she saw us and she skipped through the throng to fall into Charlie's arms. They kissed in the French way and then it was my turn! We had been so looking forward to seeing her and we were not disappointed. The weeks slipped away and our feelings confirmed the way we had felt about her during the interim.

"I so pleased to see you!" said Mathilde, and the three of us went into a three-way hug that partially blocked the arrivals exit!

I took her bag and steered the still hugging pair of them to the short-term car park.

It was after nine o'clock by the time we arrived home and Mum and Dad received a warm embrace almost as strong as ours.

Dad popped the cork on some bubbles and we settled down on the settees looking out to the Thames.

"Such a house," said Mathilde, clearly impressed.

"A big warm welcome to you Mathilde," said Dad by way of a toast, and we 'chinked' our flutes with each other.

After the champagne, Charlie and I took Mathilde to our wing where we all sat on my bed and Mathilde updated us on her mother's condition. She wept quietly as she spoke and Charlie and I hugged her from both sides. It was actually a first for us to share the sad emotion of an impending death amongst family or friends and we truly felt that we were sharing Mathilde's pain.

Mathilde suddenly smiled through her tears and hugged us back.

"I truly love you two, and thank you for your concern." Mathilde wiped a tear from Charlie's cheek and went into the bathroom to freshen up.

Mum had poached a whole side of salmon which she served on the kitchen island with a Russian and a mixed green salad in wooden bowls. We had a little of Pierre's gravlax left over from a couple of days ago which we served with fresh country bread. Mathilde cooed over the gravlax and tucked into the poached salmon with gusto.

Over the meal we explained our plan for the weekend and asked if she had anything special she would like to do.

"No, I am just so happy to see you all again and share a little slice of your life. The football game tomorrow sounds wonderful and I can give a full report to my parents about it!"

It was already after eleven o'clock and Mathilde was clearly wiped out, without doubt our emotional connection in my room had taken its toll.

Charlie and Mathilde kissed us all goodnight and went to our wing while Mum, Dad and I chatted over coffee.

"My heart goes out to that poor girl," said Mum. "What a sad burden for anyone, let alone one so young!"

"Perhaps she has some close friends at uni—boyfriend?" said Dad. "All we can do is ensure she knows we are here to support her whatever she needs. Has she spoken of her life after her mother dies?"

"No, and what's sad about it is that it seems she is not as close to her father as we might have expected. Just a feeling really, but Charlie and I both noticed it."

***

150

Dad had a call from the hospital early the next morning and had to miss out on our trip to Cambridge. He was on his way before the rest of us turned up for breakfast.

Flo and Pierre popped in to meet Mathilde and Flo came back after dropping Pierre off at the Le Coq. We would see them again this evening anyway as Dad had booked us in for dinner.

"Now you have a spare seat in the car, can I come to Cambridge with you?" asked Flo.

"Of course," Mum replied. "We'd better leave soon, eh?"

The Lexus seated five in comfort but Flo needed to sit up front to be comfortable with her bump. Mathilde had never been this close to identical twins before and was forever looking from one to the other in amazement.

"You should see us when neither of us is pregnant!" said Flo, and regaled us with some of the practical jokes that she and Mum had pulled in the past.

From the backseat Mum and Flo looked exactly the same. They still had the same short hairstyle and always went to the hairdressers' together.

Mathilde sat between Charlie and me in the back and the three of us held hands for the whole two-hour trip up the M1 to Cambridge.

We made one pit stop at a services on the M1 so Flo could have a pee!

"I'll be very glad when this little bugger stops squeezing my bladder!" said Flo.

After a brief stroll round Charlie's college we walked the short distance along the river Cam to the restaurant that she had booked for our lunch. We had a window table with a great view of the Cam right in the centre of the town. Mathilde was most impressed with old town Cambridge.

"How old is your university?" she asked.

"Eight hundred years!"

"Wow!"

***

Charlie just had the salad bar and an omelette for her lunch as she would be playing shortly; the rest of us had a more aggressive go at the salad bar with cold cuts and egg mayonnaise.

Charlie drove the Lexus to the playing field as she knew the town better than the rest of us.

"I have to leave you now as I'm only just in time for the pre-match briefing, a plus tard!"

"Bonne chance!" said Mathilde.

We had a half-hour wait to kick-off and strolled over to the modest spectator stand—most supporters chose to stand near the touch line but Flo needed to get off her feet.

Mum and Flo sat either side of Mathilde and nattered away; I was just happy that the weekend was going so well and that Mathilde was clearly enjoying herself. I wondered if Mathilde had made the connection that she would soon be losing a loved one and we would soon be welcoming a new one—the beat goes on!

***

The visiting and Cambridge teams jogged onto the pitch in two parallel lines carrying about six footballs between them. Small groups of players practiced with the balls to warm-up as the referee and two lineswomen followed them to the centre spot. After a short period, the ref blew her whistle to summon the two captains for the toss up; the visitors won and chose the end to our right. The teams formed up and Charlie was the half back on our side; she waved to us and then concentrated on the opening moves.

The teams were very evenly matched, with equal possession, and at half-time, there was no score. The Cambridge substitutes brought trays of quartered oranges and bottled water for first the visitors, and then their teammates. Both teams went into the customary captains pep talk huddle, arms around each other's shoulders to form a tight circle.

The second half started with great vigour by the visitors in the hope of an early goal but the Cambridge defence was well up to it. Half way through the second half Charlie made a break-out down the right wing but the Cambridge forwards were slow to keep up and Charlie had no one to pass to, instead she took a shot at a very narrow angle but the ball bounced away off the crossbar. The Cambridge supporters moaned and the captain gave Charlie a short hug, but the score stayed the same until, in the closing seconds of the game, the visiting centre forward tried an all-or-nothing long shot from centre field which miraculously got past the Cambridge goalie; the ref blew-up for full-time.

***

The mood in the pub was only a little less rowdy than usual. Maggie and Camp David made a huge fuss of Mum and Flo, they'd seen Mum a few times but this was the first they'd known about Flo. Equally, Mathilde came in for a big welcome and I sensed that they all thought she might be my girlfriend; I looked after Mathilde closely to foster the idea and gave Charlie a conspiratorial wink!

The captain tapped her glass for attention.

"There are no stars today, frankly you're all a bunch of losers! Charlie came close but even that was pretty pathetic and certainly not worthy of a down-down!" Everyone was booing the captain and laughing at the same time. She then turned to the landlord.

"A round of drinks please for my favorite ex-footballers!"

The booing turned to cheers as the captain went around the players for a comradely embrace.

Mathilde looked amazed at this bar-full of certified idiots and grabbed my arm.

"This is incredible—I just love it!"

Just as we were leaving, Camp David gave Charlie a largish envelope.

"Open it when you get home, OK?" said David.

153

CHAPTER TWENTY-THREE

LATER, ON SATURDAY

Flo drove us back to Maidenhead.

"I'll have to stop driving soon," she said. "Look, my bump is touching the bottom of the wheel with my arms straight out!"

We made the same pit stop halfway home and Flo was in a chatty mood when she returned to the car.

"I had a nice talk with Lady Helen last night. She and her young man came into Le Coq just after eleven without a booking, and Harold politely reminded her that the kitchen closed at eleven but Pierre came out just then and saved the moment."

"I've put the kitchen to bed for the night Lady Helen, but if you keep it simple…"

"Cheddar cheese on toast, toasted one-side only, cheese on the untoasted side, Worcestershire sauce and some bubbles please." She turned to the officers at their usual table. "You guys OK with that?"

Pierre went back to the kitchen and Harold brought the champagne.

"Helen asked if they could join me, she asked how I was doing and admired my bump! She insisted we drop the 'Lady' and we chatted like old mates; she's really very nice but came over as a rather lonely girl, her boyfriend didn't say much, if anything!" Flo continued, "I saw the female protection officer pop outside and then came over to speak quietly to Helen.

"'OK,' said Helen. 'But just one and he must share with the gang, no questions—just pics, OK?'

"Helen told me she had made an 'inappropriate' remark about the fox-hunting home secretary last night and a bunch of paparazzi had been chasing her all day for further comment. The protection lady went out and came back with a scruffy young photographer. Helen asked if I'd mind being 'in shot' and of course I didn't!

"'Just ignore him and behave as we were, it's Sunday the day after tomorrow and they just need some column inches for the tabloids," she said.

"'May I ask who your friend is ma'am?'

"'I said no questions!'

"'Sorry ma'am.' The photographer took some very fast pictures and left!

"Helen apologised and said the paparazzi were often a pest but they could be used to advantage on occasion."

***

It was just after seven when we arrived home and Dad looked freshly showered and ready for the evening, our table at Le Coq was booked for nine. While the girls went to our wing to shower and change, Mum and Flo told Dad how their day had been and how much Mathilde had enjoyed it, and then went upstairs to get ready.

"Why were you called out this morning?" I asked.

"Quite unnecessary actually, one of my kids just needed a tweak of her drug cocktail but they wanted my blessing! How are you two getting on with Mathilde?"

"Just fine! It's like we've been mates for ages — she was amazed by the after-match pub scene — totally outside her experience I think! I'll go and see if I can have the bathroom yet."

I knocked on Charlie's door and she opened it.

"Can I have my shower yet?" I asked. Charlie was in a bra and panties and looking very inviting! While Charlie was choosing her evening gear Mathilde came in from the bathroom wearing just a pair of panties. I covered my eyes theatrically and Mathilde laughed.

"Not to worry Nat—I have very little to see!"

I uncovered my eyes and grinned.

"What you have Mathilde looks very good to me, what more do you need? Can I have the shower now?"

Mathilde went back to my room and Charlie said,

"Well? What do you think?"

"She looks fine, all in proportion; I haven't seen boobs that small since you were twelve... maybe thirteen!"

155

Charlie laughed and gave me a big hug and I went into the bathroom before it became difficult to leave!

When I came back to Charlie's room Mathilde was sitting on the bed in skinny jeans and a designer T-shirt, Charlie was in her jeans also and held up two tops for me to choose, I chose one and she said,

"Bra or not?"

"Not!" I said.

"Nor me!" said Mathilde with a giggle. "I haven't even got one! I do have a sports bra for running though."

I thought for a moment that Charlie and I might have been a little more familiar than brothers and sisters normally are, I decided not to worry!

I dressed in my room and we all went back to the living room. Mum looked great and Flo looked as good as she could be in a copious maternity dress! The island was laid out with a cheeseboard of England's finest, some crackers and a bowl of Branston pickle; wine glasses lined-up down the centre. Dad took a bottle from the fridge and pulled the cork.

Mum was explaining the cheeses to Mathilde and the order in which to try them—mildest first then leading up to the Stilton! Dad poured and toasted Mathilde.

"*Santé* Mathilde," said Dad. "I hope this is just the first of many times we can get together—enjoy our English apéro!" We all touched glasses with Mathilde.

"Thank you Arthur, I feel so happy to be with you all again!" Mathilde welled-up and Mum gave her a cuddle. Mathilde took another drink from her glass.

"But this is French rosé," she said with a grin. Dad went to the fridge and gave Mathilde the bottle.

"But this is perfect, I never knew you had English wine!"

"What was in that big envelope that Camp David gave you Charlie?" Flo asked.

"Oh, I forgot about it! I'll get it from my kitbag."

Charlie opened the envelope on the kitchen island. Inside there were ten A5 glossy photos.

"These are the photos that Ralph took when Maggie and I had dinner at their place—I can't believe what he's done!"

The photos were all fashion magazine style shots showing Charlie in various situations typical of the genre. Ralph had changed backgrounds as well as light and shade but it was unmistakably the real Charlie in every picture!

Charlie read a short note tucked in with the pictures.

Dear Charlie,

I've played around with my photos using a professional 'photoshop' type software, but as you can see, I have not touched your lovely face except for the lighting!

My photo editor likes you! Give me a call—no pressure!

Love, Ralph X

"Oh Charlie!" said Mum. "These are absolutely stunning—you look like a supermodel!"

"That's exactly what Ralph said he'd do," said Charlie. "You can't believe anything you see these days."

"Time we were off!" said Dad.

There were six of us, so I used 'my' van to get to the restaurant!

Le Coq was packed as usual for a Saturday night; the only empty table being the one Dad had booked. Harold kissed Flo on both cheeks and led us to the table. Flo introduced Mathilde to him and Harold welcomed her in flawless French.

Flutes were already arranged on the table and Harold popped the cork and poured some bubbles for all except Flo.

"*Compléments de* Chef Pierre!" said Harold. "Welcome to Le Coq Mathilde."

"Thank you Harold." Mathilde tasted the bubbles. "Hmm… this is really nice champagne!"

Harold handed Mathilde the bottle to read the label.

"Oh no!" cried Mathilde. "You even make excellent champagne here!"

"Pierre's little joke!" said Harold, and fetched the menus.

***

When Flo brought us home last night she had asked Charlie if she could borrow Ralph's photos to show Pierre.

"He's going to love them—he always said you were too good-looking
to be a lawyer!"

***

Mum, Dad and I were first up in the morning and I made a large caffererre
for our prebreakfast coffee while we waited for the girls. Mathilde was a
little 'merry' on our return and Charlie and she had retired shortly after we
got home.

I took the opportunity to update them on Ed's A-list of flats in Oxford
and that only the newly built one had really interested me. We looked
through my three brochures and Mum said,

"Yeah, I can see why, the first two are a little dowdy in comparison."

"So, shall I tell Ed to go ahead with that?" asked Dad.

"Oh yes! Thank you so much—I'm very excited!"

"OK, your Mum and I will pop over to see it during the week—just to
see what you're getting into!"

"Not such good news from Charlie," Mum said. "She didn't like her
two, so we'll ask to see Ed's B-list for her with emphasis on any new ones,
if any."

Charlie surfaced just as we finished the coffee and made a fresh pot.

"Mathilde is still asleep so I think we should let her lay-in for a bit, I
don't think she's used to much alcohol!"

"How about I pop into town for some croissants and a baguette?" I
suggested. "We had plenty to eat last night."

"For sure, Mathilde won't fancy fried bacon on a hangover!" said Mum
with a smile.

I went out to find a baker.

CHAPTER TWENTY-FOUR

SUNDAY

Our Sunday with Mathilde was a marvellously relaxing family day. Shortly before lunch, Mathilde had a call from her mother and wandered out onto the patio to take it. She had her back toward us and walked slowly down to the river to sit on the bench. Harry had followed her and sat leaning against Mathilde's leg. We looked at each other showing our concern that there may be some bad news. Mathilde finished the call, slid the phone into her shirt pocket and leant over to give Harry a long hug.

When she came back to the lounge her cheeks were wet and Mum met her in a warm embrace. I noticed that Mum rocked Mathilde a little from side to side exactly as Charlie and I do.

After a while Mathilde pulled back and Mum kissed her on the forehead. Mum's top was wet with Mathilde's tears.

"I'm sorry," said Mathilde. "My mother sounded so weak, but all she wanted was to hear about my weekend with you. I told her all the things we had done and she was very happy. She sends her love to you all with many thanks for putting up with me!" Mathilde's eyes welled up anew and Mum took her back into her arms.

***

Flo arrived for lunch with her usual contribution of a starter from Le Coq, and two copies of *The Mail* on Sunday. Flo opened the paper to page two and pointed to a photo of her and Lady Helen; the headline read, *Lady Helen tells Home Secretary where to shove his riding crop.* Under the photo it read, *Lady Helen enjoying a late supper with an unnamed lady pal at the famous Michelin starred restaurant, Le Coq en Pate, on the banks of the*

Thames near Eton. The article went on to describe the ongoing media campaign against fox hunting to which Lady Helen frequently contributed.

We all agreed that Flo looked great and that we should get a free dinner at Le Coq for the advert!

Mathilde was clearly confused and Flo had to explain the anti-blood-sports campaign.

Mom had prepared a typical English Sunday lunch of a slow-cooked shoulder of lamb with rosemary and garlic slices tucked into small slits cut into the meat and served with minted new potatoes, baby carrots and mint sauce.

Pierre's starter was one he was experimenting with and wanted feedback from us. Flo opened the box and put six vol au vent on the table.

"It's actually quite simple," explained Flo. "They're stuffed with finely chopped lobster and mayonnaise; I had one yesterday and liked it a lot. He's also trying chopped scallops and prawns the same way!"

Mathilde brightened up and thoroughly enjoyed our meal. We would only have a light supper this evening before taking Mathilde to Gatwick on our way back to uni.

After lunch we all sat outside in the warm early June sunshine and just chatted amiably as if we met like this often as old friends. I reflected that this was only our second experience with Mathilde and how wonderful it was that our expectations had been correct and we now had such a great pal.

After a suitable period for our lunch to digest, Charlie suggested a run along the river.

We changed into running gear in our wing; Charlie and Mathilde into Lycra shorts and sports bras, and myself into cotton shorts and a vest. Both girls happily changed without modesty in front of me and it was lovely to see Charlie naked, I was missing her so much. My comment to Charlie that Mathilde's breasts were like Charlies when she was twelve, actually applied to her whole body—she was a fully grown woman in the body of an adolescent!

We ran along the river to Boulter Lock and then up through the town and around Summerleaze Lake before heading back home. Mathilde had a lovely easy stride that looked like she could run a marathon.

We joined Mum and Dad on the patio to warm-down with a cold beer, Flo was taking her afternoon nap upstairs. Dad pointed out our plan for a pool and said he hoped it would be installed by the time Mathilde next visited. Mathilde then showed us some photos on her phone of her home in the hills above Toulon.

"This is my mother's house and has been in her family for several generations," Mathilde explained. "My father has a very nice penthouse apartment in Marseille from when he was playing football, and he uses it for a few days every week now that he is a coach. My mother has not been there for a very long time and I have never been there without her. I think he 'entertains' there sometimes!" Mathilde's face darkened.

"But he seemed very attentive to you and your mother when you all visited the boat?" Mum said.

"Yes!" said Mathilde. "But my mother is also quite wealthy!"

***

We went to our wing for showers and let Mathilde go first. As soon as we heard the shower Charlie closed her door and we hurried out of our clothes for a serious cuddle. There was little chance that we had time to make love but Charlie took my erect penis in hand and brought me quickly to a lovely climax. She was hot herself but got off the bed to get a box of tissues for me.

"I actually owed you that, my love!" she said. "I'll tell you why after we leave Mathilde at Gatwick."

The shower stopped and we heard Mathilde go to my bedroom. I went to the shower first!

***

Mathilde's flight was at ten o'clock and she needed to check-in by nine. The motorway would be clear as it was a Sunday so we planned to leave shortly after eight.

Mum and Flo had prepared yet another English meal for our light supper, a Melton Mowbray pork pie, a York ham on the bone and a selection of chutneys and pickles. Dad sliced the ham with an old-fashioned carving knife and Mathilde laughed at his surgical mask and bandana that he wore for the 'operation'. Mathilde loved it all and Mum gave her a gift-wrapped box of mini pork pies to put in her bag.

Our remaining time together had flown away and the three of us went to collect our bags. Apart from the usual hugs and kisses, Mum gave Mathilde an extra-long embrace.

"We wish you bon courage Mathilde. We know you will have difficult times coming and I want you to know that you can call me at any time, day or night, if you would like to talk, OK?" Mathilde just nodded, she was struggling for control and failing fast. We all three picked up our bags and headed out to the van.

***

We parked in the short-term carpark so that we could stay with Mathilde until her flight. She had stopped crying from Mum's lovely words and was clearly very sad to be leaving us. We had hardly spoken a word as we sat on the seats outside the departure area. When her flight was called we walked with arms around each other until she had to go on alone.

Charlie and I hugged each other all the way back to the van. We truly loved Mathilde and our hearts ached for the pain she was in. We consoled ourselves with the thought that we'd given her a brief respite. We both were very impressed with Mum's parting words to her—we surely had the best Mum in the world.

***

We drove in silence out of the airport complex and onto the M25. Our drive to Oxford would take about an hour and a half and we were both lost in our thoughts.

"What did you mean when you said that you 'owed me one' while Mathilde was in the shower?" Charlie grinned, a first sign that her mood was lifting.

"I haven't had a chance to tell you about something that happened, or rather might have happened, between Mathilde and I when we went to bed Friday night," said Charlie. "Mathilde was still upset and weeping and I

162

could hear her from my room. I got up and went to console her. We were both in our nightshirts and I lay on your bed with my arm round her and we embraced as she wept. She lay with me as I do with you, her leg over mine, and I could feel her sex against me and the contact was moist. I swear I didn't know what I should do but the decision was taken away from me as she fell asleep. I think she was emotionally exhausted and her sleep was a merciful release. Now here's where I owe you one! I extricated myself from our embrace and went to my bed. I found I was really hot and thought to come and visit you but didn't in case she woke and needed me. I'm sure you know what's coming…"

"Coming indeed!" I said. "I'm getting hot myself just thinking about it!"

At that moment we saw the sign for services one mile ahead and I turned in. The car park was less than half full and I parked as far as possible from any other cars.

***

We made loving but urgent love with Charlie kneeling over me. I had reclined my seat and we had loved to the point of tears.

As we approached Oxford Charlie said she wished I had my flat so she could stay overnight.

"Soon my love, soon," I said.

Charlie wanted to talk about her self-pleasuring brought on by the contact with Mathilde on Friday night.

"You were turned on Nat just by my telling you about it, but what do you make of my turn-on?"

"I've thought about little else since our quickie in the carpark, Charlie," I said. "My first reaction was 'well, how lovely', and that's still how I feel. Then I thought, 'what if you two had gone all the way'? And I feel exactly the same! I would not feel that you had been unfaithful I don't think. I've wondered sometimes before at how girls are much more tactile with each other than men and how it might progress; maybe it's just my male mind that thinks that way, but can't see any harm in it, I wonder even if I might enjoy watching!"

163

Charlie looked at me lovingly, "It's lovely of you to think like that Nat, I was just a little worried about what you might think. You know, Maggy told me that lesbian sex on porn sites is very popular amongst men, not just lesbian women, so there, you have it!"

"You know Charlie, we both love our new friend and if the circumstances happened again you should just go with your heart."

"You're a wonderful man Nat, it will be great when we have our flats!"

CHAPTER TWENTY-FIVE

AURÉLIE

It was the Tuesday evening after our weekend with Mathilde and I was going over in my mind our conversation about Mathilde. I remembered the occasion when I had seen them both topless and could easily see them cuddled up together, and further, how could there not be some sexual dimension to that, or was I just thinking like a man again? My phone rang to break my reverie; it was Charlie.

"Hello Nat," I could hear Charlie sobbing as she tried to speak. "Oh Nat, I'm so sad, Mathilde just called… her mother died today…" Charlie broke down and all I could hear was her crying into her phone. I waited for her and swallowed my own sadness.

"Nat?"

"I'm still here sweetheart. I'm so sorry to hear that… poor girl, what can we do? Does she have someone with her—besides her dad I mean?"

"Yes, her aunt Anne, on her mother's side, is there and she and Alain are doing all the needful. She will know tomorrow when the funeral will be and asks if we can come over."

"I think we should, what do you think?"

"Of course," said Charlie. "I'll call Mum now and tell her the sad news."

Charlie called again later to say that Mum would phone Mathilde's landline in the morning and hopefully speak with both Mathilde and Alain.

Mum reported back via a conference call on our WhatsApp group the next day; she explained.

"It was the aunt who answered, Alain was not around, she's called Anne and sounds just like Aurélie, she was very friendly over the phone and gave me all the details for the funeral and said how she looks forward to meeting you two. I then had a very tearful conversation with Mathilde.

She seemed very pleased to talk to me and asked if I could come as well—we did connect very well over our weekend, but what do you think?" Charlie and I agreed.

"Actually, it would be great for you to be there, both for Mathilde as well as for us. This is our first funeral after Granddad," I said.

"OK, the funeral is on Saturday, can you take Friday off?" We both said we could and Mum said she'd make our arrangements.

***

Charlie picked me up outside my hall and we were home for dinner by half past seven on Thursday evening. Mum explained all the arrangements she had made.

"We fly from Gatwick at ten-thirty tomorrow, I've booked a car, a Citroën C4 like at Easter, and a hotel a little to the south of their village, which is called La Revest-les-Eaux… what else? Oh yes, I spoke with the funeral director, or Pompes funèbres, and ordered some flowers, he told me that it would be quite a big affair and that we could view Aurélie's body at home until noon when they would put her in the coffin ready for the funeral at two!"

"Wow Mum—you're fantastic!" said Charlie.

"What's all this about seeing her body at home?" I said.

"Yes, they still do that in France rather than at a funeral parlour, don't worry, there'll be no smell, she will have been embalmed very shortly after her death and made very presentable," Mum replied.

When Charlie and I went to our rooms we found that Mum had laid out my only suit, a sombre mid-grey, with a white shirt and black tie from Dad's wardrobe.

On Charlie's bed was her black 'power suit' and silk blouse.

Mum turned up while we were packing our 'wheelie-bin' carry-on bags.

"Have I forgotten anything?" she smiled.

"Absolutely nothing Mum!" Charlie replied.

"You've both got black shoes and I've given them a quick polish."

Charlie called Mathilde before dinner and gave her our arrangements. She was a little more composed than the last time and very pleased that

166

Mum was coming. She asked Charlie to call when we were settled in our hotel.

Flo arrived to have dinner with us and stay the night so she could take us to Gatwick in the morning.

***

Mum's arrangements went perfectly and we arrived at the hotel at half-past two on Friday afternoon. Charlie smiled as she hung up her clothes and my suit.

"Look how things have changed in such a short time. Mum has actually booked us into a double hotel room—how's that for a leap forward!"

Charlie called Mathilde when we were settled and she asked if she could come to see us right away.

Mathilde tried to smile as we hugged each other in greeting but it was a miserable failure; her red eyes told the story of her distress. Her tears flowed freely and both Mum and Charlie welled up.

We sat in the easy chairs in the reception area and Mathilde explained that she badly needed some time away from home. We invited her to join us in the hotel coffee shop while we had a light late lunch.

Mathilde eventually dried her tears and explained the practicalities.

"You can come to see my mother with me this afternoon or tomorrow morning," she explained. "But now is better as there is no formality. I will see you at the church tomorrow and you can come to our house after the funeral."

Mathilde gave us each a folded printed card with the order of the catholic service. On the cover was a lovely photo of Aurélie from her ballet days.

We freshened up in our rooms and rejoined Mathilde downstairs. She drove a tiny Smart car and Charlie went with her and Mum and I followed up through the beautiful hilly countryside to her house. The house itself was a revelation: all on one level with a terracotta tiled roof over Provençale pastel-coloured walls. It fitted the environment as if it had grown there.

Mathilde's aunt was a younger version of her mother, slim and elegant, with similar short cropped hair much like Mathilde's. She welcomed us warmly and we followed her and Mathilde to the room where Aurélie lay.

For Charlie and me it was the first time that we had seen a dead person and we were uneasy at the prospect. In the event however, the experience was calming and tasteful, not in the least distressing.

Aurélie was dressed in a white gown from neck to ankles, her hands clasped at her waist and a rosary entwined with her fingers. Small white flowers had been formed into a crown around her head and her face made up as if she might awake from a deep sleep, a hint of a smile on her lips. On her feet were a pair of ballet slippers.

Mathilde was holding hands with Mum and Charlie and smiled even as a tear ran down her cheek.

"She looks lovely," said Mum. "A beautiful picture for you to keep in your heart."

We sat on a row of chairs in silent contemplation. Only then did I notice the flowers in the room; a stunning array of red roses surrounded by the same white flowers that Aurélie had in her hair.

The aunt had left us when we sat and rejoined us a little later.

"We can take coffee on the patio if you wish," she said, and we all followed her outside.

***

Alain joined us and we went through the *mes condoléance* routine again. It was noticeable that Mathilde barely acknowledged his arrival. After coffee Mathilde took us for a tour of the house and grounds. The house itself was much bigger than it appeared from the front and had several out-buildings which included a small detached cottage in the same style as the main house. Mathilde explained that they had a housekeeper/gardener couple living there and that they had been virtual co-parents to her as she grew up.

Mathilde cracked open the front door.

"Cou cou!" she called.

The same lady who had served our coffee opened the door fully and embraced Mathilde who then introduced us; her name was Angèle. We sat on plastic garden chairs in the small yard and were shortly joined by her husband, Georges.

Georges was a tall, robust, ruddy man, probably in his early seventies, whilst his wife, somewhat younger, was a petite, pretty woman of around sixty, her grey hair pulled into a tight bun. Without asking, Georges produced a chilled bottle of rosé and five glasses!

Georges lightened our mood, his ready laugh welcome after our rather sombre afternoon.

"By the way," said Georges. "We really enjoyed the pork pies you sent with Mathilde, thank you!"

"Sorry! I should have thanked you earlier!" said Mathilde.

With the bottle empty, Angèle returned to the house with us, explaining that they had several guests for dinner this evening. Mathilde invited us to join them but Mum declined.

"I think you have enough to do without worrying about us!" She said, "We'll see you at the church tomorrow."

We went straight to our car without encountering anyone and returned to the hotel.

***

Mum came with us to our room and we went through the program for the funeral that Mathilde had given us.

"Did you see the date of her birth under the cover photo?" Mum asked.

"Oh no!" Charlie cried. "She was only forty-seven!"

We were so shocked; nobody spoke for a while. Charlie broke the silence.

"Mathilde told me earlier that our apéro on board in Le Lavandou was the last time her mother had left the house!"

"It's always sad when someone dies so early," said Mum. "Sometimes I wonder how your father handles all the tragic childhood deaths he sees."

We opened our funeral programs and saw that Alain was to read a passage from the bible, Anne would give the first eulogy, followed by another from the former director of the most prestigious ballet school in France, the Opéra national de Paris, where Aurélie had trained and achieved fame.

***

When we arrived at the church there was a crowd of several hundred already waiting outside. Mathilde saw us and came to greet us. She was wearing a medium-grey trouser suit the same as mine. She asked us to join the family as they would be the first to follow the coffin into the church. We were introduced to Anne's husband as well as others whose names were instantly forgotten.

The coffin was slid out of the hearse and carried into the church to rest on preprepared trestles, and we followed it in with Mum and Charlie on either side of Mathilde and were directed to sit immediately behind the family and next to Angèle and Georges.

The MC from the Pompes Funèbres placed a larger version of the photo of Aurélie, that was on our programs, onto the coffin, and surrounded it with floral tributes. The largest bouquet bore the logo of the cosmetics company that Aurélie had modelled for. Mum pointed out our flowers and we could read the card, *Avec nos meilleurs souvenirs—Famille Cooper*. Four large candles were placed with their stands at the four corners of the coffin and the service started.

***

Amidst the religious mumbo-jumbo of the catholic rites, two things stood out. The first was the eulogy by the lady from the Opéra national de Paris, who spoke with such genuine warmth about Aurélie's dedication to her art and the joy she brought to others.

The second was Mathilde's contribution towards the end of the ceremony. The priest approached Mathilde with a burning taper and Mathilde rose to meet him and take the taper. She then lit the four candles one-by-one. At the first candle her hand was shaking so much that we feared she wouldn't manage. The concentration on her little face finally overcame her nerves and she lit it and the remaining candles without trouble. After that we all had to walk round the coffin and shake a tea strainer-like wand, dipped in holy water, over the coffin in the sign of a cross. The candles were extinguished and removed along with the photo and flowers from the coffin. We all followed the coffin through the church yard to Aurélie's family tomb. The two iron gates were open and only Alain, Anne and Mathilde followed the coffin down a few steps and into the tomb. When the gates were closed the photo and flowers were arranged in front and we wandered around them in appreciation. The crowd had started to break up into smaller groups and wander off. It was interesting to see that very few wore anything other than normal day-to-day attire; many of the men had open-necked shirts.

We had been invited back to the house with the family and principal mourners for the *veillée funèbre*, or wake to us. Mathilde came with us in our car and we made our way to the house.

Mum sat in the back with Mathilde and asked her how she was feeling.

"I feel relieved that the funeral is over but I hate the idea of my mother lying in that box. I know it is just her body…" Mathilde could not say more and Mum put her arm around her.

"It's not your mother in that box Mathilde: your mother was the light and the love that you shared and that will live on in you with all your memories. The body in the box is just the vehicle." I could see in the mirror that Mum had welled up as she spoke and the pair of them hugged without further words until we arrived at the house.

***

The wake was being held on the expansive patio in front of the house. Trestle tables with white cloth covers were loaded with a tastefully presented wide ranging buffet. A catering company's uniformed waiters and waitresses helped guests fill china plates while a separate bar filled glasses.

We first went to see Alain and Anne to compliment them on the organisation of this sad event. Alain seemed a little out of it and quickly retreated to a group of his close friends from the football club. Anne's eyes followed him with barely concealed disapproval. A sense of relief seemed to prevail in the gathering and small groups sat eating and drinking at rattan tables and chairs around the limits of the patio. Mathilde stayed with us as much as she could and the lady from the Opéra national de Paris joined us to enquire as to our connection with the family. She wanted to practice her English and we were happy to oblige. She was called Olga and of Russian heritage. She told us that she had joined the Opéra as a teacher over thirty years ago and grew through the organisation to be its director up to her retirement. She had been Aurélie's mentor and her eyes misted over as she related the experience. Her heroine was the English prima ballerina, Dame Margo Fontain. As she left us to do the rounds, it was clear from her gait that the elegance and poise of ballet had never left her.

I had elected myself to be the designated driver and drank only one glass of local Provençale white wine. Georges had joined our small group and he and Mathilde explained the close, almost family, relationship between him and Angèle and Aurélie and Mathilde.

***

As the group thinned out we bade our farewells and Mathilde walked us to our car. She invited us to join her for lunch tomorrow at a restaurant high up in the hills overlooking a lake which had been a favourite of her mother's. She suggested a little tour of the region on the way so we arranged that she would pick us up at eleven.

***

We packed our bags, loaded the car, and checked-out straight after breakfast so that we could leave promptly after our lunch. Our flight was not until six o'clock but we needed to be on the road by four to be on the safe side as we also needed time to return the hired car.

Mathilde picked us up in a late model Peugeot five-series promptly at eleven. She was quite transformed from the sad girl we had left at the wake yesterday. Her smile on greeting us was definitely trending toward her old self, and her gay summer frock matched her improving mood.

Our drive took us further up and east through the foothills of the Massif des Maures which we could see through the hazy sunshine well to the east. The landscape was beautifully varied; great white rock formations interspersed with picture-book pastures and grazing sheep.

***

Mathilde leaned back in her wicker chair on the terrace of the restaurant, the midday sun shining directly on her pretty little face, her eyes closed.

172

One could almost see some of her cares and woes slowly drifting away. We three kept silent until she opened her eyes some minutes later and smiled at us.

"We only have a few hours left and I want to tell you that your love has given me the strength to get through this awful time. Your words of love and wisdom Paris have been the same as my mother would have used in similar circumstances. I must thank you all from the bottom of my heart!" Mathilde's tears flowed unashamedly but the smile never left her lips.

"You are family," said Mum.

We were all quite misty as we held hands across the glass topped circular table. Charlie coughed away the lump in her throat.

"We are very lucky to have you as our friend Mathilde, you are precious to us."

A waiter appeared with menus and recommended the fish soup. Mathilde said the restaurant was famous for this dish and we all ordered it. The waiter left only the wine list and Mathilde ordered a Provençale rosé.

"This wine is very similar to the English rosé we had at your house— we can compare them!"

The wine arrived as we returned from the salad bar and Mum asked what would happen over the coming days.

"Our *avocat de famille* will be here on Tuesday to read my mother's will. Our house here has been our family country house for a very long time. We also have a split-level apartment in the sixteenth arrondissement of Paris where my mother lived with her parents while she was at the Opéra. I never knew my grandparents, they died together in a multiple car accident on the A6 motorway on their way here long before I was born. When my mother left the Opéra she moved here permanently and the flat was leased to the American embassy. Both properties are held in a complex trust which ensures they remain in the family—that's just my aunt and me now."

"What about your father?" I said.

"When he married my mother he had to sign an attestation renouncing any claim to the properties in return for a calculated sum if he survived my mother or they divorced, so the lawyer will settle that with him."

The wine had arrived while Mathilde was talking and Charlie did the tasting. Mum was designated driver and had just a half glass during the meal. I thought the wine was so-so and no match for ours! A large terrine of the fish soup and the accompanying croutons, grated Gruyère cheese and rouille arrived and Mathilde explained how to combine them for best taste. As we enjoyed the meal, Mathilde continued her story: it seemed that she needed us to know how things were with her.

"I must tell you that I no longer have any regard for my father. My aunt and I have known for some time that he has a young woman living in his flat in Marseille and that she is pregnant with his child. We kept this from my mother, as well as some other things about him, and he agreed to play his part; but I have told him that I never want to see him ever again after the settlement." Mathilde sighed, "So that's my story, I have no secrets from you! I should also tell you that I am not at all sorry that he will be out of my life after this coming Tuesday!"

It was now after three and we had a quick coffee before Mathilde drove us back to our hotel. On the way, Mathilde told us she was taking the week off from her course and that she had been commuting on a daily basis in the latter stages of her mother's illness, Aix was a little over an hour's drive away in her little Smart car. She had a rented studio in Aix where she would stay during the week in future. Her aunt, Anne was in the process of divorcing her husband and would base herself in the house until things were resolved; she and her aunt got along very well.

Mathilde promised to keep close contact with us and we all gave her a warm hug and kiss before heading for the airport.

CHAPTER TWENTY-SIX

FLATS

Charlie and I decided not to drive back to uni on Sunday evening but to leave very early on Monday morning. We both felt the need to reconnect with each other after such an intense and emotional weekend with our love and attention rightly focused on Mathilde. We had not even made love in the huge hotel bed. We needed this night to ourselves.

Dad and Flo had made a proper English dinner of Cumberland sausages, mashed potatoes and onion gravy which really was very welcome!

"Bollocks to haute cuisine!" said Flo and giggled as we tucked-in!

We related our sad weekend and how we felt that we had helped in some small way. Dad was amazed that Aurélie had only been forty-seven.

"This cancer is such a curse, sometimes I wonder if we'll ever get on top of it," said Dad. "Talking of which, Annie seems to be in slow decline I'm afraid."

Harry seemed to prick up his ears at Annie's name and looked around before walking to the patio doors to be let out.

"Looks like we've got ourselves a dog," said Dad.

***

Charlie and I went to our wing as soon as it was polite to do so. After I'd shaved we had a long shower together before cosying-up in Charlie's bed. We were in slow motion love mode and took our time caressing lightly. We could have carried on like that — it was so nice and loving — but forces were at work!

I slid down a little to kiss and softly suck Charlie's left breast while stroking the other with the soft hairs on my forearm; Charlie loved that, and

I felt her appreciation grow in my mouth and under my hand. She quivered as I moved my hand down to brush her pubic hair lightly. Charlie pressed her vulva up into my hand and I felt the glorious heat and moisture of her.

"Come inside Nat…"

I slid on top, and Charlie guided me in with her hand. It was the greatest feeling to be so far inside this woman whom I loved so much. I moved slowly and felt the rising tide of her passion as she soon started to shudder and spasm. Charlie arched her back and pressed her wrist to her mouth as her orgasm burst and I ejaculated into the very core of her.

***

On the short drive to Oxford Charlie remembered that she owed Ralph a call about the photos and tapped a memo on her phone.

It was still very early in Oxford when Charlie slipped into the driver's side of the van outside my hall.

"That was so lovely last night Nat, I think I'm still glowing!"

"We deserved it, my love. I think it'll last me all week!"

We smiled, kissed, and Charlie moved off for her two-hour drive to Cambridge.

***

Charlie rang on Tuesday with news that Ed had arranged for her to visit a show flat in an unfinished low-rise apartment block. The agent had emailed her with the various floor plans, and she was quite upbeat about the possibilities—more news tomorrow after seeing the show flat.

Charlie had also spoken with Ralph to thank him for the pictures, and he had passed the phone to his boss who wanted to talk to her. She was called Lucy and asked if Charlie would be interested to visit their office and studio in Bedford for a chat and maybe some test photos.

'I told Lucy I could visit on a Saturday morning and asked if you could come as well, and she said that would be fine.'

"What do you think?" asked Charlie.

"Sounds fun, how about this coming Saturday?"

176

"I'll ask Ralph if that's a good time. By the way, I just forwarded the email to you that has the flat plans—see what you think!"

As promised, Charlie rang again later on Wednesday evening.

"Oh Nat, I'm just back from seeing that show flat. It's in a four-storey block and is being built by the same developer as yours, I even think it's exactly the same design. I told the agent that I wasn't allowed to make a definitive reservation, but I wanted the last one bed flat available on the top floor; he's going to ring Ed first thing tomorrow and I'm calling Dad straight after this call."

"That's absolutely great," I said. "When will it be available?"

"September or October. The developer will concentrate on flats that have already been sold off-plan!"

"Call Dad!"

***

Dad rang Charlie on Thursday to say that Ed had done the needful regarding Charlie's flat and confirmed that it was indeed the same developer that had built mine. Ed had leveraged the fact that we were now buying two flats from the same developer to ensure that Charlie's would be the first on the top floor to be finished. Charlie was over the moon!

When Charlie and I arrived home on Friday evening we were pleasantly surprised to see a mini-digger, and various other pool installation kit on the lawn, and the site of the pool and geothermal trench, already marked out with tape.

***

That weekend we had a 'newsy' email from Sophie in Mahon. The boys were asking when their 'trainer' would visit and she and Pau asked if we had any plans for the summer holidays yet. Pau and Pedro were taking good care of Mathilde and were running the engine up to temperature once a week. Pedro was also hosing the deck after each time the Sirocco southerly wind had dumped a layer of the fine red Sahara dust on Menorca. Jaime sent his best regards.

177

Sophie's email prompted us to give some serious thought to our summer hols. Uppermost in our minds was the fact that Flo and Pierre had yet to exercise their fifty-percent ownership of Mathilde. Flo's C-section, scheduled for early July, would preclude her going to Mathilde this year, but what about Pierre?

Mum stepped into the breach with an offer to stay at home with Flo and baby later in the summer holiday period so Pierre could enjoy some time on Mathilde.

"Let me run this past Flo first," said Mum. "Let her decide what she wants. Then we can start thinking about dates. I guess you two will want to be out there like a shot!" Mum smiled as she looked straight at Charlie and me with this closing comment.

"Not entirely," I said. "I've got a flat to fix up for the start of my second year and Charlie's may be ready by then as well. Charlie's flat will in fact be an exact mirror image of mine so there's plenty of scope to make plans that suit both of us."

Dad chipped in, "Ed called today to say that the transaction on your flat Nat will be completed by the end of this month with occupancy from the first of July."

"That's fantastic Dad!" I got up and gave Mum and Dad a big hug. "I can't thank you enough!"

Dad's teaching commitments obviously all fell during the academic year and he would only need to discuss with Great Ormond Street to organise his summer holiday. His new freedoms meant that he would likely be able to have more time off than previously. Mum would speak with Flo during the week, and we would do some serious scheduling next weekend.

Little did we realise then that our talk of summer holidays and student flats would be completely overwhelmed by the events that would unfold during the coming week.

CHAPTER TWENTY-SEVEN

PIERRE AND ÉLODIE

During the lunch break on Thursday, Charlie and I got a call from Mum on our WhatsApp group.

"I'm very glad to have you both on the line," said Mum. "Let me just explain things first and then we can talk." Mum's voice was noticeably shaky as she continued. "Flo was with me at home for lunch today, as usual, when she got a call from Le Coq; Harold told her that Pierre had had a heart attack at work and been taken by ambulance to Windsor A & E. Your Dad knows the cardiologist and will call me when he has news. Unfortunately, that's not all, Flo was so shocked that she collapsed and went into premature labour and I've brought her here to Windsor A & E as well, where I'm calling from. The obstetrician has given Flo an injection to stop the contractions and is consulting with Flo's doctor at Slough Hospital where she's scheduled for her C-section next month. I've just stepped out of Flo's room to call you, but everything seems stable, she, and indeed the baby, are hooked up to monitors and no one seems particularly worried. The main concern is Pierre of course. I'll go up to the cardiac ICU after this to see if anyone can tell me anything"

"I'm so sorry to hear that, Mum," I said. "Would you like us to come home?"

"The answer is yes, I would, but on a practical level there's actually little you can do…"

Mum let out a huge sob and could not speak, Charlie broke in and said, "We're coming home Mum, what do you say Nat?"

"Of course we are, call me when you're close Charlie and I'll wait outside the hall for you. Mum, call me if there's any more news—Charlie will be on the road."

"Thanks, you two, whatever happens it will be better if we're all together—speak soon!"

***

Mum called when Charlie was probably about halfway to Oxford.

"Hello Nat, just a quickie to say that Pierre is weak but stable in the ICU and has more tests to undergo; I was not allowed in to see him. I've told Flo and she is a little relieved. You can come directly to the maternity unit to meet me and see Flo, OK?"

"We'll do that Mum, give our love to Flo and we'll be there as soon as we can, and love to you!"

***

Flo was looking better than we had feared and seemed to have come to terms with the situation somewhat, she even managed a weak smile on seeing us. We both gave her a kiss and a hug and had hardly said anything when the obstetrician came into Flo's room. He was all smiles and asked Flo if she would prefer to hear his news on her own or with all her visitors.

"We're all family thanks, from your smile I assume I'm not at death's door!" said Flo with a hint of her old humour.

"I've consulted with your obstetrician in Slough, and we agree that you should have your baby first thing tomorrow morning by C-section, what do you say?"

Mum and Flo both burst into tears and Flo just about managed to nod her assent whilst crying and smiling at the same time.

"It's a little premature, maybe four or five weeks, which is just on the borderline for the definition of premature. We'll take a bit more care of him or her for a while, but no problems are expected!"

Mum and Flo regained some of their composure and the doctor continued.

"Your husband is indisposed at the moment and will be unable to attend the event, so, you have the option to appoint a substitute hand-holder or, as our cousins in California might say, someone to 'share the experience'."

The doctor smiled at his quip and Flo pointed to Mum.

180

The doctor went on to detail the procedure and left us to share Flo's excitement.

"I'll see you two ladies at six o'clock sharp, OK?"

Dad arrived a little later with Pierre's cardiologist and introduced him to us and vice versa, he was called David.

"First thing to say is that Pierre is out of immediate danger and in a stable condition under a mild sedative to keep him relaxed while we run our tests," said David.

"We've just now conferred with your obstetrician, Doctor Baker; by the way, his nickname around here is bun-in-the-oven! Baker, get it!" David allowed us a moment to relax with his joke, then continued, "Pierre is not aware of your condition, Flo, and Arthur and I agree that it would be wise not to inform him and give him anything else to concern him until we have completed our diagnostics, do you agree?"

"If Arthur agrees then so do I," Flo replied. "But I am sad that he can't be with me for the birth."

"OK," said David. "I'll leave you now and keep you updated as our work on Pierre progresses. Try not to worry, just concentrate on your big day tomorrow!"

Flo's dinner tray arrived, and we left her to it while we went in search of a pizza joint for our own evening meal.

After our pizza, mum went back to spend the rest of the evening with Flo and I drove us home in the van.

We three, Dad, Charlie and I, had a strange evening; half the time worried about Pierre and the other half excited at the prospect of Flo's baby. Dad gave us a little more detail about Pierre's heart attack which had not yet been shared with Mum or Flo.

"When the paramedics arrived at Le Coq, Pierre's heart was just fluttering, and he was unresponsive. The paramedic defibrillated him, and the heartbeat was restored. He's responsive now but being kept under mild sedation. Flo can present him with a fait accompli when he's feeling a little better!"

***

We all rose very early the next morning, and Mum, Charlie and I drove to the hospital in the Lexus.

We arrived in Flo's room at twenty-to-six and had just enough time to kiss Flo before Charlie and I were shooed out while Flo was prepped.

Charlie and I went to the waiting room with a dreadful coffee from a vending machine.

At seven-twenty Mum came to fetch us, a huge grin on her tear-streaked face.

"Come and meet Élodie!"

CHAPTER TWENTY-EIGHT

PIERRE

Charlie and I decided that there was no good reason for us to miss any more days at uni. The immediate crisis was over and so we left after dinner on Sunday as usual.

Baby Élodie was kept under close monitoring in the 'preemie' unit and only taken to Flo for feeding. Flo herself needed to rest in hospital for up to a week after the C-section, which was, after all, a serious operation. Flo was making plenty of milk and Élodie had no adverse symptoms from her slightly premature birth. After four days in the preemie unit, Élodie was moved to Flo's room and after seven days they were discharged.

On the day before, Flo had a surprise visitor—Lady Helen! Flo told us how much she had enjoyed her visit and how genuinely upset she had been over Pierre's heart attack.

***

When Charlie and I arrived home, Flo and Élodie were comfortably installed in the spare bedroom upstairs and there was a huge hole in the lawn next to the patio! Mum had kept us up to date with all the news which was all good except that Pierre's condition had only marginally improved.

We had all agreed that Flo and Élodie should come and live with us for as long as it took for her to recuperate fully, and for Pierre's prognosis to be fully understood.

Mum had visited Pierre on Monday, three days after the heart attack, and gently explained to him all that had happened and that Flo and baby Élodie were both in great shape. She explained that she would bring Flo and baby Élodie to him in a wheelchair only because Flo had a bunch of stitches that needed some time while the incision healed.

On the evening that we arrived, Mum described the scene when Pierre saw his baby for the first time.

"His face completely crumpled as I put Élodie in his arms. There was barely room for her with all those electrodes over his chest and the cannula in his arm, his monitor alarm went off and an ICU nurse quickly came over. 'Too much excitement here!' she said as she reset the alarm, 'now cool it—OK?'" Mum beamed at the recollection of the scene. "And then I left them to it!"

***

On Saturday, Mum took all of us in the van to visit Pierre.

Mum had warned us that he looked poorly but it was still a shock to see him so diminished. He looked older and his normally ruddy complexion was replaced with an unhealthy pallor. He was, however, very pleased to see us and showed some spirit with a complaint about the food! He held Élodie for the duration of the visit and she slept contentedly in his arms amongst all his wires and tubes. Charlie took some photos of the scene and then remembered that we had arranged to visit Ralph today at his Bedford studio. When she called him to apologise, he said he already had news of the events via Camp David and Maggie, not to worry and to reschedule when she had time.

***

Over dinner Dad brought us up to date regarding Pierre's condition.

"He's on a cocktail of the usual drugs, ACE inhibitors, Beta blockers and antiplatelets which all aid the heart function. He's also had angioplasty to install stents in three of his coronary arteries. It was the blockage in one of those, and partial blockage of the other two, which caused the heart attack. The likely prognosis is that he will slowly improve but not back to his old self entirely. An echocardiogram has shown that an area of his heart muscle has deteriorated through lack of oxygen during the blockage in the coronary arteries. This all adds up to a lowering of his exercise tolerance, breathlessness if he overexerts himself, and easier fatigue. In other words, he'll have to take life a bit easier in the future."

"Not exactly the best condition to commence fatherhood, eh?" said Flo.

"Look, Flo, we're all in this together," said Mum. "We'll share the load at all times and when you move back home, we'll be just a phone call away to help in any way we can."

Flo was silently weeping, and Mum held her until the tears subsided. She knew all that Dad had said about Pierre and I think she was mostly tearful because of the love and solidarity of our family.

Élodie had been sleeping in a portable cot next to the nearest settee and woke conveniently as we finished our dinner. Flo got up to feed her, but Harry beat her to the cot and rested his head on Élodie's lap; the crying stopped even before Flo had her breast out!

The ICU nurse had asked us to limit the number of visitors to two at a time until Pierre was out of intensive care, so only Mum, Flo and Élodie visited on Sunday morning. Mum left them alone after the first five minutes! Harold had rung from Le Coq for them to pick up a food parcel for Pierre's Sunday lunch which really lit up his day!

***

Charlie, Dad and I spent Sunday morning with a planning chart for the summer holidays. For Charlie and me, the break lasted three months from the beginning of July so that was the period under discussion. Our first thoughts were for Pierre and whether he would be fit enough. Dad said he would monitor Pierre's progress with David, Pierre's cardiologist, but he was quietly optimistic that he would be up to it if he limited his activities to helming, cooking and sunbathing! Élodie would still be too young, which precluded Flo of course, but Mum had already volunteered to stay with Flo if Pierre took a break on Mathilde. Dad sensibly said that he should be on board with Pierre if indeed he was fit enough to travel, and Dad pencilled-in a two-week holiday with Pierre for the first two weeks of August; Charlie and I would complete the crew.

Mum was basically a free agent and could take a break anytime except for when Pierre was away, and Dad had no teaching commitments for the summer, due to the university holidays, and could arrange his work at Great Ormond Street with plenty of leeway.

185

Charlie and I had talked about inviting Mathilde for a holiday on board and Dad suggested the earlier part of the summer would be best. We'd only spoken with Mathilde once over the two weeks since her mother's funeral and Charlie would call this evening with the offer and an update on current events in our family.

Charlie and I went to visit Pierre later in the afternoon, but the nurse told us he was fast asleep and best not to disturb him.

***

Interestingly, Mathilde had no plans for the summer and had secretly kept all her options open in case we invited her. We were very happy to hear that, and our delight was reciprocated in spades by Mathilde.

"Just send me dates and I'll be there!"

Charlie and I now had a problem. With Mathilde on board for two weeks there was little chance of hiding the physical aspects of our love. We had done so for the weekend of her visit by abstaining, but two weeks was another thing entirely.

We decided to be open with her and actually had no expectations of any adverse reaction from her. We were sure that the love between the three of us could handle the situation without judgement.

I wanted the first week of July to sort out my flat, so we could be on board Mathilde from the start of the second week, that gave Mathilde a three-week window for joining us before Dad and Pierre's projected holiday.

Charlie emailed all this to Mathilde who replied within the hour; she would arrive in Mahon on the ninth of July!

CHAPTER TWENTY-NINE

THE ACCIDENTAL MODEL

Charlie had missed a game last Saturday and there was no fixture for the coming weekend. She called Ralph and rescheduled our visit to his studio for this coming Saturday.

"Hmm… this is getting interesting," said Charlie after the call. "Ralph asked if I'd bring a swimming costume with me—I'm beginning to wonder what sort of studio this is!"

"Not to worry, I'll be there, and anyway, if you're going to be the next Kate Moss, they'll need some idea of what your carcass looks like!"

***

Time seemed to have moved into a higher gear as the year progressed. To think that it was only six months since our 'coming out' last Christmas, and all that had happened since; life was busier than ever!

The week flew past; I was enjoying my course more and more and we had good news about Pierre; he was out of ICU and on a regular cardiac ward. Twice a day he was doing gentle physiotherapy and slowly improving. Flo had agreed to Pierre going on holiday with Dad if well enough, and the prospect seemed to have a highly beneficial effect on Pierre's motivation.

We arrived home for dinner on Friday to find a much happier Flo and a baby Élodie that seemed to have grown in just a week—was that possible?

The pool had been delivered and rested on its cradle close to the hole. The plumbing and electricity tubes were in place and the trench partly filled in.

Mum held up a small bunch of keys and dangled them in front of me at the dinner table.

"Ed managed to get us the keys to your flat a little ahead of time so we can do a bit of planning. I thought we could all drive over on Sunday to mull over some ideas."

"Sounds good, let's do it!" I said. "I'll bring a tape measure and notepad and we can take lots of photos."

***

After breakfast on Saturday, Charlie and I took the van for the hour-and-a-half drive up to Bedford for our appointment with Ralph and his boss, Lucy. We were both surprised when the GPS delivered us to a light industrial estate on the outskirts of town. The studio was a detached, one-storey, almost windowless building; the sign on the wall just read, '*Shoots*'.

Ralph greeted us and took us straight to Lucy's office. Her office had the only window on the front of the building and was surprisingly well appointed considering the bleakness of the building. Lucy was about Mum's age, in great shape, and casually dressed in jeans and loose top that matched her jet-black hair. She seemed make-up free, but her wide spaced eyes and high cheek bones really didn't need any.

We shook hands and Lucy directed us to a comfortable sitting area around a low circular conference table. Lucy opened the conversation.

"Firstly, I must thank you for taking the time to visit us, I hope you'll find it interesting. As Ralph has told you, we are in the fashion business and act as agents for models used in photos for magazines, online retail and video for TV ads. Young Ralph here has a remarkable eye for talent spotting and now that I've seen you in the flesh Charlie, I can see why he was so taken with you. How about some coffee?" Without being asked, Ralph left the office.

"The system works like this. We get loads of letters with often dreadful photos of wannabe models and about one in every five hundred gets invited here for an interview. Of those, about five percent are invited to create a portfolio for our clients to view. We also do a little talent spotting ourselves and that's why we're all here today."

Ralph came back with a nice coffee set and placed it on the table.

"Every now and again we strike gold, or think we have! Sometimes it's the slightest nuance of a facial expression, or posture, and both Ralph and I think he has captured something of that nature in one of his shots of you, Charlie." Ralph went to the desk and brought a very large print of one of his photos of Charlie. "Help yourselves to coffee before it gets cold." Lucy pointed to Charlie's mouth in the photo. "This is it, your grin! That's what Ralph saw, it's in the mouth and the eyes, it's quite special!

"I know from experience that you are sitting there wondering what this is all about. You're a first-year law student at Cambridge and not at all looking for a job! All we're suggesting at this time is that Ralph take some more shots of you so that we can perform a more serious analysis of your potential. If that pans out, we will offer to create a full professional portfolio, at no charge to you, to show to clients. If a client wants you for a shoot, we will negotiate the fee on your behalf and take a handsome twenty-five percent of any fee up to ten thousand pounds, and thereafter on a sliding scale to a minimum of ten percent. Of course, any interested clients will be told that your availability will be limited to weekends and university holidays." Lucy smiled. "That's the end of my little speech, if you're still interested, Ralph will now do his bit."

***

Ralph showed us around his impressive domain. He flicked switches on the control panel next to his seat behind the camera and had Charlie sit on a stool a few meters away. Much of the light on Charlie was indirect, reflected from under huge white umbrellas.

"The first shots are for reference only and you should try to maintain a neutral expression. I need clean shots of head and shoulders so would you mind removing your top and just keep your bra on please." Charlie did as instructed without expression. "Now could you take your arms out of the shoulder straps—I need clear shoulders." Charlie complied again and Ralph adjusted his lighting and started shooting, full-on, left profile, right profile, chin up, half turned, mouth open, teeth together, suddenly Ralph screamed, and Charlie spun on her stool to face him. In the second it took her to spin round Ralph took a continuous stream of photos. "Sorry about that, just a little trick for a shock expression! Let me tell you a little story; this can be a dangerous job sometimes! I once approached a lovely looking lady on the platform at Waterloo station and told her who I was. She turned to me, smacked me across the face, and told me I needed a better line than that!" Charlie was following Ralph's story and her smile broadened as she foresaw where it was going. All the while he was talking, Ralph was continuously holding down his remote camera control.

"We talked in the office about your grin, or smile, Charlie; can you do it now, on command, while I pull funny faces?" Charlie grinned at the silly idea and Ralph took another stream of shots as she did so.

"OK, now the bit we've all been waiting for; would you change into your swimming costume behind the screen, please?"

Charlie looked great in her bikini, as usual, and Ralph again took loads of shots in all postures.

"That's it! How about some lunch, Lucy's treat."

***

We knew that Mum and the rest of the gang had planned to visit Pierre in the morning, so we diverted slightly to go via Windsor and see him on our way home after lunch.

He was just back from his second physio session of the day when we arrived and was rather tired. It looked to us like afternoon nap time for him, so we didn't stay too long. He asked us about Mahon and Menorca in general but dozed off halfway through our response!

***

Our garden looked like a building site, but everyone was out on the patio regardless, and soaking up the early summer rays when we arrived. Charlie asked, "How many beers?" and all except Élodie raised a hand. We went to our wing to change into shorts and picked up the beers on the way back. Flo was very pleased to have the odd glass of wine or beer now but kept it to just a couple a day.

"So, how was your first 'photo shoot'?" Dad asked.

"Quite interesting," Charlie replied. "Ralph and Lucy told us over lunch how there was now a massive market for online shopping models, but competition was tight and fees low. Lucy's agency was trying to concentrate on TV video ads for cosmetics, lingerie, swimwear and famous-label fashion, where fees were high for the select few who fitted the bill. I told them that I didn't think the online stuff sounded very interesting. Lucy agreed and said that they could fill their studio anytime with 'clothes horses' for their 'bread and butter', but their roving eye was focused higher." Charlie took a swig of her beer. "Ralph said that they needed faces rather than bodies, and both in the same model if at all possible, hence their interest in my facial expressions."

"You do certainly have the face in my opinion," said Flo. "But can the camera catch it?"

"Ralph had some crazy antics to get my face animated," said Charlie. "And took masses of shots at an incredible speed in the attempt, let's see what he got out of it."

***

The next day, after a leisurely breakfast, we all piled into the van and went to Pierre's hospital in Windsor. Only Flo, Mum and Élodie went in so as not to overcrowd the ward; the rest of us would visit later.

We drove straight from Windsor to Oxford to see my flat and I parked in the designated slot. I had been worried that the van might be a tight fit, but it was just fine.

Charlie had seen the flat once before with me but this was Flo's first time. It felt great to have everyone there and all wandered around giving their opinion on how the spaces could be utilised. Mum brought the meeting to order!

"OK, let's go from room to room, give our opinions and let Nat make the decisions—however wrong they might be!" I laughed at Mum's quip, and we started in the kitchen, which was the easiest as it was fully equipped!

There was no gas supply to the building in anticipation of forthcoming regulations banning fossil fuel, so everything was electric. The hob was a three-burner induction over an electric oven, and hot water was by immersion heater in the airing cupboard.

Flo said, "You need Pierre to see this and make a shopping list for pots, pans, cooking tools, crockery and cutlery. He'll love that and it'll give him a project for when he comes home. He can even start while he's in hospital. Take some photos for him, Nat."

"How about four bar stools for the breakfast counter?" Charlie offered.

I finished my kitchen photos and added 'bar stools' to the kitchen page of my notepad.

The bedroom too was easy; the built-in cupboards had all the drawers and hanging storage I could possibly need, I just needed a nice big bed and headboard to rest against when I read or used my laptop in bed, and a couple of nightstands; perhaps a rug for the parquet floor. I measured the room, it would comfortably take a one-metre-forty wide bed.

The bathroom just needed towels, a bathmat, toilet paper and wet wipes.

The living area was where some suggestions might help. I'd already noted the essentials: sofa bed, desk and office-type chair, smart TV, stereo speakers, a couple of easy chairs and a coffee table. Mum and Flo were in deep discussion looking at the space from the balcony French doors.

"How about this for a layout?" Mum said, and went on to point out their ideas. "And if you think of anything else you can easily move things around." I sketched the layout in my notes for reference.

Job done; now we just had to accumulate all this stuff!

I suggested lunch by the river at the Old Trout and Charlie gave me a loving smile as we both remembered our reunion.

***

Charlie was our designated driver and drove us home after an excellent lunch. We dropped off three of our girls, leaving Dad, me and Charlie to visit Pierre. When we arrived on the ward, he was away having his physio, so we waited by his bed. We watched him as he walked unaided to his bed and Dad commented on his progress.

"They say I can come home in a couple of days," said Pierre. "How about that?"

"That's great Pierre, but best if you come to us for another few days, so you can find your feet first, eh?"

"Sounds good to me, Arthur, and many thanks for all you're doing for us!"

"We're just pleased that we can," said Dad. "And now that you're getting back into shape, we have some work for you!"

We described how Flo had offered his services for my kitchen and he smiled broadly.

"I'd love to do that, and it will be our treat, our contribution to the flat!"

On our drive back home, Dad commented on how well Pierre was recovering.

"Not much doubt in my mind," said Dad. "That if he carries on like this, he'll be OK for a relaxing holiday on Mathilde by the middle of next month!"

***

When we got home, Dad described our visit to the hospital and gave his opinion of Pierre's progress and his agreement to spend some time with us before going home.

Charlie and I went to get our stuff together for the drive back to uni after dinner.

"I so enjoyed lunch at the Old Trout, Nat. It reminded me of the happiest day of my life!" Charlie's eyes were swimming as she smiled, and we embraced with a special tenderness. Charlie led me to her bed where we undressed and very gently made the sweetest love.

***

We were now starting the last two weeks of our fresher year and spent time preparing for the end-of-year exams. We also finalised our plans to fly to Mahon on the Friday of the first week of the holiday.

I ordered a BBQ like Pau and Sophie's from a French online chandlery for delivery to the club and Mum rang Sophie with our plans for the summer. Sophie asked for Charlie and my flight details and said she'd pick us up.

The days sped by and on our final weekend before the holiday we arrived home to find the pool installed, Pierre relaxing on the patio, and the trench backfilled. All that remained was the non-slip tiling around the pool and installation of the pool cover—it looked like we would have our inaugural swim before flying out to Mahon!

193

***

During the last week of term, Charlie rang to say that Ralph had called. He and Lucy were very pleased with the results of our visit to Bedford and would like to invite Charlie back to do a full professional portfolio shoot.

"He suggested the morning of the first Tuesday of the holiday, what do you think?"

"Fine by me, sounds quite exciting!"

"OK, I'll call him back. There's also something else he mentioned which I'm a bit unsure of. He would like to include nude shots of me just standing, no posing, just front, back and sides. With his software he would place a black rectangle over my pubic area and eyes, and black squares over my nipples; what do you think?"

"It's very little more than you expose yourself in a bikini, and we know that Ralph is unlikely to be aroused by you in the buff!"

"Yeah, that's what I thought, I'll tell him, thanks Nat—love you!"

"Love you too!"

***

As expected, Charlie's exams were more exacting than mine, which were not in fact a great stretch, but she felt that she had done rather well.

When we arrived home on Friday, we found the tiling finished and the pool very slowly filling. The cover was installed and the semi-circular sections 'nested' at the deep end ready to slide out and form a tunnel over the pool. The underwater lights were on and the whole thing looked absolutely great! Everyone was extremely pleased and looking forward to the first swim the following day!

Pierre was going from strength to strength and had cooked one of our favourite dishes for dinner, slow cooked lamb!

Mum and Dad had suggested to Flo and Pierre that they stay with us until after Pierre had come back from his holiday on Mathilde, they had agreed with minimal reluctance, and we were all very pleased!

We spent the whole weekend in or next to the pool and invited Frank to join us for a BBQ on Sunday. He was the happiest we had ever seen him and spent nearly all the time, when he was not eating, holding baby Élodie;

he was, without doubt, fulfilling in his mind the grandfather role he had alluded to at our Christmas meal in Le Coq!

***

On Tuesday, Charley and I left home early for our appointment at Shoots. Besides Ralph and Lucy there was also a costumière who took a precise record of at least thirty of Charlie's measurements!

Lucy participated in the direction of the shoot and clearly knew her stuff. The shoot took over an hour and ended with the nude shots that Charlie had agreed to. It was in fact utterly sexless to see Charlie naked in this way.

Back in the office, after the shoot, Charlie was invited to sign a management contract with Shoots which we both read and found nothing to object to, but to be on the safe side, we said we'd run it past Frank Stokes and send it back as an email attachment. Ralph showed us some shots of the first shoot, and it was magic to see how he had captured what he and Lucy had seen in his original shots from the dinner party.

Lucy looked pensive for a moment, then said,

"We have a swimwear and lingerie client who has a new line— I'll tell them I have a new model!"

CHAPTER THIRTY

MAHÓN

As promised, Sophie was there to welcome us off the plane with an all-enveloping hug for the pair of us! We were genuinely delighted to see each other again and on the short drive to the club we told her that Dad and Pierre would be arriving for a holiday early next month as part of his convalescence.

"That's great, I'm so looking forward to meeting your father. I think I've read all his papers in the medical journals! I'm going to take him to our hospital to show him off!"

When we arrived at Mathilde we found Pau sitting in the cockpit and all the deck hatches open to air the boat. More greetings followed and Charlie and I dumped our wheelie-bins below before joining them in the cockpit.

We'd taken a mid-afternoon flight from Gatwick and now, with the one-hour difference, it was not too early to invite them to the clubhouse for a beer.

Over cold San Miguel's we told them of Mathilde's arrival in three days' time and the tragedy in her life.

Sophie and Pau invited us to join them for dinner at the club as we had nothing on board, and we happily accepted.

*****

Back on board, we made up our bunk in the fore cabin and switched on the fridge ready for a shopping run tomorrow morning.

Menorca, in common with the rest of Spain, basically shuts down for siesta and only starts to come alive again after five in the afternoon. Charlie and I decided to go 'native' and went below!

Charlie's Easter tan had not completely faded and she looked wonderful as she lay on top of the light blue sheets of our bunk. I took a long moment just enjoying the sight of her before lying on my side next to her.

"What were you looking at, Nat?"

"Firstly, your face, and I thought I might like to kiss you; then your breasts, and I thought they might be nice to cuddle a little; and then my eye went on down further looking for something to tickle!"

"Where are you going to start?"

"Here!" I said, and slipped down to tickle Charlie's feet. She screamed and pulled her leg up to escape and in so doing exposed something else that I thought would be nice to tickle. Charlie giggled as I slid up to rest my head on her thigh and part her hair with my finger.

"How do you know I'm ticklish there?"

"I don't, but I'm about to find out!" I playfully flicked my finger just above Charlie's opening and she giggled some more.

"Hmm… that's fairly ticklish," Charlie squirmed slightly. "Can you tickle with your tongue?"

"I can try!" I rolled my face onto her and flicked my tongue lightly over where my finger had been, and Charlie squirmed some more.

"Mmm… that's a lovely tickle, Nat… mmm… that's the best tickle… I'm tickling my nipples too…"

After some more tickling with my tongue Charlie was hot and wet and moving against my face…

"Tickle me inside Nat… please…"

I rose up and just entered her with the tip of my penis and tickled her a little like that. I was resting on my elbows and kissed her smiling lips. I felt her heels pressing on my buttocks…

"Tickle me deeper Nat…" Charlie's head went back and she flicked her nipples ever more quickly. She gripped me inside, as she does, and started to climax with faster thrusts of her hips; I fully entered her and just lost it completely with a huge orgasm that pushed Charlie to hers as well. We stayed in that wonderful state until my penis decided it was siesta time.

"I didn't know I was so ticklish Nat!"

***

We decided to order a mixed seafood and chicken paella from the club for dinner with Mathilde when she arrived in two days' time and invited Pau and Sophie to join us.

Charlie made up one of the aft cabin bunks for Mathilde and we did a good general clean-up both on deck and below; Mathilde was looking good!

CHAPTER THIRTY-ONE

MATHILDE'S STORY

Mathilde was due to arrive at five in the afternoon and we were both looking forward to seeing her again. We'd talked about her visit and how it might pan out. The yacht was closely associated with her mother, and we expected some nostalgic tears. Charlie wondered if we should wait until after our dinner with Pau and Sophie, before we had the conversation about our relationship. It had to happen today, because we would share the fore cabin tonight, and we were certainly not about to change that. I agreed with Charlie; we'd talk after dinner.

*****

Mathilde positively bounced from the arrival hall and into our arms! Her happiness at seeing us transcended all else and we hugged this girl/woman with unusual fervour. I would ponder this moment later, it was in some ways unusual and a first for me, and I wanted to understand it.

We caught the bus back to town and waited for Mathilde's reaction when we arrived at the club. She stood still on the pontoon when she saw the yacht and we could see her eye moving along the deck and then up into the rigging.

"She looks more beautiful than I remember," she said. "I had hoped she would." She was clearly quite misty, but in a happy way, and I was happy to see that.

"Shall we take her out tomorrow?" she asked.

"Of course," said Charlie.

*****

We had invited Pau and Sophie for a glass of champagne on board to welcome Mathilde before going up for dinner. Charlie had mentioned Mathilde's recent loss to Sophie and her connection to the yacht. Over our drinks, Mathilde told us that she and her mother used to take Mathilde out on their own quite often, and that Aurélie had been a competent and well experienced sailor from childhood. Mathilde became very quiet for a while, as her composure showed signs of slipping; Sophie gave her hand a motherly squeeze and a tear escaped down Mathilde's cheek.

***

The paella was just as good as we remembered and the friendly conversation around our table even better. Charlie's two football fans were eagerly anticipating seeing her this weekend and were hoping for another 'training session'.

***

Back on board, the girls settled in the cockpit while I went below to make coffee. Charlie started the conversation that we needed to have with Mathilde about our relationship, but Mathilde stopped her in mid-flow.

"I think I already know what you're saying, Charlie," she said. "Ever since our weekend at your house, I have understood that your love for each other was the deepest I have ever seen; that you are brother and sister is as nothing compared to that, and my love for you both is the best thing in my life right now."

I looked from Mathilde to Charlie, and both had tears in their eyes. There was nothing to say and the three of us went into a three-way embrace that reminded me of our 'love-ins' with Mum.

We went below, all three of us quite spent from the emotion we had shared. The girls stripped out of their shorts and T-shirts without false modesty, and I to my boxers; we lingered over a warm embrace and kissed each other good night. It was a first for me to hold two topless women against me!

Mathilde went to her aft-cabin and we to the fore, where we removed our pants and climbed into the bunk. We were both a little aroused—how

200

could we not be, but as we started to cuddle-up, Charlie put a finger to my lips, and we listened; we could hear muffled sobs coming from Mathilde's cabin and Charlie slipped out of bed to go to her. I could not make out what was being said softly between them, but Charlie came back after a couple of minutes with Mathilde, and they both climbed into our bunk, with Mathilde on the outside next to Charlie. Charlie held her tightly and the sobs faded away. Our bunk was wide enough for us all as Mathilde took up almost no room at all lying on her side in Charlie's embrace.

Charlie kissed Mathilde on the forehead in a motherly way, and Mathilde raised her head to kiss Charlie on the mouth before replacing her head on Charlie's shoulder. I was on my side and Charlie turned her face to me for a long and loving kiss. I ran my hand up Charlie's thigh and found that Mathilde was straddling Charlie's other leg, a gentle motion in progress, much as Charlie liked to do with me. I ran my hand up to Charlie's breast only to find Mathilde suckling one and caressing the other. I put my hand on the small of Mathilde's back and gently stroked her there and down to her tiny buttocks which were moving rhythmically, as a series of urgent panting sounds started escaping her. I continued to stroke her back until she started to climax and moved my hand to Charlie who was hot and very wet to my touch, her climax a matter of seconds away. She came as Mathilde's climax carried Charlie along with her. Charlie turned her head to me and we kissed again as she moved her hand down to my solid erection, with her other hand she urged Mathilde to slide on top of her and then over to me. For the briefest moment I hesitated but Mathilde was already there and Charlie was guiding me to the inevitable.

Mathilde lowered herself slowly, as if testing, and I felt the tightness of her. I tried to limit my penetration in case I hurt her, but she pressed down and cried out as I went deeper into her. Her climax built again, and I could not stop my own from bursting within her. Charlie took my hand and put it on Mathilde's tiny breast, and I moved my other hand to caress the other. Her breasts were indeed small, but her hard nipples pressed beautifully into my palms. Charlie turned her face to me and kissed my lips. In the faint light I saw Charlie's beatific smile and tried to banish the thought that we had just crossed a line, maybe a magic line, but definitely a line.

Mathilde returned to her cabin and Charlie and I embraced. I don't think either of us could have articulated our feelings at that moment, but there was not time anyway; Charlie was hotter than I had ever known her and mounted me urgently. She had to press my penis to her clitoris as I stiffened and entered her. Her nipples were wonderful to my touch and she seemed to be in continuous climax, whimpering all the time until an even stronger wave took her I knew not where. I must have climaxed at some point but could not recall as I was so stunned at my lovely Charlie's devastating orgasm. We were still and silent while Charlie's breathing came back to normal, but I could still feel her twitching somehow around my penis. Charlie's eyes focussed on my face, and I moved my hands down to her hips.

"What happened to me Nat? Are you OK?"

"I'm very OK, my love, and you've just had a monster orgasm."

***

I slept soundly and woke to find Charlie stroking my cheek, smiling as we kissed. The events of the night flooded into my consciousness, as if remembering a dream, but that lasted for just a moment and I clung to Charlie, her kiss quelling a moment of panic. My mind had wandered into unknown territory; had we not just been unfaithful to each other? I recalled my comment to Charley about her turn-on with Mathilde during our weekend at home, '… Just go with your heart!' Could we claim a greater good, or were we kidding ourselves?

We could hear Mathilde showering in the aft bathroom. Charlie took a couple of wet wipes from the box on her side of the bunk and wiped my stomach and penis.

"Oh no!" Charlie cried. "Look!" She showed me the wet wipe—there was blood all over it!

"I must have hurt her, or her period has started, or was she… was she…"

"A virgin?" Charlie finished my sentence.

We were silent for a while and then…

"Coffee in the cockpit!" Mathilde called.

202

Charlie and I gave Mathilde a hug and kiss and sat opposite to her across the cockpit table. Mathilde reached across and held our hands; she had a broad smile on her face and tears were trickling down her cheeks.

"I honestly don't know what to say except that I feel so happy!" the smile broadened. "You can't possibly know what last night meant to me. I have a long story to tell you, one I have never told anybody else, and yes, I know what you must be thinking, I was a virgin."

I think Charlie shared with me a great sense of relief at Mathilde's happiness and a strong desire to hear her story. We loved this girl, and now we had both made physical love with her. It had occurred initially out of her sadness and our compassion and ended with her obvious joy.

***

The coffee was stone cold so I went below to make a fresh pot and a simple breakfast of toast and soft-boiled eggs. I set the saloon table and called the girls down when it was ready.

Mathilde and Charlie sat across from me, there was an atmosphere of peace surrounding us, Charlie squeezed Mathilde's hand.

I broke the silence. "You'd better eat this, I'm not making it again!" They both grinned at my feeble attempt at humour, but it worked, and we all tucked in. Mathilde ate heartily and was clearly thinking how to begin. I made more toast and coffee and Mathilde started.

"I think I must tell my story backwards, at least to start with, and tell you how it has been for me at university." Mathilde drank some coffee and continued, "I used to think that I was probably asexual. I enjoyed the company of both boys and girls but when a boy got keen on me, and made a pass, I just seized up and could not let him get close to me. When I looked in the mirror, I did not see a desirable or a sexual person. I just looked childish, and undesirable from a sexual point of view. I once drifted into a low-level lesbian relationship that lasted only a short time; I was disgusted by the 'toys' she wanted to use. My only real sex life has been with myself, and I accepted that, I was even content that that was all there was for me." Mathilde silently buttered the last slice of toast and started to eat it; her eyes focused on something we could not see.

"So now I go back to my childhood. It must have seemed to an outsider that I lived in a dream world, an ideal world, my father a famous footballer, and my mother an equally, if not more famous, ballerina. In my earliest memories I basked in their fame and loved them very much. At bedtimes it was our habit for my mother or father to put me to bed with a story and a good night cuddle, and I felt cherished." Mathilde's face softened on recalling these early memories but equally quickly turned to stone.

"My mother often travelled with her ballet company and at those times my father continued our bedtime routine. As time passed my father's 'bedtime cuddles' started to become more intimate, and I grew to hate it. He used to tell me if I did not do what he wanted he would tell my mother what a dirty little girl I was, and how she would hate me…" Charlie embraced Mathilde and they both wept. I too was feeling very emotional.

"You don't have to go on with your story, Mathilde," I said. "We can see what a horrible situation you were in. I'm so upset that you suffered so much at the hands of that bastard…" I was close to tears and went to sit next to her as well. Mathilde was the first to speak.

"I won't say more about those times except to say that he never tried to penetrate me… if he had I think I would have found a way to kill him!

"I now know that I was a victim of domestic child sexual abuse, and strangely perhaps, it helps me to know that there is a name for what I went through. Of course, I now understand my feelings of false guilt and self-loathing. My mother's love was everything to me, but if I told her what was happening, I thought all our relationships would crumble, her marriage as well as the love between her and me."

"I'm heartbroken to hear what an awful life you've led Mathilde," said Charlie. "And all the more so that he's got away with it!"

Mathilde continued, "I think now that if my mother had not been terminally ill, I would have had to expose him. She had to give up her ballet career when I was in my early teens. She suffered repeated stress fractures in her second metatarsals and could not dance en pointe any longer; it's quite common in female ballet dancers. She became depressed and that lasted until she was chosen as 'the face' for the cosmetics company. After my mother's diagnosis, I confided in my Aunt Anne. We agreed that my mother should never find out, it would have broken her completely. When we were told that she was terminally ill, Anne reached an agreement with my father to have no further contact with me, and in return we would not interfere with the inheritance he would receive on my mother's death; basically, we would do anything to stop my mother knowing and ruin what little time she had left. I so hate that man, I've asked our avocat de famille to arrange for my surname to be changed to my mother's family name."

I suddenly remembered the funeral service for Mathilde's mother, and the barefaced duplicity of her father's reading from the bible; and there was more: I recalled his close attention to Aurélie at our apéro on the evening that we first met Mathilde, and all this while keeping a mistress at his apartment in Marseille! It was not hard to utterly despise this man.

"I want us to go sailing soon but I must just finish this first." Mathilde continued, "I have just completed my first two years at university, and in my whole life, until last night, I have had no real lover nor, in fact, wanted one. I loved you two from the first time we met. The love that you and your family have shown, and the physical expression of that last night, has been life-changing for me; I understand now how badly damaged I was…"

"Let's go sailing!" said Charlie.

***

Pedro came round when he saw us preparing to leave and called out something to us in Spanish, Mathilde turned to us.

"He wants to know what time we will come back?"

"How about tomorrow afternoon?" Charlie said.

"Sounds good to me!" I replied, and Mathilde spoke for a little while with Pedro in Spanish, which clearly included them introducing themselves.

"Wow, that sounds very fluent," said Charlie. "We didn't know you spoke Spanish!"

"Yes, I did both English and Spanish for my Baccalaureate, but the Spanish is quite rusty now, maybe I can brush-up a little while I'm here."

I backed us out of our slot and gave Mathilde the helm when we were clear of the moorings.

"You're captain for the day, Mathilde—we'll do whatever you wish!" said Charlie.

"Right now, I just want to sail on the wind—get back in touch with Mathilde."

As soon as we rounded the southern tip of Menorca Mathilde called for the mainsail as she took a course on the port tack in the general direction of Mallorca. I sheeted in the main and Mathilde heeled in response and picked up speed. Mathilde switched the engine off and called for the headsail which Charley and I deployed and sheeted well in. Mathilde wasn't joking when she said she wanted to sail on the wind! We made tiny adjustments to the headsail under Mathilde's instruction, and she sailed the boat as close to the wind as was possible. She was clearly an expert sailor and our speed through the water was hovering around nine knots with the north-westerly wind a steady twelve.

Mathilde positively danced over the small waves and our lovely friend was over the moon.

We stayed on that tack for over an hour and not once did Mathilde luff the headsail by getting too close to the wind.

We tacked across the wind and Mathilde ordered the sheets eased for a broad reach back to the Menorcan coast.

"OK crew!" 'ordered' captain Mathilde. "Choose a nice anchorage for lunch and give me a course, please."

Charlie and I decided to return to Calas Coves where we had first met Pau and Sophie and entered a waypoint on the plotter just outside the bay. Mathilde made a course adjustment and engaged the autopilot.

Mathilde left the helm and came to sit with us as I went below for three beers. Charlie set the bimini and we all relaxed in the shade; Mathilde had not said a word since engaging the autopilot and took it upon herself to keep watch; there was nothing anywhere near us.

I directed Mathilde to anchor in the middle of the bay and put the dinghy in the water ready to take our stern line ashore. Mathilde beat me to it and hopped into the dinghy with the stern line.

"Remember who's captain today, Nat!"

***

It was now late afternoon, the girls were sunbathing on the fore deck and I was looking at the pair of them in wonder from the cockpit. On the port side

Charlie lay topless with her bikini bottoms pulled up tight for maximum skin exposure, her lovely breasts shiny with sun oil. Mathilde, also topless, lay next to her. In her way, I could see that Mathilde was quite attractive, sexy even. With my memory of last night still achingly fresh, I relived the moment that Charlie hoisted Mathilde over me and guided my penis into her, how tight she had been, and yet I had no idea I was the first. Her breasts had fitted comfortably in my hands and her nipples had been rampant. As I looked at her now, I tried to suppress my rising desire for more of her and turned my gaze to the love of my life. Charlie was handling our new reality with apparent ease, but I still felt incredibly unsure and very nervous about what we had started last night, and how things might evolve.

To bring my reveries to an end, I climbed down to the swimming platform and dived in.

The girls had heard my splash, and both dived in from the pulpit to join me. We swam to the beach and sat on the white sand to watch the sun on its way down to the west. The girls sat either side of me and we put our arms around each other, my doubts started to evaporate, and I began to think that I should just relax into this new reality, whatever it might be. As if a decision had been made, I gave the girls a squeeze and Charlie lifted her face to me for a kiss, I turned to Mathilde, and she too was looking for a kiss with a loving smile on her elfin face—so I kissed her too!

Back on the swimming platform the girls shed their bikini bottoms for the shower and Charlie pulled my trunks down as well. I had never exposed myself in front of any other woman except Charlie and kept my back to Mathilde. Charlie took my shoulders and turned me to face her.

"You two are so beautiful," said Mathilde, and hugged us both. We put our arms around her in a three-way hug and I told her that she should realise how good looking, and indeed sexy she was.

"Shower and dinner, what do you say?" I asked, and we all took our shower on the swimming platform!

CHAPTER THIRTY-TWO

THE THREE OF US

The sun had set, and I switched on our masthead anchor light before pulling the cork on one of Jaime's red wines.

The girls were now wearing their nightshirts and putting together our dinner below while I sipped my wine in the cockpit. My mind was positively buzzing with the potential connotations of what we were doing, and I wondered what must be going through Mathilde's head; it could not be other than a total renaissance for her.

And what about Charlie and me? I really needed some time alone with her so we could talk this through.

Charlie started putting bowls of salad, a plate of Serrano ham and a few cheeses on the cockpit seat at the companionway and came up as I put our dinner on the cockpit table. Charlie kissed me on my forehead and whispered in my ear,

"In case you're thinking what I'm thinking Nat, from my side I could not love you more. What we've done with Mathilde is to include her in our love, we've done nothing less than transform her life and we should rejoice that we've been able to do that."

Before I could respond Mathilde joined us and we tucked-in to our meal with gusto! I poured wine for the girls and caressed Charlie's thigh in silent affirmation of what she had said, my mind relaxed.

Mathilde went below to make coffee and we watched the stars appear in the moonless sky. I spoke softly to Charlie,

"I so agree with what you said Charlie, and yes, my mind has been quite disturbed; and yes again, my love for you is only stronger now."

Mathilde reappeared with the coffee and sat next to Charlie.

"There's so much I want to say," said Mathilde. "But I have not the words…"

"We don't need words," said Charlie, as she embraced her. "We're both overjoyed to see the happiness on your lovely face, our love for one another can only be a blessing."

Mathilde buried her face in Charlie's neck and they held the embrace for some time. When Mathilde lifted her face, her cheeks were streaked with tears which Charlie wiped away with her thumb.

"I will go to my bed now," said Mathilde. "With the most happiness I have ever known!"

CHAPTER THIRTY-THREE

BACK TO THE CLUB

Pedro saw us arriving and rushed round to take our lines as Mathilde nosed us perfectly into our slot. Once more she had a lengthy exchange with Pedro.

"He's old enough to be your grandfather!" joked Charlie.

"He was just asking why I had the same name as the boat and I told him the story, but he is quite handsome though, don't you think?" Mathilde laughed.

Mathilde put the bimini up while I brought three beers up to the cockpit.

***

The next day we were invited to Pau and Sophie's home for lunch and met their son and daughter-in-law, Joan, the Catalán version John, and Julia, Guillem and Jordi's parents.

We liked them immediately. Joan was definitely a chip off the Sophie block with his generous proportions and ready laugh. Julia was from Cartagena originally, on the southeast corner of the mainland, and had not yet fully mastered Catalán. She sympathised with Mathilde when the others sometimes slipped into a rapid Catalán exchange!

Jaime, as expected, was also in attendance, and Maria helped the other ladies in the lunch preparation.

Joan was an architect with a firm in Palma de Mallorca and ran a suboffice for them in Mahon, Julia was the senior midwife at Sophie's hospital.

The boys claimed Charlie for their own and she willingly joined them in the garden for a kickabout.

Sophie called us all to the table and Charlie and her footballers washed their hands and joined us.

The star dish, amongst the many, was a large shallow earthenware pot of potatoes and chipirones, a medium sized member of the squid family, cooked with its tentacles in a broth made with the ink of the squid.

Charlie and I knew this dish from our holidays with Mum and Dad in southwest France, but this version was the best yet!

Jaime left for his siesta at three o'clock and we took this as a signal that lunch was over; Joan gave us our ride back to the club.

***

"I'm dizzy from all that's happening to me," said Mathilde. "All these lovely people, and we three doing what we're doing. There seems to be far more love in the world than I ever imagined. How about we anchor in a nice bay for a couple of days? We can swim, go running, and work off some calories!"

"I agree with all that," Charlie replied. "I'll pop out after siesta for a ready roasted chicken and we'll leave early in the morning."

We had all had several glasses of Jaime's wine and Mathilde in particular was ready for a nap. I stretched out under the bimini for my siesta while the girls went below; I glanced down the companionway and saw them both heading forward!

CHAPTER THIRTY-FOUR

CALA PRESILI AND THE THREE OF US

We left at nine the next morning, and headed north up the east coast. Pau and Sophie had marked our pilot with three of their favourite spots during our Easter holiday with Mum. The furthest was Cala Presili, about a two-hour sail away, and we headed for that.

The east coast of Menorca is largely in the lee of the prevailing wind, and we had to get well offshore before we found enough wind to fill our sails in the light conditions.

Our indirect route took us four hours before we dropped anchor in the most northerly of the three bays of Cala Presili. It was a beautiful open bay with white sand beach and low rocky cliffs separating it from the next bay. I put our dinghy in the water and attached the outboard motor while the girls prepared a simple lunch of aioli potatoes and hard-boiled egg salad. I opened a bottle of dry white wine.

It was too hot below for siesta so Mathilde brought our pillows up and we napped in still air under the bimini until the sun was well on her way down. We swam to the beach to freshen up and ran along the beach before returning to the boat.

Charlie and Mathilde had made appointments to have their bikini lines waxed in three days' time, so that fixed our timing for the return to the club on the evening beforehand.

***

Over breakfast the next day, Mathilde told us that she had started her period.

"I knew I was due so was not too worried, but it's still a relief," Mathilde smiled at us. "For the first time in my life I guess I need to do something about contraception!"

"We have no condoms on board Mathilde, but I have a good supply of pills if you would like to do that. I can ask Dad to bring some more if need be."

Mathilde said she would like that and thanked Charlie.

I had made love to Mathilde without protection and was heartily relieved at this development. To a certain way of thinking it normalised our activity somewhat, and a little more of my nagging doubt evaporated. I also realised that our behaviour had been more than a little immature, reckless even. What if Mathilde had become pregnant? She was clearly OK with contraception but what were her thoughts on abortion and morning-after pills?

The three of us needed to have that conversation.

Mathilde spent the nights in her cabin for the time we stayed in the bay, and Charlie and I reconnected in our special way. The three of us still shared moments of intimacy and affection so Mathilde did not feel excluded in any way.

We swam a lot, stretched our chicken to two dinners, drank another bottle of wine, several beers, and did exactly as we had planned—relaxed!

On our second day Mathilde realised that she had an interesting problem. Should she have her bikini line waxed while she was having her period? What would the beautician think if she noticed the little tampon cord? She decided not to, her bikini bottom was not so high cut anyway! She rang the salon to cancel her half of the appointment but would go with Charlie anyway in case they didn't speak English.

***

There was no one around to take our lines when we arrived at the club at sunset; Charlie brought us into our slot perfectly and I was able to just step onto the pontoon finger from our swimming platform to secure the mooring lines.

We'd had an easy broad reach back after we found some wind about a mile or so offshore, and let the autopilot do the work while we had an apéro of white wine and serrano in the balmy evening breeze.

We had virtually no food on board so had a light supper in the club before settling in the cockpit with a pot of coffee.

I brought up the subject that had been bothering me about our sexual activity and the girls agreed with my concerns. Charlie lightened the moment by saying that we must have all been on a high of love, which was of course true, but it was not an excuse.

"How would you have reacted Mathilde, if you had been pregnant?" Charlie asked, and Mathilde gave it some thought before responding.

"My knee-jerk answer would be to abort straight away, but there is something that stops me saying that," Mathilde replied. "I have never thought of having a baby, I don't even know if I ever want to have children, but that's not to say how I might feel if I became pregnant with your child Nat—what do you think?"

"Charlie and I have been each other's sole lover ever since puberty and we have always known that we can never have a baby between us. For that reason, it has never been a consideration. For all three of us this new situation is absolutely unique. We could never have imagined a three-way love affair until we both fell in love with you, Mathilde," I answered. "The more I think about it, I see that there are more considerations than I first thought, for example, what would your feelings be Charlie?"

"I can best answer that by telling you about something that happened to us on the weekend that you visited. Do you remember Mathilde that you and I had an intimate cuddle on that first night, after you became very emotional over your mother's illness? You fell asleep in my arms and I went back to my bedroom feeling very horny from our intimacy. I didn't want to go to Nat in case you woke up and needed me, so I pleasured myself. When I told Nat about it, he became hot just thinking about it and I asked what I should have done if you had not fallen asleep and we had both been turned-on, Nat had said, 'just go with your heart!' And isn't that just what we have all done. Logic screams that a pregnancy is the last thing we need, but I also think that if it did happen, our collective response may not be as simple as the knee-jerk you first mentioned, Mathilde."

Mathilde had tears in her eyes but smiled broadly nonetheless.

"I remember that night vividly," Mathilde said. "I did wake up when you left me, and I was wet as well. I was unsure what to do so I silently did the same as you; it was wonderful!"

The erotism of our conversation was having a major impact on me, as I was sure it was with the girls. I was about to suggest we all go to the fore cabin when Mathilde beat me to it.

"Can we go for a cuddle?"

We paused in the saloon to get out of our clothes and piled onto the big bed and had our lovely three-way cuddle.

Mathilde kissed us both as if saying 'good night'.

"I'm leaving now. You need a little time on your own I think."

***

When the girls returned from the beauty salon the next morning, they could hardly contain their amusement—and Charley showed me why! The waxing had removed virtually all of Charlie's pubic hair except for a fan-shaped area above her vulva; she giggled as she showed me. It was a bit of a shock, but I grinned, and yes, I rather liked it! The remaining hair was almost the same length as it was before, I looked forward to running my fingers through it.

"You'd better pull your pants up Charlie!"

CHAPTER THIRTY-FIVE

MATHILDE AND I

Charlie popped out for some basic supplies, and I realised that this was the first time that Mathilde and I had been alone together since we had started our intimacy, and for some obscure reason I was a little tense.

I dried our breakfast dishes while Mathilde made her bed. I had my back to her cabin, and she came up behind me to give me a hug.

As if prompted by telepathy, she said, "I know, Nat, I feel just the same!" I turned into her and she went up on tiptoes for a kiss. Our height difference was exactly twelve inches and I had to bend down to kiss her. We both laughed as we realised it was the first time we had shared a lover's kiss standing up! I scooped her up with my hands under her bum, her legs round my waist and arms round my neck, and we kissed some more, small kisses at first and then a long one, our tongues slowly sliding around each other. My erection was right against her sex through our clothes and Mathilde pressed against it. We could have made love there and then but Charlie's imminent return held me back; Mathilde read my thoughts, "Soon Nat… soon!"

When Charlie did return she gave me a knowing smile and a hug. "It's good Nat, no worries!"

Charlie made coffee and we decided we should call home to report on our holiday. Mathilde spoke with Mum for a short while and thanked her and Dad for letting her join us, clearly conveying her happiness.

Flo was napping with Élodie, and Dad was at the hospital, so Mum updated us on Pierre's condition; he was progressing slowly and his holiday with Dad a virtual certainty. Flo had been woken by the phone and came on to gush about baby Élodie and how well Pierre was doing with fatherhood. Mum came back on.

"I'm very happy to hear Mathilde so enjoying herself, Nat, you and Charlie have done wonders!"

Charlie took the phone below for a private few words which I knew was about Dad bringing some extra pills to replace those that Charlie had 'mislaid'!

***

I had noticed that Pau was doing some 'housekeeping' and went over for some advice about the BBQ that I had not yet unpacked.

He showed me his installation and made the point that it's better to use a small gas cylinder completely separate from the main gas supply for the cooker in the gally and I pictured my aft cockpit lockers for a suitable location.

"I'm going fishing tomorrow, Nat, just us boys—no girls allowed, if you'd like to join us," he said. "That's me, Joan, the two boys and Jaime, interested?" I didn't need to think about it!

"Absolutely, I'd love to, do you have a spare rod for me?"

"I'll bring an old one from my garage, you can have it actually, I haven't used it for years."

"Thanks a lot! What about food and beer?"

"Club cook will make sandwiches and I'll load the ice and beer last thing tonight."

"Great, please put the beer on my account!"

"Five o'clock start, OK?"

"Perfect!"

***

My ladies were nowhere to be seen when I returned, but the stripped beds told me they were on a laundry run to the club's washing machine; not surprising really, as we had changed the fore cabin sheets three times since Mathilde's arrival!

I rigged a clothesline with the gib-sheets tied to the shrouds for when they returned and went in search of some small sachets of wasabi, the hot Japanese mustard-like paste, that I knew we had in one of the lockers over

217

the fridge. If we caught tuna tomorrow I would make some sashimi to have with our lunch.

I went to find Pedro and unpacked our BBQ that he had kept in his workshop for us, and walked back with the girls who had left the washing machine to finish its cycle.

When Mathilde saw the BBQ clamped to the aft pulpit she offered to Christen it with an Indonesian chicken or pork dish called satay, which sounded delicious when she described the peanut butter and chili sauce.

***

"I'm off in the morning for a boys-only fishing trip with Pau, how about doing the satay in a couple of days' time?"

"Out all day, huh!" said Charlie. "Not to worry! We'll find something to amuse ourselves!" the girls both grinned and 'high-fived'!

"Thanks a lot!" said I, and smiled with them!

***

It was over an hour before we had any hint of sunrise. Pau had his boat up on the plane doing twenty knots in the general direction of Sardinia until he arrived at his favourite tuna fishing area, about thirty-five miles off the Menorcan coast. Pau had his radar on the whole time, because at that speed, another boat just out of sight over the horizon, was less than fifteen minutes away!

Pau slowed down gently to ten knots as the boat settled down from the plane and into displacement mode.

He had four fishing rod sockets across the width of the stern and I was allocated one of the central ones for my antique gift rod! It was actually rather beautiful, the rod itself was made of wood whereas the others were all fibreglass. The reel on mine was also made of wood with brass mechanism and reinforcing where needed; it just cried-out to be nicely sanded and revarnished!

Pau's two grandchildren, Jordi and Guillem, were appointed my 'advisors', and we deployed our line at a somewhat shorter distance than the outer lines to avoid entanglement. Joan, Pau's son, made a large pot of coffee after taking the other inner position and Pau and Jaime the two outers.

We had hardly settled down with our coffees before my rod bent alarmingly; Pau slowed the boat to just enough to maintain steerage and I started to reel the line in. I was told to pause every few seconds for the fish to catch-up before taking in more line.

When the fish was visible we saw it was a very good tuna, over half a metre in length. Joan helped the boys land it onto the swimming platform with a gaff hook and Jordi killed it instantly with the alcohol spray straight into the gills. Jaime used a lethal looking filleting knife to decapitate and clean out the guts before putting the fish into a huge Ziplock bag for the ice chest. Pau used the swimming shower to hose off the detritus and we resumed fishing; the whole thing over in about ten minutes! It was only just after seven, if we carried on like this we would have enough fish to feed the five thousand by lunchtime!

As it happened, we did not carry on like that! After catching two more tuna over the next hour, smaller than mine, there was no further excitement until noon when Pau declared it was lunchtime. I asked Pau if Jaime could cut me a fillet from one of the small tuna and I went below to mix my soy sauce and wasabi, and thinly sliced the tuna for sashimi. I arranged my slices around a large plate, with my bowl of sauce in the centre, and took it up with a handful of forks.

Joan was the only one who had had sashimi before and the others looked on with great suspicion as he and I showed how to dip the slices into the sauce before eating. Each took a tentative nibble at first but only Jaime didn't like it; the plate was cleared in very short order!

After our sashimi, sandwiches and beer lunch, Pau suggested we head back at fishing speed to see what else there might be to catch. Tuna, he said, mainly fed at sunrise and sunset.

With no further action, the boys got a little bored so we brought our lines in and Pau took the boat up to planing speed for the remainder of the trip home.

***

The girls were in their bikinis under the bimini when I arrived and both had news for me.

Mathilde had two items. First, her period was over, and second, she had an email from her Aunt Anne to say that the avocat d'famille had finalised her name change, she was now Mathilde Dovergne

"Do you like it?" Mathilde asked.

"I like both," I replied with a smile. "And anything is better than your father's name! What's your news Charlie?"

"I have a nice email from Ralph. He says that Lucy showed my portfolio to the client she mentioned when we were in her office and she's very interested. They have a new line of swimwear, and their assistant creative director wants to come out with Ralph, bringing some stuff for me to wear for a trial shoot. They want to come out sometime over the next few days and take some of the shots on-board if it's convenient, what do you think?"

"Wow! You're going to be a star!" I joked. "It sounds like fun, but before you answer him, what about your holiday, Mathilde? Is there something special you would like to do, you have less than two weeks left?" Mathilde laughed.

"Something 'special'?" she replied. "These last few days have been the most 'special' I can remember!"

"OK, let's fix Ralph's visit and we'll work around that for our holiday, eh?"

Charlie went below for pen and paper and called Ralph from the saloon.

Mathilde moved next to me on the cockpit seat and held my hand.

"Thanks for thinking about me, Nat, but I'm enjoying every day, whatever we do. This modelling thing with Charlie is very exciting and completely new for me, I'm sure to enjoy it. You're a wonderful person, Nat… and I love you dearly!" She squeezed my hand.

Charlie came back up after her call with Ralph.

"OK, that's all fixed…" Charlie stopped in midflow and looked at Mathilde and me… and smiled, "I think you two should go below… I'll join you in a few minutes!"

We hurried out of our minimal clothes in the saloon and were in the big bunk in no time. Mathilde was hot and twitching as I put my tongue gently on her labia and up to her clitoris. She held my face to her, her hips moving on me. She was very close, "Oh Nat, I'm coming… coming now…" Her knees came up and I sucked on her clitoris as she climaxed, her juices almost squirting over me. I came up and entered her and then saw Charlie watching us. Our eyes locked onto each other. She was naked, one hand to her breast and the other moving between her legs: I hardly missed a beat and followed Mathilde's climax until I could not stop myself, never taking my eyes off Charlie.

Charlie climbed onto the bed, still holding herself and kissed Mathilde, who disengaged from me to care for Charlie who climaxed almost immediately and we relaxed into a magical embrace.

***

I woke up to an empty bed sometime later and could hear the girls talking in the cockpit. I put on my shorts and went to join them. They were freshly showered, sweet smelling, and held their noses as I passed to get to the swimming platform shower! I just ignored them! Ten minutes later, equally sweet smelling, I rejoined them.

"So where were we?" I asked. "Oh, yes! You were about to give me some news, Charlie."

"Well, actually, I've got two pieces of news now!" she said. "The first is that it's nine o'clock and we're both starving waiting for you to finish your beauty sleep! Which, incidentally, has not worked! So before the rest of the news, you have to take us up to the club house for our supper!"

I was pleased to do so of course, and we went arm-in-arm up to the club for the cook's 'gourmet' cheeseburgers and salad!

***

I finally got the main news over coffee in the cockpit after supper!

"Ralph will try for Wednesday, that's three days away, and will email confirmation after speaking to Heather, the client's assistant creative director. They will spend two days here and ask if we can all go sailing for some of the shots. We'll be suitably compensated!" Charlie went below for her laptop and looked in her inbox.

221

"OK, it's confirmed. They arrive on the midday flight from Gatwick and a hotel car will pick them up. They've booked a two bedroom suite and will use the sitting room for work. They will call when settled and ask me to join them for some fittings and trial shots in the afternoon and later to come and see the boat. How about that?"

"Sounds great, we'd better do a little cleaning and polishing, eh!"

CHAPTER THIRTY-SIX

CHARLIE'S SMILE

The call came at two o'clock on Wednesday afternoon. Charlie had made some sensible preparations: a very light salad lunch to avoid a full-looking tummy, nails neatly trimmed, and her lovely ash-blonde hair shiny from conditioner. Mathilde and I walked Charlie to the bus stop and wished her luck with a kiss from both of us.

Back on board we cleared our lunch stuff from the cockpit and did a last-minute check on deck that all was shipshape. Over the last three days we'd given the top-sides a thorough scrubbing and polished the brightwork; she looked great!

We'd opened every deck hatch, but it was still very hot below. We both took off our T-shirts and just wore our pants as we did the washing up and tidied the saloon.

*****

Charlie and I had still not quite convinced Mathilde of her attractiveness. Her self-doubt of such long standing still persisted, although at a much reduced level.

I watched her as she stretched over the saloon table, her panties had ridden up to uncover one cheek and she looked utterly desirable! I put down the tea towel I'd been using and came up behind her to put my arms around her. I'd grown to love her tiny breasts and cupped them now as I pressed against her buttocks. My cotton briefs doing nothing to hide my arousal. I slipped my penis out to rub it gently against her and Mathilde lowered her head and pressed herself back to me, her legs opening. I pulled her panties aside and she held me to her vagina to move a little with me.

We stayed just doing that for some magic moments before I turned her to me and lifted her up for a long kiss. Without guidance from either of us my penis entered her, and she sighed deeply, putting her head against my neck. Neither of us wanted to move but I could feel a gripping sensation in her tightness. She put her face to my cheek, "I am so in love with you, Nat… can we lie down please… I want to be on top…"

I walked to her cabin and sat on her bunk before lying on my back, my penis still deeply loving her inside with her astride me. The look of love on her slightly parted lips, and eyes moist to the point of tears, squeezed my heart. Without breaking eye contact Mathilde slowly lifted a little and then down. Her tightness reminding me that it was just a few days since I had broken her hymen and she still moved a little tentatively with this new sensation. This was quite wonderful and indeed the first time we had made love truly alone. Mathilde clearly wanted this to last and limited her movement; I was totally with her, and we read each other's desire perfectly. Her breathing was becoming deeper as she pressed a little harder and I suppressed as best I could my own mounting passion. Her mouth was now forming a circle as she breathed out and I fanned her amazing little nipples and took my eyes from hers to watch those nipples slipping between my fingers. Her breathing quickened with her movements, and she climbed to orgasm in just a few seconds. I tried to delay my own climax to prolong hers but could not hold back. I could feel the limit of her, but she still pressed down, her head back, a silent scream of ecstasy on her lips as I ejaculated. When Mathilde lowered her head to look at me her face was wet with tears, and she was sobbing without restraint. I pulled her down to me and she straightened her legs; I caressed her neck and back until the sobs subsided.

***

After showers in the club bathroom, we remade Mathilde's bed and sat in the cockpit in the shade of the bimini. I had a cold beer and Mathilde a glass of iced water, and we regained our composure.

It was nearly five o'clock when a smiling Charlie returned with Ralph and the lady who must be Heather. Ralph was in 'long' shorts and T-shirt and Heather a crop top and skinny jeans. They stopped on the pontoon as Charlie pointed out our boat and Mathilde and I waved to them.

With introductions made we sat around the cockpit table and Mathilde fetched beers for Ralph and Charlie and another glass for Heather to share Mathilde's bottle of water. Heather was clearly impressed with the boat.

"Hey, Ralph, was this boat just made for shoots or what?"

"It's better than I had hoped," said Ralph with a smile.

Charlie was clearly bubbling from her afternoon with them at the hotel.

"I've tried on loads of swimming costumes and some very sexy undies, and every one fitted perfectly. I liked a lot of them but I'm not sure if the thong type suits me!" Charlie grinned, "I think things might get a bit sore if you wore one all day!"

"Plenty of girls do these days," said Heather. "Including me—anything to avoid a pantie line!"

"So what's the plan?" I asked.

Ralph turned to Heather.

"Heather calls the shots, literally! So what do you say, Heather?"

"Mainly I'd like some stationary shots on deck, but without other boats around, Like at anchor, with a nice beach in the background. I'd also like some action shots of Charlie sailing this lovely thing, if possible."

I checked my weather app.

"There's basically no weather tomorrow, just a light variable breeze mainly from the north. We can motor-sail into whatever wind there is to fill the sails, and there's more chance of that on the west coast; I would propose we go that side and anchor in a nice bay that we know quite well. It has a white sand beach in between some good cliffs."

"Sounds good to me," said Ralph. "What do you say boss?"

"Oh Ralph, this is such a treat. Charlie, this yacht, the weather, I wish every shoot got off to such a good start. I agree with everything Nat said."

I wondered how old Heather was, I was definitely picking up some vibe there! I thought she was a good bit closer to Mum's age than mine, but still very easy on the eye. Of course, she knew I was Charlie's brother and certainly Mathilde must look far too young for me—so what was she thinking I wondered!

"What time would you like to start tomorrow," I asked.

Heather looked to Ralph.

"Can we say nine o'clock?" Heather asked.

We all nodded our assent.

"Fine, I'll bring hotel packed lunches for us all, any allergies?"

"No, we're all OK on that," said Charlie.

"Good, one last thing Charlie, please don't wear any bra or panties tomorrow, they leave marks which can show up on the shots. OK, nine o'clock then!"

Charlie took them out to catch the bus but found the hotel car was waiting at the gate for them!

"What a waste of money!" said Charlie. "Oh, and talking about money, Ralph is offering us four thousand pounds a day for the use of the boat, and I'm to get three thousand a day, how about that!"

"Wow!" I said. "But come to think about it, if they were to hire a crewed charter yacht it would likely be a lot more than that! What about your three thousand?"

"It seems like a lot, and especially so as I'm having fun, but like you say, if this was my full-time job, I'd need to do a lot of shoots for a reasonable yearly income. Ralph said three thousand is a normal fee for a model's try-out shoot, but I can expect a lot more if this line takes off; and all because I can grin like an idiot!"

***

We were all showered and fed by nine o'clock when Ralph and Heather arrived. As instructed, Charlie was just wearing one of my shirts and nothing else. Their driver and Ralph needed two trips to the car to bring all their gear, and Mathilde and I helped bring it all into the cockpit. Charlie was frightened to bend over so was excused from this effort!

When everything was safely stowed below, I started the engine. We'd agreed over breakfast that I would be skipper for the day. Mathilde and I took our lines in and I put her on the helm. I saw Heather's eyes widen when Mathilde backed us out and bow-thrusted us round to exit the moorings. She did look smaller than usual behind the big wheel, her arms at almost full stretch to hold both sides. I'd put her on the helm for that very reason, so that our guests understood that she was a full member of the crew despite her diminutive stature.

I took our fenders in and stowed them in the foredeck locker, rather than on the lifelines, as I doubted Heather would want them in view and took down the bimini for the same reason.

Charlie and Heather were below, and I could see that Charlie had put on her first bikini and Ralph had his kit ready for action. I handed out life vests as we motored down toward open water explaining that they could be removed as and when required for the shoot. Ralph and Heather both said they were competent swimmers.

As expected, the sea was calm and the breeze very light.

Heather directed Charlie for various poses, mainly as if sunbathing on the foredeck and then looking wistfully out to sea from the pulpit. Heather asked if Charlie could take the helm and I told Mathilde to engage the autopilot. The pose I liked the most was when Charlie had to remove her bikini top and hang it on her left forearm, still on the wheel, and her right arm across her breasts, as if protecting her modesty, while she helmed the boat. Heather called out the facial expressions required and asked for 'amused shock' for the arm-over-breast shots. The shots were repeated with little variation for each of the costumes and I was most impressed with Charlie's performance. Heather was very professional in her direction of both Ralph and Charlie and mostly got what she wanted without repeating her instructions.

I asked if they would like the sails up and explained that we could motor-sail into the light breeze to fill the sails as if we were actually sailing. Heather asked us to wait while she and Ralph went below to review the work so far on a laptop.

"Looks great so far! Well done, Charlie, you're a natural!" said Heather. "So, let's see how things look with the sails up please. I rolled the main out first and sheeted it in tight. Mathilde knew exactly what to do and took a course with the breeze just off our starboard bow and I unrolled the head sail. The wind speed over the boat was now about ten knots, six from the engine and four from the breeze, but it kept the sails full for the camera.

Ralph and Heather walked around framing possible shots with their hands while Charlie sat with us in just my shirt.

"What do you make of it so far?" asked Charlie.

"It's very interesting and you look great in most of the costumes," Mathilde replied.

"It was getting a little repetitive before Heather called for the sails, but you looked stunning in some of them, can you keep any?" I asked.

"I'll ask, after all they were made for me!"

***

Ralph used some clever tricks with light filtering through the sails and the new shots were far more interesting than before.

After an hour, Heather asked where we could have our lunch.

"Right here if you like," I answered. "Or we can anchor in the bay I mentioned."

"OK, let's anchor in the bay," said Heather. "Sounds like we can do some shots in the water and maybe the beach as well."

I furled the sails and showed Mathilde the waypoint for Calas Coves on the plotter. She took her course, engaged the autopilot and came to sit at the cockpit table with us.

"How about a cold beer?" said Charlie.

"Great," said Heather. "But only one for you my girl. No gas filled tummies allowed!"

I put the bimini up and we relaxed under the shade with our very welcome beers for the trip to the bay. Heather was sitting next to Mathilde and asked her what school subjects she liked the most! Mathilde burst out laughing and told her she would be starting her third year at uni after the summer break! Heather was mightily apologetic, but Mathilde smiled broadly.

"It happens all the time, Heather! I know I look only about thirteen, so no need to apologise, it's quite funny most of the time!"

Both Ralph and Heather were flabbergasted, and the mood lightened. Heather pointed to me and then Mathilde, "Now I get it!" And we all smiled. Heather told us of an interesting problem that the fashion business faced regarding modelling clothes for adolescent girls. There was much negative press concerning the sexualisation of children, and models in that age group had to have a parent or guardian present during shooting. The trouble was that the parents often did not object to questionable shots thinking that their children may become famous models a little later in life! Any model over the age of consent who looked younger could make serious money in that niche!

As we arrived off Calas Coves, Mathilde took over from the autopilot and dropped the hook well away from two other yachts that were anchored as close as possible to the beach. I swam ashore with our stern line and made it fast.

I stayed in the water enjoying my swim and Charlie and Mathilde joined me, both just wearing their bikini bottoms. We could see Ralph and Heather taking it all in and conferring for the later shots. Heather was also topless and held her arm across her breasts for the jump off the swimming platform.

We all congregated around the anchor chain and Heather said what a little paradise this was and how she and Ralph were looking forward to the afternoon shoot.

"How about some lunch?" Ralph suggested, and we queued-up at the swimming ladder. Charlie had had the foresight to put a stack of towels at the aft end of the cockpit. Heather suggested that Charlie rinse off the salt water as her hair might look sticky after it dried. Heather watched Charlie shower and indicated for Ralph to look also.

"That's a lovely shot right there!" said Heather, "Maybe another cheeky one, with a booby blurred by the shower!"

Mathilde went below and passed up our packed lunches and beers for everyone except Charlie!

The afternoon was spent entirely on the boat with me rowing the dinghy for Ralph to take shots from the water when required.

With Heather being virtually naked from lunchtime onwards I had to revise my estimate of her age. She was probably mid-thirties and the less she wore the better she looked! Not as much so as my Charlie, or as interesting as Mathilde, but a very nice addition to this celebration of the female form—and to think we were being paid for this!

***

At the end of shooting for the day we all enjoyed a swim as the sun headed down toward Mallorca. After showers I popped a chilled bottle of white wine and Charlie and Mathilde passed up some impromptu little dishes for our apéro; Ralph took some 'holiday snaps' of our happy little gathering.

***

We were invited to their hotel for dinner and a review of the day's work in their suite beforehand.

Ralph had connected his laptop to the smart TV in their sitting room. The recording was unedited of course but there were truly some lovely shots of Charlie. My favourite was the cheeky topless shot with Charlie at the helm, her arm across her breast allowing a cheeky glimpse of underboob, her pseudo-shocked grin lighting up the scene magically. The shower shots were also cheeky, with Charlie's naked form blurred by the shower and her bikini hanging on the stern pulpit. There were pictures of Mathilde and I that we hadn't noticed Ralph taking; the ones of Mathilde, in particular, superbly captured her natural look of elfin joie de vivre!

Room service arrived, and we were treated to a glass of bubbles before taking the lift up to the rooftop restaurant for our dinner.

***

The relaxed conversation around the table started with profound thanks from Heather to the three of us for such a happy and fruitful day, and to Ralph's superb efforts in capturing it all. Charlie came in for special praise for her ability to project the casual fun and light-heartedness that was exactly the mood required for the promotion of the line of swimwear.

Ralph commented on the natural light in the bay as we left just before sunset, and proposed to Heather that we take advantage of it tomorrow for some of the lingerie shots.

After dinner, Heather and Ralph came down with us to the entrance where Heather asked the concierge for a car to take us back to the club and we all kissed goodnight.

***

On our return I filled our water tank while Charlie made coffee and we enjoyed the cool night breeze. We all agreed that we had had a great day.

"Did you notice Nat, that Heather definitely has the hots for you?" asked Charlie.

"Yes! But her coming to the conclusion that Mathilde and I were an item, has got us out of a potentially difficult situation," I replied. "But she is quite attractive nonetheless!" Charlie and Mathilde punched me playfully from both sides!

"We can't blame her for that now, can we?" said Mathilde!

CHAPTER THIRTY-SEVEN

BACK TO CALAS COVES

Our new day started much the same as yesterday. Heather wanted us to head straight for the beach at Calas Coves, before it got busy, to finish the swimwear shoot.

I motored without any attempt at sailing and anchored much closer to the beach. One of the yachts from yesterday had spent the night there but otherwise the bay was clear.

While Mathilde attended to our stern line, Heather and Ralph assembled their kit to take to the beach.

We loaded up the dinghy with all their stuff, which included four of the enormous hotel swimming pool towels that Heather had borrowed.

This shoot was a lot less complicated than yesterday; Charlie sunbathing on her front, her back, on her side reading, sunglasses on, sunglasses off… and repeat for each of the several costumes Heather had brought. Then shots of Charlie in thigh deep water sending up spray with her hands that sparkled in the sunlight… and repeat… etcetera. I rowed the dinghy out so that Ralph could shoot towards the beach for some of the shots.

I took Heather and Ralph back to the boat to review their work which Heather declared very satisfactory. I told them to help themselves to drinks while I went back to collect the girls and all the gear.

After our packed lunches things got a lot more interesting! Heather and Ralph planned the lingerie shoot with pictures taken below, where Charlie dressed and undressed more times than I could count, and in the cockpit, relaxing under the bimini. Charlie, nor I for that matter, had ever been much into ladies' underwear, so it was a revelation to see her wearing thongs with just a small triangle of material above her bum, and cleverly engineered bras that were barely there. Heather called them 'sheepdog' bras, as they rounded-up the breasts and pointed them in the desired direction!

Although the underwear covered basically the same geography as the swimwear, it seemed a lot more intimate, vulnerable, intrusive almost—perhaps that was the unspoken desired effect.

When we reviewed the shots over a cold drink, I noticed a rather curious thing; on the screen was Charlie in the most intimate of clothing, holding our attention as if viewed through a keyhole, while Heather, Mathilde, and now Charlie, were all topless, just wearing bikini bottoms!

***

We had a couple of hours to kill before the sundown shots, which Heather and Ralph planned down to the second, as the sun's descent was relentless.

In preparation for the shoot, I took down the bimini and Ralph rigged a small spotlight next to the companionway. The spot had several filters for various colours of light. Ralph asked Charlie to stand in different positions across the stern and angled the spot ready for the shoot. He looked through his camera at Charlie from the side decks, the mast and halfway down the companionway steps, making notes on his clipboard as he went.

These were of course lingerie shots and Heather laid out just five sets next to the spotlight, for quick changes.

Charlie had showered and rinsed her hair with conditioner to brighten it under the spotlight and we all watched the sun, waiting to start the shoot.

Heather wanted a calm, serene, closed mouth smile, Charlie practised for her and 'got it' immediately!

When the time came the warm colour of the sunlight made the cliffs stand out and the white sand shimmer. Ralph's coloured spot made Charlie look fabulous, she glowed, a touch of the Walt Disney perhaps!

The moon was not yet up so we slowly motored back with the radar set to just a one-mile range and the plotter constantly showing our position on the electronic chart. We invited them for supper in the club, but they declined, saying that they had to review the two days' work and plan the edit. They wanted Charlie at the hotel for some bedroom lingerie and sleepwear shots, starting at nine o'clock, and then for us all to join them for a light lunch before going to the airport.

***

Mathilde and I went back to bed after breakfast with Charlie having left to catch the bus to the hotel.

We'd had a lovely and loving night. Charlie and Mathilde had really got into each other. The girls thought they were neglecting me, but I found their love-making incredibly erotic to watch and feel. After Charlie's climax with Mathilde, she climbed on top of me and Mathilde slipped out of bed to go to her cabin. Charlie reignited rapidly to come almost immediately in what was in reality the second wave for her. I was massively aroused by their love-making and Charlie's orgasm went on intensifying with my penis deep inside her until I exploded. Charlie had stifled her scream with her wrist, but her vagina continued to spasm around me for some time after.

Charlie fell asleep almost immediately after she slid off to my side and we stayed in that embrace till the alarm went off at seven-thirty.

***

Mathilde and I were a little early at the hotel coffee shop and enjoyed a fresh orange juice while we waited.

We'd had a long and touching conversation in bed about our relationship after the holiday. I told her that Charlie and I loved her unconditionally and that our fondest wish was for that to continue in every way possible. However, we were not oblivious to the possibility that, with her sexuality now restored, she may eventually be attracted to someone else and that she should not feel in any way inhibited, we would no doubt be saddened, but her happiness was our first concern.

Now, in the coffee shop, she spoke of her sexuality, and I reassured of how desirable she was.

"We'd better change the subject Mathilde," I said. "I'm getting a stiffy just talking about sex with you!" Mathilde's face broke into her lovely grin.

"I can feel some tingling down there too!" And she squeezed my hand. "You and Charlie have changed my life, Nat, and I cannot think of ever falling for anyone else. I understand why you said the things you said in

234

bed, and it was very wise; but I cannot think of that now, I will love you forever, I promise."

Charlie, Heather and Ralph arrived with news of an excellent morning's work. Charlie held up a hotel laundry bag.

"And I've got lots of sexy undies and bikinis too!"

"We're a little pressed for time," said Heather. "So let's hit the salad bar and talk over our lunch, please!"

When we returned with our plates Heather continued,

"The shoot has been a joy for me, Charlie, and I'm certain we'll be in touch after the team at home see our results. I also hope to see the three of you in the not-too-distant future."

"We've had a lot of fun too, Heather," I said. "I never knew I had such a sexy sister!"

On that note Heather looked at her watch.

"Come on Ralph, our car's waiting."

As the car pulled away, Charlie told us that the money we had earned would be held in her account with Shoots until she told them where to deposit it.

"I'll ask Dad to get advice from Frank about that."

***

Back on board we let out a collective sigh and had a three-way hug.

"So, tell us about your morning, Charlie," I asked.

Charlie emptied her laundry bag onto the cockpit table and showed us her goodies.

"I've also got a thumb drive of my best shots—according to Ralph that is!"

"If you ever wear any of these undies in my presence they won't last two minutes," I joked.

"And that goes for me too!" said Mathilde.

"I'm off for siesta," said Charlie. "I've been prancing around all morning with half my bum hanging out of these ridiculous undies and I need to come back to my home planet. If either or both of you care to join me you'll be most welcome!" And with that Charlie was off!

Mathilde and I gave Charlie a few minutes to get settled and then followed.

We could hear Charlie purring from the bottom of the companionway and quietly went to Mathilde's cabin where we cuddled up in a very fond embrace, Mathilde's arm across my chest and my hand comfortably cupping one of her buttocks, and we too took our siesta.

Charlie woke us with a kiss to our heads.

"Come on you cuddle bums, I've coffee in the cockpit!"

CHAPTER THIRTY-EIGHT

BACK TO OUR HOLS

Over coffee we decided to call home, but I suggested that we have some plan for the remainder of Mathilde's holiday before doing so. Our main topic would, of course, be the shoot, but we also needed to talk about our mooring at the club. Jaime had decided to sell his boat and would keep it on the hard for any survey that a prospective buyer might need. Pau had said that he and Sophie hoped we would take over the mooring and use the club as our home base. Charlie, Mathilde and I had talked it over and strongly agreed. Menorca was perfectly centred in the western Med within easy sailing of mainland Spain, Italy, Sardinia, Sicily, and of course, the Balearics themselves. We thought it was a 'no brainer', especially considering how cheap the club was compared to commercial marinas anywhere else. Charlie fetched a notepad to list the topics; we also needed Dad and Pierre's dates so that Mathilde could arrange her return. This last item dampened our mood considerably!

***

We were of course looking forward to seeing Dad and Pierre, but we were much saddened by the prospect of losing Mathilde. We talked about how our love for one another had bloomed massively from the very first day of this holiday, and Mathilde could not hold back her tears in once again trying to explain how wonderfully transformative it had been for her.

Charlie made the call, and it was Flo who answered. Everyone was round the pool except for her who'd come in to feed Élodie.

"She's actually at my left breast as I speak," Flo giggled. "And she's getting too heavy to hold like this! Pierre's in the pool doing 'lengths' at the moment but I can tell you he's doing very well and so looking forward

237

to coming out. They've delayed their departure for three days for an appointment with his cardiologist so they will arrive in exactly two weeks. They're taking the British Airways morning flight from Heathrow so that they can fly business class; your dad wants to make it all as stress-free as possible."

Charlie had the phone on loudspeaker and we smiled at Mathilde who's face had lit-up at the news of the delay!

"I'll just put the phone on loudspeaker and call your mum and dad. I'll say goodbye now and sit where I can see Pierre—I'm still a bit nervous about him being alone in the pool; lots of love!"

Mum and Dad came on and the three of us shouted our greeting. Charlie related all her news about the shoot and what fun we'd all had with it. She laughed as she told them how much she had made just by enjoying herself and asked them to speak with Frank about where to put it. Mathilde put up her hand to say, 'me now'!

"I just wanted to say 'hello' and tell you how happy I am and to thank you again!"

"You don't need to keep thanking us, you're family now!" said Mum.

I leant over the phone for my turn and explained to Mum about the club mooring and how Pau and Sophie hoped we'd base ourselves here and take over Jaime's slot. I told him how much Charlie and I liked the idea.

"We'll talk it over with Pierre and Flo, Nat, but my gut feeling is very favourable; I'll text you tomorrow. I'm taking the phone out to Pierre, he's just drying himself. See you soon!"

"*Bonsoir mes petits, et toi Mathilde, ça va?*"

"*Très, très bien Pierre, merci!*" chirped Mathilde.

"Nat, your dad and I have delivered all your cooking and eating kit to the new flat, hope you like it, and Charlie, I have yours too, just waiting for the keys to your flat!"

Charlie and I both thanked Pierre and said our goodbyes.

***

Duty done, we turned to our own plans. Mathilde's joy at her holiday extension was infectious and we went into our three-way hug.

"So, we have two weeks," said Charlie. "What options shall we consider, Mathilde?"

I opened the pilot book to the general chart of the Balearic Islands, and we all spent a thoughtful minute pondering our options.

"You first Mathilde!" I said.

"I would really like to do some sailing, to go somewhere. I love all these beautiful bays and beaches, but I so love to be at sea as well. How about Ibiza, or go east instead to Sardinia?" More pondering!

"I think both options are exciting," said Charlie. "But I was reading that the passage across to Sardinia can be quite rough. It's also about two-hundred and fifty miles, i.e., two nights at sea each way. If we were caught out and needed to wait for a weather window to come back; we could be late for Dad and Pierre. I favour Ibiza, only one night at sea direct or anchor in southern Mallorca to avoid sailing at night, how about that?"

"I think Ibiza is the best option," I said. "And remember, it's the party island!"

"That's great!" said Mathilde. "And I prefer a stopover in Mallorca— more cuddles that way!" And we all grinned our agreement!

***

I called Pau to say that we'd have an answer about the mooring tomorrow and of our plans for Ibiza. Sophie came on to ask for Dad and Pierre's arrival details and instructed us not to plan anything for dinner on that day!

We made our plan to be back in Mahon a few days before Dad and Pierre arrived and studied the pilot for our stopover in Mallorca.

We chose Cala Marmols, the southernmost bay on the east coast and the closest to a direct line from Menorca to Ibiza.

Dad called the next day while we were shopping for our trip and told us to go ahead with the handover of Jaime's mooring. I also told him of our invite for dinner on the day he and Pierre arrived.

"Yes, your mum told me about Sophie being in the trade, I look forward to meeting them and bon voyage for tomorrow!"

***

We left at seven the next morning and had a magic twelve knot northerly wind on our starboard beam all the way across to arrive off Cala Marmols at exactly five o'clock in the afternoon.

The bay was deserted with no sign of any touristy development, and we anchored in five metres. The bay was open from the east round to the south, and I checked my weather app to see the forecast; this would not be a good place in a southerly! There was no change in the forecast.

I was so happy for Mathilde! She was skipper till lunchtime and did not stop smiling the whole time.

As soon as the anchor was set, we all jumped in for a cooling skinny dip. The girls had been topless all the time at sea and I could not be happier. My Charlie was the more classic beauty of the two with her lovely face, full breasts and slim hips. Mathilde was completely different; she truly had the body of a thirteen-year-old, her breasts full of promise for their development over the coming years; a development that had never happened. Mathilde's breasts had come in for a lot of attention from both Charlie and I over the last ten days and we both loved them. I watched Mathilde as she dried herself on the towel and wondered if they had in fact grown a little—was that even possible? I would ask Charlie later!

We sat on the cockpit cushions after our swim and I was the happiest man on earth, gazing at these two naked lovers of mine.

"I honestly can't take my eyes off you two, I love you both so much," I said.

"Time for that cuddle I mentioned!" said Mathilde.

"You two go down," said Charlie. "This one's for you Mathilde, I'll be down shortly!"

***

So we did!

As soon as we laid down I kissed Mathilde's lips and tongued her nipples on my way down. I was afraid that I might be further along, but I needn't have worried as soon as my tongue touched her clitoris she was in motion and I quickly slid up to slip the tip of my penis into her. She was just as hot as me as she lifted to take the length of me, I was home, and Mathilde was well on her way!

There was no holding either of us, or any desire to, and Mathilde's cries in orgasm pulled me to an eruption of love deep within her.

***

Charlie had not joined us, and we found her still in the cockpit. I raised my eyebrows questionably!

"Come here you two," said a smiling Charlie, and we sat either side of her.

"It was lovely just sitting here listening to you, and it got me thinking about how we're handling our sex life. I have loved everything we have done together, both in twos and threes, but frankly speaking, our threesomes can be rather awkward, don't you think?"

I was quite shocked and saw that Mathilde was too; but Charlie had struck a chord.

"Don't get me wrong," Charlie continued. "I love our cuddles and intimacy and especially making love to both of you. It's just that with the three of us at it all together I find there's an element that's not as fulfilling as when there's just two of us—in any combination that is!"

Mathilde's eyes were swimming and Charlie embraced her.

"Is it that I'm the odd one out? Am I spoiling things for you?" Mathilde sobbed.

"Not in the least, my little love," said Charlie, lifting Mathilde's head to kiss her eyes and lips. "You're a wonderful lover and have been a massive boon to our love life, and I know Nat feels the same way; it's just that a twosome is more loving where we can give our all without trying to keep tally on where everyone's bits and pieces are!"

Mathilde smiled at last. "Actually, I agree with you, and I have felt quite awkward sometimes. I thought it was my inexperience in making love but after what you've said, Charlie, I do feel a little better! When I make love with either one of you on your own, I do feel more… hmm… competent!" Charlie and I both laughed at that.

"You are a most beautiful lover Mathilde," I said. "And I get Charlie's point completely—so how do we handle this?"

"No immediate problem," Charlie replied. "I started my period today, so you two get the forecabin for the next few days!"

After a while we went for another dip and a quiet three-way cuddle in the water, holding onto the swimming ladder.

"Much better than sailing all night, eh!" said Charlie.

****

We needed an earlier start for our sail to Ibiza. Our chosen landfall was Cala de San Vicente, high up the east coast and probably up to two hours more than we had sailed yesterday. I'd entered a waypoint on the plotter just outside the bay.

Charlie was up before the sun and the smell of coffee brought Mathilde and me up to the cockpit. She'd made toast and put butter and marmalade on the table for a quick breakfast and efficient departure.

****

After rounding the southern tip of Mallorca, Charlie took a direct course for our waypoint at Cala de Vicente. The wind was the same as yesterday after we were clear of the land effect, and just aft of our beam, a slightly slower point of sailing than yesterday.

After thirteen hours of perfect sailing, a very happy Mathilde dropped our hook at seven-thirty in the evening in six metres of crystal-clear water. There were six other yachts anchored closer to the white sand beach.

The bay was enclosed by high forest clad hills that sloped down to the pleasantly developed beachfront hotels, holiday appartements and restaurants.

The sun was well down over the hills to the west as we jumped into the water for a refreshing skinny dip. Mathilde was so happy; she threw her arms and legs round Charlie as she hung onto the swimming ladder and gave her a long kiss—and then it was my turn!

It is true to say that Mathilde sometimes acted the age she appeared, rather than the age she actually was. I figured that that was due to being robbed of the innocence of childhood that should have been her birth right; so, who could blame her for doing a little catch-up! It was an absolute delight to me that Charlie and I had been instrumental in breaching that logjam by showing her the love she so richly deserved.

***

I went below to switch on our anchor light and brought up a nicely chilled bottle of Barbadillo and some nuts for a simple sundowner. Charlie fetched the glasses and we settled ourselves on the cockpit cushions. We were happy with our own company for this evening and would venture ashore tomorrow. I think we were all quite pensive over our threesome discussion and I resolved to be particularly attentive to Mathilde over the coming days, the last thing I wanted was for her to feel the intruder.

***

I called Pau to tell him of our decision to take over Jaime's mooring, and as expected, he and Sophie were delighted. Pau asked where we were and when I told him he said we must try a restaurant here called Can Gat, which he and Sophie had enjoyed several times in their cruising days.

I opened our pilot book to the section on Ibiza so we could make a loose plan. When we left Mahon, we had thirteen days left before Dad and Pierre arrived. We'd taken two days to get to Ibiza and would need two for the return plus say three days contingency, that left just six days in Ibiza. We would spend tonight here in Cala de San Vicente, leaving five days. Although Ibiza was small, just twenty-six by sixteen miles, we needed to limit ourselves to, say, two more locations before heading back to Mahon. We let Mathilde make the call and she studied the chart for a couple of minutes

"OK, leave here after lunch ashore at Can Gat tomorrow and go to Tagomago Island, and possibly another anchorage, then to Puerto de Sta Eulalia marina with the objective of leaving from there for Mahon in five days' time."

Charlie and I followed the plan on the chart.

"I think that's good, the best we can do without rushing," I said. "The island is only four miles away and Sta Eulalia another seven. If we wanted to see the capital, Puerto de Ibiza, we could catch a bus, it's just eight miles away."

***

We pottered over to the island without bothering to set our sails. We'd had an excellent seafood lunch ashore before leaving Cala San Vicente and I'd called the marina at Sta Eulalia to book a slot for our last two nights in Ibiza.

I was enormously pleased with the yacht; it had been the perfect vehicle for all that had happened since Mathilde joined us and the loving relationship that had developed. The calas were the perfect backdrop to love, to be loved, and to make love, in the privacy of the anchorages. These had been the happiest days of my life; the renaissance of Mathilde, the cherry on the cake!

As the last days of Mathilde's holiday ticked by, our sail back to Mahon would not be without some profound sadness for all three of us.

***

When I checked the forecast on my weather app there was some disappointing news. The conditions that we had been enjoying were forecast to deteriorate due to a low-pressure area forming in the Golf de Lyon, about two-hundred miles to the north; we had a three-day window to get back to Mahon!

I showed the forecast to the girls, and we all agreed we should leave tomorrow morning from Isla Tagomago to be on the safe side. We had stocked-up on essentials at the small supermarket in Cala San Vicente after lunch, so we were good to go. I phoned the marina at Sta Eulalia and cancelled our reservation.

I suggested that we sail through the night to be ahead of the weather and doubly sure of being in Mahon on time for Dad and Pierre; the girls agreed. For Charlie and me it would be only our second overnight sail and a first for Mathilde.

Dad and Pierre would arrive at lunchtime in just a few days' time; Mathilde had booked her flight back home for the late afternoon of the same day so that we could all have lunch together. There was a kind of resonance in Pierre's arrival and Mathilde's departure as we had high hopes for Pierre's further recuperation on board!

***

In the event our passage back to Mahon was as near perfect as possible. We all wore life jackets when not below and had harnesses handy if the conditions deteriorated. We worked a rolling two-hour watch system with two on watch and one resting. After two hours one of the on watch would swap with the one below and so on in rotation.

There was a three-quarter moon which was so bright we could see other traffic almost before we saw their navigation lights. The wind was just forward of our beam at a steady twelve knots until we passed under the lee of Mallorca, we put the motor on to top up the batteries until we came back into the wind, which had by then picked up to fifteen knots and slowly up to twenty-two by the time we rounded the southern tip of Menorca.

Mathilde had loved every minute of it and had stayed in the cockpit the whole time, napping once or twice on the cushions.

In total, we had covered the one-hundred and fifty miles in under a day, a handsome average speed of six and a half knots.

Mathilde expertly slid us into our slot at exactly nine o'clock in the morning!

***

Charlie rang home to report our safe arrival. Dad was away at Great Ormond Street and Flo and Pierre were still in bed after a restless night with Élodie. Charlie explained that we'd cut our stay short in Ibiza due to the weather and Mum complemented us on our seamanship in making the responsible decision.

CHAPTER THIRTY-NINE

DAD AND PIERRE

In the final days of Mathilde's holiday, Charlie and I went to great lengths to reaffirm our love for her, and although the holiday would end soon, we would spend more time together over the remainder of the summer break. The three of us agreed that we had started something wonderful and could not contemplate it ever ending. We made love often, mostly in pairs but for the occasional three-way cuddle that got out of hand! We contemplated the perfection of our triangle of love; one straight male with two bisexual women. Mathilde had triggered Charlie's AC/DC tendency and we wondered if there was a link with Mum and Flo's sexual ambiguity, perhaps genetic? In Mathilde's case her former sex life was limited to a low-level lesbian affair and masturbation. Mathilde assured us that her life was now sexually complete, more so than she had ever dreamed, and could not contemplate taking another lover.

***

Sophie called to confirm that she would pick us up at seven-thirty for our dinner with Dad and Pierre at their place. Mathilde would have already left so we would just be four.

Whilst Charlie and I were looking forward to seeing Dad and Pierre, we dreaded the departure of Mathilde. She had been an explosion of love and joy in our life the likes of which we could never have imagined.

***

The time sped by, and the dreaded day arrived. Charlie had spent the last night with Mathilde and I joined them in the morning for a loving cuddle;

Charlie got up to make our breakfast and Mathilde and I made love for the last time this holiday. Mathilde cried after her climax, and I stroked and hugged her until she smiled again.

***

We stripped our beds in the forward and aft cabins and made up the two aft cabins for Dad and Pierre. By the time we'd finished the cabins it was already noon, and time to catch the bus to the airport.

***

As planned, Dad and Pierre had flown business class on British Airways from Heathrow to ensure a comfortable and stress-free ride for Pierre; and he looked the epitome of health as he came through the arrivals hall; he'd lost some weight and even had a tan from his hours by the pool. Dad was his usual self and embraced us all warmly.

Pierre, by whatever instinct, walked to the bus stop with an arm around Mathilde and she responded warmly. In that image I saw Pierre in a more empathic light and was quite delighted.

On arrival at the club, we went first to the boat, both of them were well pleased with Mathilde's new home.

Mathilde's flight was at half past six so we would catch the bus back to the airport at around five. We took a relaxed light lunch in the club and spoke French the whole time. Mathilde had insisted that we speak English with her and had done so for her entire holiday. Now Pierre jokingly reprimanded her for speaking French with an English accent!

Dad and Pierre loved the club, and Charlie and I were greatly relieved. I had wondered if we had oversold the idea but needn't have worried; this was a great place to base a boat, with good sailing and interesting destinations. This latter point had been hovering at the edges of my mind. Whilst we had loved all the beautiful anchorages, and of course the evolution of our love affair with Mathilde, I wondered if one could become blasé in the absence of any higher purpose. The old English adage, 'too much of a good thing is bad for you', came to mind.

Mathilde dressed in the same skinny jeans and top that she had arrived in and said a tearful farewell to Dad and Pierre.

"*A bientôt,*" said Pierre.

"Come visit soon!" said Dad. "We'll miss you!"

***

We sat in the little cafe overlooking the runway; Mathilde was desolate.

"There's so much I want to say," she said through her tears. "I just…"

"Stop!" said Charlie. "I know we all feel the same. There are no words for this." Charlie was sitting next to Mathilde and embraced her. Charlie was weeping too, and I had trouble holding it together.

The flight was called, and Charlie hugged her all the way to the gate. I gave Mathilde her carry-on bag and hugged her to me.

"We will not miss any opportunity for us to be together, my love!" And we kissed. It was the first time I'd called her 'my love' and I really meant it. Charlie joined our hug.

"And that goes for me too, I love you! Now go, before I lose it completely!" Both of them smiled through their tears and then kissed. Mathilde turned to the gate and didn't look back.

We stayed at the airport until we saw Mathilde's plane take off. Now we both had tears in our eyes and hugged each other, swaying slightly, as ever.

***

On the bus back to Mahon we did our best to regain some humour for the evening meal with Pau and Sophie and comforted ourselves with speculation on when we would meet up again with Mathilde.

The 'boys' were all freshly showered and enjoying a beer when we returned. Charlie and I had just enough time for our own showers when Pau arrived a little early and joined us for a beer.

"My wife is so looking forward to meeting you Arthur, you must be careful—I think she might want to adopt you!"

***

The evening began with Dad and Pierre being introduced to the usual suspects and Charlie being hijacked by Jordi and Guillem for a kick-about in the garden. They'd rigged an impromptu goal and Charlie was teaching them the best penalty strategies, even though she'd never been called upon to take one herself!

Sophie was her normal effusive self and gave Dad a special welcome.

Dad produced a gift wrapped present for Sophie which I had no knowledge of. Sophie burst out laughing when she saw the contents and gave Dad one of her all-enveloping hugs as she thanked him. It was one of his Cooper-Hamilton retractors which he had engraved, 'For Sophie', on the widest part of the surgical stainless steel construction!

"That's just a small token for all the help you all have given our two families and especially the invitation to join your club and acquire Jaime's old mooring. This really does seem to be the perfect 'base camp' for us. Now we just need to bring Pierre back up to speed after his heart 'wobble', thanks again!"

"No thanks needed Arthur," said Sophie. "We are delighted with your lovely family and look forward to meeting your wife and baby, Pierre!"

Pau had filled our glasses and we drank to friendship.

As the tapas started to arrive, Pau called in the 'footballers' to wash their hands and join the party.

Charlie was somewhat cheered by the two boys and gave me a knowing smile which, in turn, lifted my mood and we enjoyed the happy evening, even though Mathilde was foremost in our hearts. Charlie took a call from Mathilde a little later in the evening and went outside to talk with her. She was in her Aunt Anne's car on the way home after her aunt had picked her up at the airport, and sent her love to us all with yet more thanks for her holiday.

The wind was forecast to gain strength tomorrow so Sophie invited Dad to visit her hospital so she could 'show him off', she joked. We would certainly not be going sailing.

***

As we sat in the cockpit for tea before going to bed, we could feel the wind increasing and hear some halyards slapping on masts—fortunately not too close to us!

"Good decision to come back early from Ibiza," said Pierre.

"Yeah, we had over twenty knots for the latter part and it has been increasing ever since," said Charlie.

"Let's call your mum and Flo, it's an hour earlier at home, we should check in!" said Dad, and made the call, Flo answered,

"*Bonsoir Chérie!*" said Pierre.

"*Bonsoir tout le monde!*" replied Flo, and they carried on in English, Pierre giving a very upbeat report of the boat, our evening with Sophie and family, and how they were looking forward to meeting her and Élodie. We all had our turn, Charlie and I mainly talked about Mathilde and how sad she was about the end of her holiday and Dad about his new admirer, Sophie, and the hospital visit tomorrow.

"You just watch it with that Sophie, Arthur Cooper!" said Mum. "I have my spies there! And Charlie and Nat, you must tell Mathilde she can come anytime to our place, any time at all—she's my mate too remember!"

***

The wind was gusting over thirty knots across our moorings in the morning, after a minor lessening overnight. Pierre and I added some extra lines to be on the safe side and went over to Pau's boat to check his as well. We needn't have worried, Pedro was checking every boat.

With Dad at the hospital with Sophie, Charlie and I had Pierre to ourselves, and it was nice to get his take on recent events in the family. Our new pool had become his health spa and a physiotherapist from the hospital at Windsor had advised on his exercises in the water.

He and Flo were over the moon with parenthood; his only worry being his health and the possibility of not being around long enough to be a significant part of baby Élodie's life.

Pierre admitted that their current living arrangement with Mum and Dad was working so well both he and Flo, especially Flo, weren't looking forward to returning to their own place!

Flo too was working hard to get her body back to pre-maternity shape with aqua-gym in the pool and floor exercises.

Pierre said that Dad had been fantastic in helping his rehabilitation, but he had been advised, in no uncertain terms, to avoid stress at all costs. His heart was damaged and his arteries in general were not in the best shape.

"Now, after all that dreary stuff, show me what we can do in this hallowed birthplace of mayonnaise!"

***

Dad arrived with Sophie at lunchtime while we were studying the pilot that she and Pau had marked-up for us.

"One thing's for sure," said Sophie. "Your cruising area today, and tomorrow at least, is limited to the club bar!"

Pau had been doing some housework on their boat and joined us for a fish soup lunch in the club house.

After Sophie left us to go back to work, Pau took Dad and Pierre down to the office for introductions and mooring handover paperwork.

Pau came back for coffee with us and 'consulted' on our BBQ and gas bottle installation. He told me where I could buy a gaff hook, a rod holder that would clamp on the aft pulpit, and that Sophie would 'contribute' a spray bottle of clinical alcohol.

Charlie stayed at the club to do the laundry from Mathilde's visit and Pau gave us three boys a lift to the fishing gear shop and then left us to our own devices.

***

Mahon is a small town of maybe thirty thousand. The view down the harbour from the narrow streets of the old town is stunning and the low-rise pastel-coloured buildings reminiscent of the Provençal coast of southern France. To the west, you can see the San Antonio estate, where Admiral Lord Nelson lived during his tenure here.

We had a beer on a cafe terrace overlooking the water, a yacht marina to our right and the naval base to the left. The strong wind was bringing up a good chop on the water even in this most sheltered of harbours.

251

"I like this place a lot," said Pierre. "And the club is the best of all possible worlds yacht-wise. We've really fallen on our feet, and it's you, Charlie and your Mum we have to thank—well done the lot of you!"

"What shall we do for dinner, any ideas?" Dad said.

"We haven't got much on board," I said. "But the club does a great gourmet cheeseburger!"

"Sounds good to me," said Pierre, and we caught the bus back to the club!

***

Charlie had been a little gem while we'd been away. There was a neat stack of washing on the saloon table, ready to put away, and a tempting array of olives, serrano and anchovies for our apéro ready to take up to the cockpit. The only problem was that Mathilde now had a permanent list to port, due solely to the wind, which was now steady at forty knots—a full gale: far too strong to sit in the cockpit.

Charlie cleared the washing away and set the table with the nibbles and glasses, then pulled a bottle of Barbadillo from the fridge. I watched the others, wondering if anybody else was feeling as nauseous as me with the motion of the boat and was saved by Charlie.

"I'm feeling a bit sick with this motion," she said. "How about we save the wine and go to the bar now?"

The water was quite a sight; spray flying off the wavelets within the moorings and the open water beyond an impenetrable wall of foam cutting visibility to just a few metres; even the pontoon we were walking on was in motion; the sound of halyards slapping masts now a cacophony!

The stability and quiet of the clubhouse were most welcome.

***

The gale took a further three days to blow itself out and the sea to calm down, that left just ten days holiday for Dad and Pierre out of their fourteen.

We spent a lot of time in the club house while the gale was at its strongest and used the time to plan our itinerary and diet to cater for Pierre's health requirements. The cheeseburger in the club was an exception and the last red meat that Dad allowed for the duration!

Charlie and I took the opportunity to improve our fitness as well, and ran every day, either along the inlet or up through the old town. We'd wear our small backpacks and pick up minor shopping items for Pierre's magic concoctions in our small galley. There was a great wet-fish market in town, near the fishing harbour, where Pierre would shop every two or three days.

Dad and I took the opportunity to install our BBQ and rod holder ready for our first sail into open water and stowed Sophie's alcohol spray next to the gas bottle.

***

On the fifth day of Dad and Pierre's holiday we ventured north up the east coast. Like Mathilde, Pierre was a keen sailor, and we took a north easterly course after clearing the mouth of the inlet into open water. The sea still had some chop left over from the gale and the wind now a steady northerly at twelve knots. We stayed on a close reach for three hours with the wind just forward of our port beam and a broadly grinning Pierre at the helm most of the time, and then tacked, the wind now on our starboard beam, in the direction of the northeast coast of Menorca.

We had a waypoint at Cala Presili, where we'd been before with Mathilde, and headed for that. The bay offered perfect protection from anything with a northerly component, being under the lee of Cabo Favaritz.

We anchored well outside the swimming area, which was marked by a line of red buoys, and quickly had the bimini up and cold beers on the cockpit table. Pierre was over the moon and unable to wipe the silly grin from his face!

"Boy! I so enjoyed that!" he said. "This is all so much more than Souffle, I had the feeling we could just sail all the way round the world in this boat!"

Dad was allowing Pierre one beer at lunchtime and a glass of wine with dinner; Pierre was a good patient, knowing full well that his rehabilitation depended on the discipline that Dad was imposing.

Pierre took a nap after lunch and then we all swam to the beach for a walk south along the bay to the next beach, Playa De Capifort. Pierre walked slowly at a measured pace, and we rested for a while before returning to Cala Presili where we rested again before swimming back to the boat.

Dad explained, over afternoon tea, that, when at anchor, Pierre would have a session of aqua-gym after breakfast close to shore with the water at about chest level, and that Charlie and I were welcome to join in. The swim ashore twice a day were part of the regime as was the afternoon walk.

After dinner on our first evening at Cala Presili, Charlie treated us to a showing of the thumb drive that Ralph had made of Charlie's fashion shoot. Had Charlie and I seen the drive beforehand we might have deleted a couple of the lingerie shots!

"Oh wow, Charlie," said Pierre. "Some of these could be in Playboy!"

Dad was equally impressed. "You look absolutely gorgeous Charlie, your mum will love these, but where do you think all this is leading?"

"I'm not sure," said Charlie. "At first it seemed just a lark, but after this shoot there seems to be some potential for me to do some serious part-time fashion modelling. I don't intend to actively pursue it as a career, but it might be a fun thing to do on the side. Ralph and Lucy think that my smile is somehow marketable!"

"That's no surprise to me," said Pierre. "I've always thought your smile was something special, and now I'm not the only one!"

We stayed in Cala Presili for three days and Charlie and I did the morning aqua-gym with Dad and Pierre every day. He was a surprisingly good instructor, led the exercises in a very professional manner, and both of us, as well as Pierre, got something out of it.

We made love one afternoon, instead of doing the walk, in the belief that the exercise value was about the same!

We were shy of making love at night, but on our second night in Cala Presili we couldn't help ourselves. We stifled our cries as best we could but that only triggered fits of laughter that were much louder!

Over breakfast the next day Pierre asked if we would share the joke and all four of us cracked-up!

***

On the evening before we left Cala Presili, we called home to check in. Mum had an idea that Dad could stay with us when Pierre flew home and that she could fly out to join us after a couple of days. Dad said he and Pierre would discuss it but saw nothing wrong. It would be nice for Flo, Pierre and Élodie to have some time together before returning to their own place.

After the call, Dad and Pierre had their chat and neither came up with any reason why Pierre should not fly home alone; he was going from strength to strength and Dad was monitoring his blood pressure daily. His only luggage was a carry-on 'wheelie-bin'; he was good to go!

Dad called home straight away to say that he and Pierre were happy with the plan and looked forward to Mum joining us.

After aqua-gym the next morning we weighed anchor and headed south. This was the eighth day of Pierre's holiday—just six to go!

***

The wind was directly behind us and we sailed wing-and-wing, the mainsail out as far as it could go on one side and the full headsail on the other. It was the slowest point of sailing, and I deployed my fishing line to see if I could catch our supper!

As we rounded up into the Mahon inlet the wind was still with us, and we sailed close-hauled all the way up to the club. Outside the moorings we started the engine, rolled up the sails and I reeled in my fishing line—the fish clearly not hungry at this time of day! Pierre had the helm all the way up to the club and brought us into our slot very slowly and with great accuracy, a first for him.

***

Over a late salad lunch in the cockpit, we planned the remaining days before Pierre's departure. Our obvious choice was to confine ourselves to the water between Menorca and Mallorca. The only shoreside attraction of any great note was the Caves of Drach at Puerto Cristo on the east coast of Mallorca, which afforded the opportunity for a good long sail in each direction. He'd also like to see Cala Coves, which we'd all raved about.

I checked the weather; the northerly wind was forecast to remain unchanged for several days. Dad phoned the marina at Puerto Cristo and was lucky to book a slot for two nights starting tomorrow, this being the busiest season. So our plan was set; one day-sail across to Puerto Cristo, visit the caves the next day and sail back to Calas Coves the next and stay there until the day before Pierre's flight. This ticked all our boxes; Pierre got the maximum sailing time in, which we would all enjoy, and a nice relaxing wind-down in Cala Coves, which would be new for both Dad and Pierre.

Dad went online to defer his flight home to a date yet to be determined and then called home.

Mum answered and was happy to be planning her trip to us in a few days' time. The most exciting news was that Harry had fallen into the pool and proved to be an excellent swimmer!

Pierre spoke to Flo with good news of his progress and how he looked forward to when Flo and Élodie could come out and enjoy the boat with him.

Pierre made up a shopping list for the coming days and Charlie and I took the bus into town for the supermarket. We took the opportunity to call Mathilde, without Dad or Pierre realising that our relationship was somewhat deeper than they knew.

Charlie and I had talked about this and whether we should tell Mum and Dad how things were between the three of us. We had decided not to tell them as this was still very early days, maybe in a few months, and probably to Mum first as she had first-hand experience of something very similar.

It was lovely to hear Mathilde; she said she missed us but was still on a high from the wonders of her holiday with us. We talked about when we could next be together and thought she could come back to the boat after Mum and Dad went home, or when we were all back home. We had no fixed dates to plan around except that it would be as soon as possible. Like us, she had no fixed commitments before the start of the new academic year—we were free agents!

***

When we got back from shopping, Dad told us he'd invited his new 'girlfriend' and her husband to join us for a paella dinner in the club the night before Pierre flew home.

There was not much to plan for our sail across to Puerto Cristo; the distance was just under sixty miles, the direction south-of-west. With the wind in the north, we could expect a nice reach all the way with the wind a little aft of our starboard beam; we would take ten hours maximum and planned to leave at six in the morning to ensure a timely arrival.

***

Charlie and I set our alarm for five-thirty to make breakfast but were woken by the smell of fresh coffee at five o'clock instead, Pierre had beaten us to it and was making scrambled eggs with smoked salmon. It was a touch chilly in the cockpit so we ate in the saloon.

While Dad did the washing up Charlie and I topped up the water tanks and started the engine. Charlie put a note in the log to discharge our holding tank sometime around midday and we all put on light sweaters for the first hour or so until the sun was up.

We left at ten-to-six and motored with full navigation lights down the inlet. As we headed for the southern tip of Menorca, we were treated to a glorious sunrise directly astern and unrolled our mainsail ready for when we came out from under the lee of the island and into open water.

Conditions at sea were exactly as forecast and we set a course for our waypoint near the harbour entrance at Puerto Cristo.

This was perfect sailing; engine, navigation lights and sweaters all off; sails trimmed and autopilot on! Pierre was grinning like an idiot and Charlie took a number of candid shots with her phone.

After four hours Charlie emptied our holding tank and I noticed my fishing rod bending a little. When I reeled in the line I saw that I had caught a small tuna, less than two kilos, but I was very proud of my first catch! Pierre beheaded and gutted the fish in a bucket and washed it in sea water; dinner solved!

***

When we arrived in Puerto Cristo the marina was full and our berth not available for another hour; the Capitainerie told us to moor at the fuel dock, so we topped up on diesel while we waited. We were in fact over an hour early on our estimated time of arrival having made a very quick crossing at an average speed of seven knots.

After we were settled into our slot Pierre went to his cabin for a siesta. He had been on deck all the way across, and the mixture of sun and excitement had taken its toll. Dad said he would insist that Pierre rested more on our way back.

Our neighbour was another French yacht, out of Nice, and I chatted to the owner as I prepared our BBQ for the tuna. When he saw what I was doing he politely told me that BBQs were generally not permitted in marinas, and when I thought about it, I realised it should have been obvious because of the fire risk and cooking smell.

Charlie and I went for a run but it was too hot to go far. Pierre was still asleep, and Dad was reading in the cockpit under the welcome shade of the bimini when we collected our towels for a shower.

Pierre slept for a solid three hours and was still groggy when he surfaced from the heat of his cabin. Dad gave him a large glass of chilled water from the fridge and his midday medication which we had forgotten while we were at sea.

When Dad and Pierre came back from their shower Pierre was back to his usual self and I told him of the BBQ problem.

"I should have seen that one coming," he said. "It makes sense; I'll fillet the tuna and freeze what I can."

"Leave a fillet for me please," I asked. "And I'll make sashimi for apéro."

The sun was heading down over the town and a welcome onshore breeze brought additional relief from the heat of the day as I popped the cork on a bottle of Barbadillo. I put the sashimi on the table with the soy/wasabi sauce and we tucked in.

Pierre suggested we either eat in the town or have a simple salad with some chicken drumsticks he'd made in the oven yesterday. Charlie said she was quite hungry so why not save the chicken for our lunch at sea on the way back and eat ashore this evening; so that's what we did!

***

Charlie and I decided not to visit the caves with Pierre and Dad the next morning. We'd had a lovely cuddly night and hopped straight back to bed as soon as they left for the caves after breakfast!

We carried on from where we had left off earlier and soon triggered our mutual arousal. We made gentle love and tears rolled down Charlie's lovely cheeks to her smiling mouth and our love enveloped us. I gently caressed her swaying breasts and felt the nipples stiffen against my palms. I felt myself beginning to rise to the occasion again, and so did Charlie. Her smile turned to a grin as she started to move on me… gently… as I grew again inside her.

"Oh Nat… I'm coming very soon… Ahhh… can't stop it…"

I was in ecstasy just watching Charlie's face in her moments and my own release almost took me by surprise.

Charlie lay down on me, and one by one, put her legs between mine without me slipping out. She kissed my nose and said she loved me, and we relaxed, still united.

Charlie showered in her bikini on the swimming platform, and I followed. We sat on our towels and held hands across the cockpit table and just loved each other.

***

Charlie made some open sandwiches for lunch and I topped-up our fresh water tanks from the dock hose while we waited for the boys to return.

Pierre was visibly tired when they got back, and Charlie brought up our lunchtime beers and open sandwiches before Pierre could nod off under the bimini.

After lunch, Pierre laid a sheet on the saloon settee for his siesta and was snoring happily as soon as his head touched the pillow. The large deck hatch in the saloon had a wind scoop which caught what little breeze there was to make it habitable below.

The three of us stayed in the cockpit finishing our beers and the half bottle that Pierre had left.

Charlie and Dad lay on the long cockpit seats and I on the seat by the companionway hatch. Charlie was gently purring and Dad on one elbow reading his Kindle when I dozed off.

I awoke with the sun on my face just after four o'clock, alone in the cockpit. I looked down the companionway to see Pierre still sleeping nicely. There was a note on the cockpit table, under an empty beer bottle, that I hadn't noticed. It was from Charlie to say that she and Dad were off for a walk round the marina and to keep an eye on Pierre.

Pierre joined me soon after I'd peeped below.

"Boy! I needed that." he said. "I'm beginning to understand my limitations now. I'll take it a bit easier tomorrow on the sail back. How about a glass of water?"

Pierre brought up a cold bottle from the fridge and two glasses. We finished the bottle just as Dad and Charlie returned.

"How're you doing, Pierre?" Dad asked.

"Good thanks, Arthur, but I was just telling Nat that I'm beginning to realise my limitations now!"

"Your endurance will improve over time, Pierre, but we must keep up the physio. This heat is also a factor, I think we're all feeling it. The Spanish have the right idea with their siesta!"

"What about our dinner tonight, Chef?" said Charlie.

"Well, BBQed tuna will have to wait till tomorrow in Calas Coves; so, the chef's suggestion is fish a la plancha… ashore!"

***

We had checked out after dinner and made a fairly early start the next morning for our return to Menorca. We already had a waypoint at Cala Coves and took our course after exiting the pretty S-shaped inlet of Puerto Cristo. The wind remained as predicted, from the north, and forward of our beam as we headed northeast; a comfortable and fast close-reach point of sailing.

We ate Pierre's drumsticks with tomato salad at midday and Dad sent Pierre down for siesta shortly thereafter.

Dad called Pierre on deck as we arrived at Calas Coves to admire the beauty of the cala as we entered. There were several yachts anchored with lines ashore and we dropped our anchor to seaward of them all. Charlie swam to shore with our stern line and I erected our bimini. Pierre was most impressed.

"Wow! You saved the best till last—this is just perfect!"

***

We all enjoyed our stay in Calas Coves but for Pierre it was quite special. Dad kept up his physiotherapy regime and we were asked by two Spanish couples if they could join us in Dad's aqua-gym sessions, which of course he agreed to.

On the second day Charlie and I tried to make love in the water while I hung on the anchor chain, but we found that Charlie's natural lubricant washed away too easily. I solved the problem by getting the tube of Vaseline from the first aid box and a whole new world opened up for us!

***

Pierre used our new BBQ for both our dinners using different marinades for the tuna, all very delicious, but in all honesty, Pau and Sophie's was the simplest and best of all!

We weighed anchor after an early lunch on the third day of our idyllic stay in Calas Coves. The north wind was still with us but down to eight knots. We might have motored if Pierre hadn't insisted on sailing, and we broad reached gently down the coast until we lost it on our turn for the run up to the Mahon inlet. The short distance from Calas Coves to the club took over four hours and we eventually tied up at six o'clock. Our dinner in the club with Sophie and Pau was booked for eight-thirty with drinks beforehand on-board Mathilde at eight.

After showers we rang home and swapped all our news. Pierre and Flo chatted in French for a change, each looking forward to their reunion tomorrow. Dad and us two were equally looking forward to Mum joining us in four days' time.

***

Pierre and Charlie prepared some finger food for our predinner drinks with Sophie and Pau while Dad and I discussed some options for when Mum arrived. Dad was good for ten days after Mum joined us, and Charlie and I until the new academic year started in the first week of October, in about six weeks' time.

Charlie and I had mulled over the idea of Mathilde joining us after Dad went home. Of course, we had a similar problem as before, how could we conduct the intimate aspects of our relationship with Mathilde with other family members on board? If it was just Mum with us, we thought she would be the most sympathetic. The problem would not arise at home, as all we had to do was tell the family that Mathilde was 'in the loop', regarding Charlie and me, and we could all stay together in our 'wing'. We'd give it more thought when it was just Mum and us on board.

***

Sophie was once again a vision of voluptuousness in a cloudlike sun dress of printed cotton; her magnificent cleavage easily capable of acting as a bike rack! Dad was first in the pecking order for Sophie's embrace, followed by Pierre, me and Charlie.

Pierre popped the cork on our last bottle of Mumm champagne and the evening was off to a great start!

Our mixed seafood and chicken paella was as stunning as ever and Pierre had Sophie act as translator when Sophie called the cook to our table to describe his recipe. Pierre actually made notes on a napkin, and the cook glowed with pride when Sophie explained Pierre's position in the profession.

The evening was a great way to end Pierre's holiday. Over coffee in the cockpit after dinner, Pierre was quite misty in his thanks to Dad and us two for making it possible. He was sorry it was over but equally looking forward to seeing Flo and Élodie tomorrow. Pierre's British Airways flight was at eleven in the morning, and we had declined a lift to the airport from Pau as we usually liked to stay at the airport until the flight had taken off, just in case there was a delay or cancellation.

***

Charlie and I made a light breakfast of toast, marmalade and coffee; we had all overindulged with the paella last night!

Pierre had showered before breakfast and had only a carry-on bag which was already packed and in the cockpit. We needed to be at the airport by ten o'clock and took a leisurely walk to the bus stop at half-past nine.

BA had a fast check-in counter for business passengers and Pierre was processed in no time. We took Pierre along to the coffee shop overlooking the runway and chatted mainly about family stuff.

"I think I'll have to drag Flo back to our place, she's very attached to the pool and Paris has been a great help with Élodie," said Pierre. "Not to mention all your help with my rehab, Arthur!"

"You can treat the pool as a common facility, Pierre, it's there for all of us."

The flight was called at twenty to ten and we said our goodbyes with hugs all round at the departure gate. Charlie had her phone ready as a smiling Pierre turned to give us a final wave before entering the departure lounge.

We went back to watch Pierre's plane take off. I pictured Pierre's welcome at Heathrow and smiled for his reunion with Flo and baby. Back on board, we talked about Mum's arrival in four days' time. She would have an open return ticket, but Dad needed to be back ten days after that. We were all smiles as we looked forward to Mum's arrival and tossed around some ideas for an itinerary.

"I know what Mum would say if we asked her," said Charlie. "Something about getting her bum brown on a nice sandy beach!"

It was just after twelve and we went up to the clubhouse for a draught San Miguel before a snack lunch.

***

Dad's phone rang at twenty past two, it was Mum.

"Hello love, has our boy arrived OK?" Dad listened for a moment, and we could hear the panic in Mum's voice.

"Yes, of course, we watched him pass into the departure lounge and the plane took off on time." We could hear Mum explaining that she and

Flo were waiting in the arrivals area and all the passengers had come through except Pierre.

"Maybe he's come in for some special attention in customs," said Dad, looking very worried.

"Hang on a minute, Arthur, there's someone from BA who wants a word with us… I'll call you back…" And the line went dead.

"I don't like this one bit," said Dad. "He's either been arrested for something or been taken sick, and I fear the latter!"

Fifteen minutes later Mum called back.

"Pierre's dead, Arthur! He passed…" Mum broke down and another voice came on the line.

"Hello, my name is Christine from British Airways, may I ask who I'm speaking to?" Tears were streaming down Dad's face.

"Eh… yes, I'm Arthur Cooper, Pierre's brother-in-law…"

"Hello Mr Cooper, I'm most terribly sorry to bear such sad news, but your brother-in-law passed away on our flight from Mahon this morning. Our staff are taking care of your family and the formalities at this moment, can I help you in any way?" Dad took a deep breath and tried to collect himself.

"Yes… eh… when is your next flight from Mahon please?"

"There's one this evening at seven-thirty-five, how many tickets?"

"Three, and I already have an open business return."

"Names please?"

"Myself, Arthur Cooper, and my two children, Charlise and Nathan, both adults."

Christine was clearly sitting at a computer terminal.

"OK, just bear with me a moment… OK, good, you and your children are booked on that flight, please go to the business check-in an hour before take-off where your children's tickets will be waiting for you and present your return ticket."

"Thanks very much for your help, Christine, we'll be there."

"One last thing, Mr Cooper, your wife and her sister want to go home to Maidenhead, and I've arranged for a car to take them. There's a BA counsellor with them and she will stay with them until you return, and indeed, for as long as you think she can be useful. Is all that OK with you and is there anyone I can call to be with them as well?"

Dad looked at us and we both shook our heads after a moment's thought.

"Yes, they should go home and thanks for arranging everything… there's no one else to call, but thanks for the consideration."

"OK, I let you get on with your preparations Mr Cooper, and once again, my condolences for your loss."

We three sat in stunned silence, tears on all our cheeks; Charlie and I moved to sit next to Dad and we held a long embrace until Dad spoke.

"What a terrible thing, he looked so good when he left us…"

"What do you think happened, Dad?" I said as my composure started to return.

"My guess would be a stroke, a big one! His arteries were in poor shape, and this was always a possibility I'm afraid. It could have been days or decades in coming, and Pierre knew that he told me he just wanted to live until he died!"

"And that's exactly what he did, isn't it?" said Charlie.

CHAPTER FORTY

TWO MONTHS LATER

These last two months since Pierre's death were a kind of limbo for all of us. We were all in agreement that Flo and baby Élodie should stay for as long as they liked; indeed, we'd always loved Flo as the closest possible family member and had all 'adopted' baby Élodie; it was only natural that we should all live together.

Flo's sadness at Pierre's loss was without dimension and I could not imagine how she might have come through it without Mum's total empathy; it was as if they had merged and I recalled Mum's attempted explanation of their identical twin relationship last Christmas.

***

Frank Stokes had been amazing; in his fatherly way he loved Flo and had made all the funeral arrangements and legal necessities so that Flo didn't have to think about them.

Pierre had, of course, left everything to Flo, and Frank had arranged for the French version of his will to be registered with the Notaire Public in Biarritz. The change of title of the flat from Pierre to Flo involved a substantial inheritance tax which Dad paid without mentioning to Flo; it could be sorted later, or indeed, not at all.

Dad had written a sincere and heartfelt letter to British Airways to thank them for their superb and sympathetic handling of the whole tragedy, with special thanks to Christine, and Pamela, the councillor who had stayed with Mum and Flo until we returned.

Mum and Charlie had collected Flo's clothes to bring home and packed all Pierre's clothes into two cardboard packing cases which were left in the hall at their place.

***

Charlie and I returned home for the third weekend of the Michaelmas term as usual and were pleased that Frank was there to have dinner with us. After the meal, Charlie and I strolled down to the river to enjoy the fresh night air and Frank joined us shortly afterwards.

"How are you two doing in your flats?" he asked, and we told him how much we were enjoying our new independence.

"I'm glad to have this opportunity to talk to you away from the family," said Frank. "I have a confidential matter I need to discuss with you; by confidential I mean just that, please do not share this with the rest of the family; after our discussion you will understand. It would be best if we could meet in my office—perhaps on a Sunday on your way back to uni would be best as you can have all week to digest my information."

Charlie and I looked at each other in bewilderment.

"Can't you tell us now Frank?" I asked. "You've got us worried!"

"It would be better to have some time to ponder the information between yourselves—but you need not be unduly worried."

"I want to know sooner rather than later," said Charlie. "How about this Sunday, we normally leave around seven after an early dinner?"

"Sunday it is then, I'll be in the office from seven-thirty."

***

Fortunately, we were quite busy on Saturday. Our flats were very minimalistic and we only added stuff as need arose. We went shopping with Mum in the morning to buy microwave ovens and I wanted a pair of side tables for the sofa bed in my living area. We left our packages in the van and swam several lengths of the pool before lunch. Flo was sitting on the steps at the shallow end with Élodie playing a splashing game. Charlie took the baby so that Flo could swim lengths with me. Flo was trying hard now to regain her figure and we all saw that as a good sign.

Charlie and I did a long run together in the afternoon and just filled the time as best we could; what we really wanted was for it to be half-past-seven tomorrow evening!

Charlie and I spoke long into the night, as we had last night, but there was nothing we could think of except perhaps something to do with our own personal relationship—but what could that be?

***

Charlie came to my bed early Sunday morning and snuggled in as close as possible.

"We haven't made love all weekend Nat. We mustn't let Frank's mystery spoil things!"

Charlie lay in my arms in her favourite position with one leg over my thigh. After a while I felt her increase the pressure on my leg and I moved my hand from her shoulder to her lower back and she closed her hand around the base of my penis. Charlie did not move against me nor stroke my penis, but very gently squeezed my leg and penis in unison. I could actually feel her heat on my thigh and felt an overwhelming desire to be inside her. Charlie and I knew each other's feelings so well that we moved as if by telepathy; she slid over and took the length of me in a single silken movement until I felt the limit of her; my heart swelled with love.

We stayed like that, unmoving, just looking into each other's eyes. Charlie had tears on her cheeks and my sight misted over also. The beginnings of a grin came to the corners of her lovely mouth as she shifted down slightly to increase the pressure of my penis on her clitoris, and only then started to move on me. Each early stroke returned me to the limit and Charlie pressed her clitoris harder against me. I already had a gentle hold of her breasts and now flicked her nipples as she rose toward her climax. Her hand flew to her mouth and her head arched back as she screamed in ecstasy. I came massively as Charlie pressed down and the spasms of her vaginal muscles gripped and released me repeatedly.

Charlie lay down on me and I held her in firm embrace as she continued to spasm with slowly diminishing echoes of her orgasm.

I turned her onto her back and slid down. Charlie was very wet as I pressed my face against her. She raised her knees and rotated her hips as my lips found her still swollen clitoris. Charlie moaned and rocked a little from side to side, my tongue following her every movement.

Charlie suddenly went rigid as she climaxed again, without any warning, and cried out with a massive sob. I moved up quickly to re-enter her and she kept on coming as I lost control and came again.

We looked at each other lovingly and suddenly Charlie laughed.

"What's so funny?" I asked.

"Your face looks like a glazed ham!" she replied, and now we both laughed.

***

The day yawned ahead of us, but we managed to fill it with baby games in the pool with Flo and Élodie and a lengthy run before lunch. I didn't like the idea of secrets from Mum and Dad regarding our planned meeting with Frank, and again worried about what it could reveal.

Against all odds the time did pass, and Charlie and I packed our bags before an early dinner.

***

Being a Sunday, it was very easy to park the van close to Frank's office in Eton. We were ten minutes early and waited in the van; we had a view of the entrance to Frank's office and waited till seven-thirty before ringing his bell. Frank buzzed us in, he must have arrived early, and we climbed the stairs to his first-floor office. Frank was dressed in his version of casual attire—corduroy trousers, suede loafers and button-up cardigan.

"I fully understand that you must be a little worried about our clandestine meeting and I will therefore get to the point without further ado."

At that point, Frank opened his desk drawer and took out two envelopes. The first was addressed to Charlie and I and the second to Frank.

"These letters are from your late uncle Pierre," said Frank. "He gave them to me soon after being discharged from hospital following his heart attack, with instructions for me to give you that envelope two months after his death. I believe that my letter is just a copy of yours. I should add that I am aware of the subject matter, but not in any great detail." Frank placed a letter opener on our envelope and got up from his chair.

"I'll leave you now to open your letter and I'll open mine in the outer office. Take whatever time you need to digest the contents and call me when you're ready."

"You open it Nat!" said Charlie, as if something horrible might jump out.

I slit the envelope open; inside was another smaller envelope and a letter. I set the envelope aside and unfolded the letter in front of us.

Chers Charlie et Nathan,

This is such a strange letter to write, it is indeed a letter from the grave, as I have asked Frank to give it to you two months after my death. Of course, I have no idea when that might be, I hope it will be a very long time so that I can see baby Élodie grow up, but I was advised by my doctors, after my heart attack in June, that my heart was quite weak and that another, likely more serious, event could happen without warning.

I must start right at the beginning, otherwise my information will not be in the context needed to fully understand what I will tell you.

We can start with the Christmas holiday of your fresher year at university. Flo and your mother have never had any secrets from each other, and Flo knew everything that occurred between your mother and yourselves regarding your relationship—not that that was news to Flo and me. We also knew how Paris explained her history with Flo as a way to mitigate things. Equally, Flo and I have no secrets from each other, so I knew everything as well. We also know that your mother did not quite tell you the complete story of her and Flo, so I must bring that into play, as it were!

We must now go back even further, to the time before Flo and I met.

Flo would often accompany your parents on their summer holidays, and it was in those days that your mother and Flo played the biggest practical joke of all the tricks they played as identical twins. I wouldn't say they took it in turns to sleep with your father, but something approaching that! At that time your mother was not taking the pill but Flo was, so no problem there! I have no reason to think that your father knew anything of this!

I hope that you will not feel at all judgemental over this revelation, I certainly do not, but you need to know this, as you will see.

We must now fast forward to when you were about ten years old Charlie. It was not long after you had moved into the big house. It was a Monday, my usual day off from Le Coq, and your father and I were doing a BBQ lunch for your Granddad's birthday. I remember how much he enjoyed it. Your Mum and Flo dressed identically, and we played a game where we asked your mother or Flo different questions to try to find out who was who.

You were growing up fast Charlie, and had lost your childhood chubbiness so that the beginnings of your future adult features were starting to appear; you were clearly going to be a beauty, just like your mother, and of course Flo. I was quite fascinated watching as you played happily. At one point I saw you grinning at something and suddenly I realised what it was that had caught my attention; your grin reminded me of my late brother Damien. You may recall that Damien was a soldier in the French army and was killed by a booby-trap bomb while on an anti-terrorist operation in the Sahel. He was my hero and I have never for a moment forgotten him. I was very happy to be reminded of him in this way and watched you often to see if it would appear again, and on several occasions it did.

Time went by and you two grew up into fine young adults and started your university courses.

One day, Charlie, you come home after your football match with some amazing photos that a friend of yours had taken of you at a dinner party, and Flo borrowed them to show me. We sat with a drink at our coffee table as I went through them. Suddenly it seemed that I had been struck by lightning, Flo thought I was having a heart attack; I was rigid, with tears flooding down my face and unable to speak. Flo put her arms round me and asked what had happened. I pointed at the photo in front of me, "It's Damien!" Flo didn't understand so I fetched a photo of my brother and placed it next to yours and then she understood; you were absolutely the very image of each other and I could not contain my emotion.

After that experience, I became used to seeing my brother in you and it made me very happy.

However, after a while, a seed of doubt started to grow in my mind which would explain this apparent family resemblance; had the girls been up to their 'old tricks' all those years ago? Was it possible that I was your father, Charlie?

I thought about this and little else for many days. I would be overjoyed to have such a daughter as you, Charlie; but if it were true, the ramifications for our families might be upsetting, especially for your dear father, Charlie, my closest friend and the man you have always considered to be your father.

I thought to confront Flo but decided it was not a good idea as she had given birth so recently.

I seemed to have two options: I could confront your mother instead of Flo or do nothing!

I chose to do nothing!

Well, not quite nothing. I decided I wanted to discuss my dilemma with a trusted friend, and I chose Frank Stokes. Not only is he obliged by law to maintain client confidentiality, but he is a trusted friend and always a wise counsel.

Frank listened patiently to my story and pondered the options. Frank logically explained that the options were not so much mine, Charlie, as yours. Under UK law, everybody has the right to know who their birth parents are, even adopted children who may not have even known that they were adopted. As it was only a possibility that I was your father, Frank proposed the following.

That I should have my genome sequenced and that he, Frank, should hold the relevant documentation.

That after you have read this letter, he, or a subsequent holder of his position, would offer to arrange for you to have your genome similarly sequenced, in that way you would know with certainty whether I was your father.

Frank explained that, in this way, you would have three options:

Do nothing.

Have your genome sequenced to compare with mine and know for sure if I am your father, and keep the result to yourselves.

As above, but confront your mother with the result. After all, she would have known all along if the possibility existed.

In all of this my Charlie, I want you to know that niece or daughter, I have loved you whatever.

I'm sure that it has not escaped either of you that, if I am indeed your father Charlie, then you and Nat are not full siblings, and that that may be significant for you.

Whatever you decide, please give great consideration to your 'father's' feelings, they would likely be very complex indeed.

You two good people have been one of the greatest loves of my life and I close with nothing but the warmest of feelings for you.

Pierre.

Charlie opened the small envelope and laid the two photos on the desk. Then Charlie and I embraced and our tears ran freely at what we saw.

THE END

NAUTICAL TERMS USED IN THIS BOOK

BOATS

Bow	front of boat.
Stern	back of boat.
Fore	at the front.
Forward	toward the front.
Aft	toward the back.
Beam	maximum width of the boat.
Port	left-hand side of boat looking forward.
Starboard	right-hand side looking forward.
Masthead	top of mast.
Forestay	multi-strand stainless steel wire supporting the mast from the bow.
Backstay	as above but from the stern.
Shrouds	as above but from the beam, both port and starboard—typically three each side.
Cap-shroud	middle shroud of the three each side supporting the masthead. The other two shrouds, set a little fore and aft of the cap-shroud, support the mast at about halfway up.
Cockpit	command and social centre, typically at the stern of a single masted yacht.
Helm	steering wheel.
Bimini	collapsible, pram-hood type sun-hade, over cockpit.
Galley	kitchen.
Head(s)	toilet.
Holding tank	tank to hold the output of the head for later discharge at sea.
Companionway	stairs from cockpit to saloon.

Companionway hatch lockable hatch to secure the companionway.

Pulpit stainless steel welded tubular frame attached to the bow providing the forward anchor points for the life-lines.

Aft pulpit or push-pit as above but across the stern.

SAILING

Foresail/jib/genoa triangular sail attached to a furling mechanism installed around the head-stay.

Mainsail triangular sail attached to a furling mechanism inside the mast, and to the aft end of the boom.

Rope there is only one rope on a boat and it is attached to the ship's bell 'clanger'! All other 'Ropes' have specific names as follows:

Sheets two 'ropes', attached to the free corner of the foresail, which are led back, each side of the boat, outside the shrouds, to the cockpit to control how far out the foresail can be when sailing. Similarly, the mainsail sheets, attached to the aft end of the boom, provide the same function for the mainsail.

Halyard a 'rope' run from the base of the mast, over a masthead pulley, and attached to the top corner of either foresail or mainsail, used to hoist the sail. In modern yachts, the halyards are typically run inside the mast and exit at about chest height for the crew to handle. In older yachts, the halyards ran outside the mast and tended to 'slap' against the mast in a wind.

Rode the chain or 'rope' from the anchor to the bow.

Painter the 'rope' from the bow of the dinghy to the yacht.

Points of sail a yacht can sail in any direction, relative to the wind, except directly into the wind.

Reach a yacht is said to be reaching if the apparent wind is on the beam, i.e., at ninety degrees to the direction of travel.

Close reach	the apparent wind just forward of the beam.
Broad reach	the wind aft of the beam.
Run	the wind astern, and the slowest point of sailing, as the yacht cannot exceed the wind speed.
Wing-and-wing	on a dead-run the sails are deployed with the headsail on one side and the main on the other.
On the wind	sailing up-wind.
Close hauled	sailing close to the direction of the wind, the fastest point of sailing.
Hard on the wind	sailing as close as possible to the wind direction.
Tacking	a yacht sails up-wind in a series of zigzags, or tacks, when close hauled. At the end of each tack, the bow must cross the wind and the sails deployed on the other side.
Going about	crossing the wind.
Port tack	wind from the port side.
Starboard tack	wind from the starboard side.
Easing the sheets	the sheets are at the tightest when close hauled and progressively 'eased' or loosened, as the wind comes aft.
Jibe	on a broad reach, the yacht can tack downwind, in a series of 'jibes', the downwind version of 'going about', i.e., the wind crossing the stern, often preferable, and faster than a dead-run.
Pilot or Sailing guide	book of information relevant to a specific sailing area, containing charts, harbour plans, anchorages, shoreside facilities, local weather patterns, etcetera.

www.ingramcontent.com/pod-product-compliance
Lightning Source LLC
Chambersburg PA
CBHW061534210726
48287CB00006B/1945